THRILL SQUEAKER

A SQUEAKY CLEAN MYSTERY, BOOK 11

CHRISTY BARRITT

RIVER HEIGHTS

COPYRIGHT

Thrill Squeaker: A Novel

Copyright 2016 by Christy Barritt

Published by River Heights Press

Cover design by The Killion Group

COMPLETE BOOK LIST

Squeaky Clean Mysteries:
#1 Hazardous Duty
Half Witted (Squeaky Clean In Between Mysteries Book 1, novella)
#2 Suspicious Minds
#2.5 It Came Upon a Midnight Crime (novella)
#3 Organized Grime
#4 Dirty Deeds
#5 The Scum of All Fears
#6 To Love, Honor and Perish
#7 Mucky Streak
#8 Foul Play
#9 Broom & Gloom
#10 Dust and Obey
#11 Thrill Squeaker
#11.5 Swept Away (novella)
#12 Cunning Attractions
#13 Cold Case: Clean Getaway
#14 Cold Case: Clean Sweep
#15 Cold Case: Clean Break
#16 Cleans to an End

While You Were Sweeping, A Riley Thomas Spinoff

The Sierra Files:
#1 Pounced
#2 Hunted
#3 Pranced
#4 Rattled

The Gabby St. Claire Diaries (a Tween Mystery series):
#1 The Curtain Call Caper
#2 The Disappearing Dog Dilemma
#3 The Bungled Bike Burglaries

The Worst Detective Ever
#1 Ready to Fumble
#2 Reign of Error
#3 Safety in Blunders
#4 Join the Flub
#5 Blooper Freak
#6 Flaw Abiding Citizen
#7 Gaffe Out Loud
#8 Joke and Dagger
#9 Wreck the Halls
#10 Glitch and Famous
#11 Not on My Botch

Raven Remington
Relentless

Holly Anna Paladin Mysteries:
#1 Random Acts of Murder
#2 Random Acts of Deceit
#2.5 Random Acts of Scrooge
#3 Random Acts of Malice
#4 Random Acts of Greed

    #5 Random Acts of Fraud
    #6 Random Acts of Outrage
    #7 Random Acts of Iniquity

Lantern Beach Mysteries
    #1 Hidden Currents
    #2 Flood Watch
    #3 Storm Surge
    #4 Dangerous Waters
    #5 Perilous Riptide
    #6 Deadly Undertow

Lantern Beach Romantic Suspense
    #1 Tides of Deception
    #2 Shadow of Intrigue
    #3 Storm of Doubt
    #4 Winds of Danger
    #5 Rains of Remorse
    #6 Torrents of Fear

Lantern Beach P.D.
    #1 On the Lookout
    #2 Attempt to Locate
    #3 First Degree Murder
    #4 Dead on Arrival
    #5 Plan of Action

Lantern Beach Escape
    Afterglow (a novelette)

Lantern Beach Blackout
    #1 Dark Water
    #2 Safe Harbor
    #3 Ripple Effect
    #4 Rising Tide

#4 Bound by Trouble

#5 Bound by Mayhem

Vanishing Ranch

#1 Forgotten Secrets

#2 Necessary Risk

#3 Risky Ambition

#4 Deadly Intent

#5 Lethal Betrayal

#6 High Stakes Deception

#7 Fatal Vendetta

#8 Troubled Tidings

#9 Narrow Escape

#10 Desperate Rescue

The Sidekick's Survival Guide

#1 The Art of Eavesdropping

#2 The Perks of Meddling

#3 The Exercise of Interfering

#4 The Practice of Prying

#5 The Skill of Snooping

#6 The Craft of Being Covert

Saltwater Cowboys

#1 Saltwater Cowboy

#2 Breakwater Protector

#3 Cape Corral Keeper

#4 Seagrass Secrets

#5 Driftwood Danger

#6 Unwavering Security

Beach House Mysteries

#1 The Cottage on Ghost Lane

#2 The Inn on Hanging Hill

#3 The House on Dagger Point

School of Hard Rocks Mysteries
>#1 The Treble with Murder
>#2 Crime Strikes a Chord
>#3 Tone Death

Carolina Moon Series
>#1 Home Before Dark
>#2 Gone By Dark
>#3 Wait Until Dark
>#4 Light the Dark
>#5 Taken By Dark

Suburban Sleuth Mysteries:
>Death of the Couch Potato's Wife

Fog Lake Suspense:
>#1 Edge of Peril
>#2 Margin of Error
>#3 Brink of Danger
>#4 Line of Duty
>#5 Legacy of Lies
>#6 Secrets of Shame
>#7 Refuge of Redemption

Cape Thomas Series:
>#1 Dubiosity
>#2 Disillusioned
>#3 Distorted

Standalone Romantic Mystery:
>The Good Girl

Suspense:
>Imperfect
>The Wrecking

Sweet Christmas Novella:
    Home to Chestnut Grove

Standalone Romantic-Suspense:
    Keeping Guard
    The Last Target
    Race Against Time
    Ricochet
    Key Witness
    Lifeline
    High-Stakes Holiday Reunion
    Desperate Measures
    Hidden Agenda
    Mountain Hideaway
    Dark Harbor
    Shadow of Suspicion
    The Baby Assignment
    The Cradle Conspiracy
    Trained to Defend
    Mountain Survival
    Dangerous Mountain Rescue

Nonfiction:
    Characters in the Kitchen
    Changed: True Stories of Finding God through Christian Music (out of print)
    The Novel in Me: The Beginner's Guide to Writing and Publishing a Novel (out of print)

CHAPTER
ONE

I STARED at the decrepit iron gate in front of me. The black, ornamental barrier hung lopsided on its hinges, and the words "Mythical Falls" were welded into the intricate, almost medieval, design. If a flock of ravens landed anywhere remotely close, I was running for the hills. Pronto.

I had parked my brand new Honda sedan in front of the gate and stepped into the afternoon sunlight to call my friend Chad. Unfortunately, I had no cell phone signal here in the middle of the wild and wonderful West Virginia mountains. I'd driven just over five hours from my home in Norfolk, Virginia, so I could help him with a big job he'd accepted here at the former theme park. An old friend of his was restoring the place.

I had no idea why.

Something about it being a "resort destination."

As I peered through the iron bars, I spotted an old booth with "Tickets" emblazoned across the front. It lay on the ground with grass and weeds trying to eat it alive.

A disaster destination was more like it. In my opinion, at least.

I rattled the gates. The way they screeched on their hinges

sent a shiver up my spine. This place was spooky. More than spooky.

I pressed my face into the slats, trying to figure out how to find Chad since, without any cell service, calling him was out of the question. But all I saw was a place where nature tried to reclaim what mankind had taken from it.

Nature was winning.

Graffiti bruised a large building in the distance. Trash littered the ground. Old flags that probably appeared cheerful at one time now drooped, faded and ragged along the edges of the area. Saplings and mold covered the dilapidated roofs of abandoned buildings.

"This looks like a whole lotta work," I muttered to myself.

Everything about this place screamed, "Go back now before it's too late!"

"Gabby!"

I gasped and jumped back at the unexpected sound. That's when I spotted someone walking down the path toward me.

"Chad . . ." The word tapered into a chuckle.

Overreact much, Gabby?

He grinned from the other side of the fence. "Didn't mean to scare you. I figured you probably didn't have reception so I decided to swing by."

He fiddled with the lock across the gate and finally pushed it open. I waited for the normal greeting of "How are you?" or "How was your drive?" Instead, he pointed at my cheek. "You've got some rust there."

I rubbed my skin. That gate. That's where it must have come from. A glance at my hands confirmed the theory. My fingers and palms were now orange.

I wiped them on my jeans—I'd worn old ones that I didn't mind getting dirty. At least I hadn't gotten anything on my shirt. Right there on the lapel were the words "Squeaky Clean Restoration Services," the name of Chad's company. At one time, it had been my crime-scene cleaning and restoration business, but I had since ventured into other pursuits and Chad had taken over. I still helped out whenever I could, though.

It wasn't my cutest shirt. I really liked ones with sassy, snicker-worthy sayings across the front. My newest favorites were: "Please Don't Make Me Adult Today" and "Forensic Mopologist." But I thought I'd try to look professional when I showed up. For most of the rest of my visit I'd look grubby, trading perfume for the scent of oil, makeup for grease and dust, and nail polish for grime. No one would be singing "She's a Lady" when I was around and deep into clean-up mode.

Chad turned and followed my gaze.

"So this is Mythical Falls," he started. "You're in for a real treat."

He'd arrived a week earlier to sketch out what needed to be done, work on getting permits, and buy some supplies.

I glanced at the ticket booth corpse again. "It looks like quite the destination."

"Believe it or not, at one time this place was a hopping theme park," Chad said. "It closed down twenty years ago, but now my friend Nate wants to open it back up again."

"Your friend Nate might be a little crazy."

Chad smiled, like he knew something I didn't. "You have no idea."

At that moment, a jacked-up oversized truck pulled behind my sedan, dirt and dust from the gravel road flying up all around it. A man hopped out, his feet landing with a bounce on the ground. He looked to be the same age as Chad and me, and he had a scruffy brown beard, oversized work boots, and a gleam of mischief in his eyes.

This had to be Chad's longtime friend Nate Reynolds. Apparently, in a past life, Chad and Nate had been ski instructors together in the winter, as well as whitewater rafting guides in the summer. My initial impression of the man was that he was an adrenaline junkie, someone who would rather be poor and have fun than be tied down with an office job. I'd have to wait and see if I was correct.

"Hey, man!" Chad held up his hand, and the two did a little high-five/handshake/hug thingamajig. "This is Gabby, my former business partner and all-around hard worker."

Nate's eyes traveled from my head all the way down to my feet in a manner I didn't appreciate. He didn't even try to hide his obvious interest, nor did he show any shame as he let out a low whistle.

"Not what I expected, but welcome, pretty lady." He winked. "I've always had a thing for redheads. And blondes. And brunettes, for that matter."

"She's taken," Chad interjected, his eyes sparkling. "Married for that matter."

"That's up for debate," I muttered. Chad got a kick out of my predicament.

It was true that my ex-boyfriend, Riley Thomas, and I had accidentally gotten married a few months ago. Since then, we'd rekindled our relationship, and we planned to really get married if we could ever nail down a date. But that was a long story for another day.

Nate raised his hands and stepped back. "I get that. No harm in looking, right?"

I crossed my arms and changed the subject, not wanting to waste any time talking about Nate's lack of manners. Life was too short to give this guy too much thought or attention. "So tell me about this project."

I desperately wanted to ward off the uncomfortable feeling in my gut about spending a week on these grounds. Maybe I should have said no to this project. However, Chad had been desperate, and I just happened to have two forensic training workshops in West Virginia that I'd been able to arrange this week.

"It's going to be awesome. Awesome!" Nate exploded his

hands in the air, spreading his fingers like fireworks bursting in the air. "People love stuff that's abandoned. *Love* it."

I could already tell that Nate was a repeater. I repeat: he was a *repeater*.

I mentally rewrote the lyrics to the song, "I'm a Believer," changing the chorus to "He's a Repeater." Now that was going to be stuck in my head for the rest of the day.

"All the rides, for the most part, are history—they have to be taken down, or I have to put up a fence around them so no one gets hurt," Nate continued. "But I really need your help fixing up the rest of this place in time for the grand opening. I'd like to be done by Halloween. Anyway, I'm converting the old buildings into cabins people can rent. Of course, at Halloween, we'll have a big blowout because, let's face it, it's spooky here. *Spooky*!"

"I see." *I see*, I repeated silently.

"You want to give her a tour?"

Chad nodded. "Yeah, let's take her around the grounds. Time is money, right?"

Nate laughed. I wasn't even sure what was so funny, but I did know that his extended chuckle was clipped in machine-gun like syllables. It reminded me of a cross between a woodpecker and a broken record. And it made me want to burst my eardrums so I wouldn't have to hear it.

"Let's go then! Onward, ho." He glanced at me. "That's an expression. I wasn't calling names."

I squirmed and bit my tongue, feeling a mix of annoyed and embarrassed—not for myself but for Nate. "I realize that."

"Just making sure. Don't want any hard feelings or anything. You know what I'm saying?" He turned his head and widened his eyes as if he desperately wanted me to take him seriously. But his comical expression only made me want to roll my eyes.

He didn't break his gaze until I responded with, "Got it."

"Excellent. Let's leave our vehicles here. You'll have more of the full effect of this place on foot. Believe me. This will be an experience you won't forget."

Oh, I believed him. This place would give some people nightmares.

The gate creaked as Nate pushed it open farther, and I shivered. All of my instincts screamed that I should go back to Virginia and resume normal life, which was strange. I wasn't superstitious. But I had a major case of the creeps right now.

Could it be because nothing but miles and miles of rugged mountainside surrounded us? This place seemed like a monument to days of the past, a stark reminder of how life could change from fun and games to sorrow and devastation. It could represent my life, for that matter. At least things had been looking up lately, but I was just waiting for the next ball to drop. I could trace that pattern back for years and years.

Things went well. Things went horribly wrong. Things went well. Things went horribly wrong. That was my life in a nutshell.

It's a job, Gabby. A job. Stop reading too much into this.

On a positive note, the foliage around us was beautiful. Gorgeous. Full of autumn glory. The place even felt like autumn. Maybe it was the brisk wind and the scent of decaying leaves or the way the sun hung low on the horizon, casting strange shadows with its warm, orange glow. I loved this time of year, and the mountains were the perfect place to fully enjoy the season.

I stepped through the gate and paused, getting an unobstructed view of Mythical Falls. The large building dead in front of me boasted a sign reading, "The Bermuda Triangle." To my right was a rusty old dumpster, also turned on its side. In the far distance, tucked into the mountainside, were the remains of an old rollercoaster, which lay like ancient dinosaur bones. At my feet on the crusty asphalt were old tickets, a set of vampire teeth —the kind a child might play with, and an old park flyer.

"This place, back in the day, was a sight to behold," Nate said. "People from all over the country came here on family vacations. My parents talk about the candied apples and cotton candy and the time Kiss played on the main stage. It was totally a big deal. Like a *big*, big deal."

I watched my step as I strode across the grounds. The cement walkway below me looked like it had been quaint at one time, but now it was uneven and hazardous. Nate must have noticed my caution because he frowned.

"Yeah, we have to get that fixed. We can't have anyone suing us," Nate said. "Lawsuits are bad. *Bad*. Anyway, come on. I'll start in my favorite part of the park. Bigfoot Woods."

"Bigfoot Woods?" I repeated.

The question had slipped out. I hadn't had much time to research the place before I came. I was too busy with working. Truth was, I'd been keeping myself especially busy lately. It could have something to do with avoiding uncomfortable topics.

Like setting a wedding date. At one time, I would have flipped over backward to do such a thing. But, lately, fear had crept in—fear of something else happening, fear of getting my hopes up, and fear of having my heart broken again.

"Yeah. So the park is divided into different areas, each one based on different mythical creatures or legends. We've got Bigfoot Woods, Loch Ness Lake, Area 51, the Bermuda Triangle, and Pharaoh's Tomb. "

"Pharaohs weren't mythical," I said.

"It was probably the lamest section of the park. It features ancient mythology." Nate continued to lead us down the path toward the woods in the distance. "We're not going to actually open that area. Not in the beginning. I just want to focus on Bigfoot Woods, the Bermuda Triangle, and Area 51, to start with."

I wanted to stop and soak in every detail—to locate the Ferris wheel that was now concealed by trees. To let the broken "concessions" sign stain my memory. To envision families bonding over kettle corn.

We passed a big pavilion—I would guess it was where shows

were held at one time. Perhaps it was where Kiss had performed. Right now, part of the roof looked like God himself had stepped on it.

Directly ahead of us, on a wooden sign that stretched above the narrowing walkway, was the warning, "Enter at your own risk." That sign really should be plastered all over this place.

"Here we are," Nate continued with a grand sweep of his hands. "Bigfoot Woods."

My throat went dry at the thought of venturing into those woods. I wasn't even sure why. I just felt like this was some sort of overblown haunted house where monsters were waiting to jump out and scare me to death.

Come help me, Chad had said. *It will be fun.*

He had failed to mention that the area could double as the set for a really bad 80s horror flick.

Thanks to my dear friend, I was now in the middle of crazy town where no one would hear me scream for help. That was awesome. Sarcasm dripped from my words, even when they were spoken silently in my head.

"Bigfoot Woods had a couple of rides," Nate said. "One picked you up and dropped you down real fast. It was called the Yeti Smash." Nate let out that woodpecker laugh again. "*Yeti Smash.* Isn't that terrible?"

I gave Chad a pointed look, and he shrugged. Nate and Chad might just be cut from the same cloth. Both were laidback and rugged in their own ways. Chad usually had a soul patch below his bottom lip, one that he sometimes let grow too long. He was on the shorter side but lean with light-brown hair streaked blond by the sun.

Since Chad's baby, Reef, was born three months ago, he'd changed from Mr. Carefree to Mr. Responsible—not that he hadn't been reliable before. I mean, the man had been a mortician at one point in his life. But I supposed fatherhood had simply upped his grown-up factor.

I shivered again as I walked farther down the trail. Tree limbs grew over the walkway, reminding me of bony, skeletal arms reaching out to form a canopy and lord over anyone who entered the area. Shadows flickered across the footpath with the breeze, and a bird of prey squawked overhead.

Perfect.

"There are some more old concession buildings here and some shops," Nate continued. "I want to turn them into cabins. People will pay big bucks to come and stay here just for the experience."

"You think?" I asked.

He nodded, dead serious. "Absolutely. Do you know how many people have tried to sneak in here and steal parts of this park?"

"I can't say I have any idea." And there was a big difference between breaking in to steal things and paying to come here and stay. I kept that thought silent. I wasn't a consultant, after all. I was hired to help, to simply follow directions.

"It's been a real problem," he said. "Especially with college students. The fraternities and sororities must get a huge kick out of daring each other to sneak in here. We've had severed heads— fake ones, of course—stolen. Signs have been taken. Graffiti has been left. It's been a real shame."

I wondered where Nate had gotten the money to buy this place. Just the land alone had to be expensive. How many acres did this cover? I'd guess at least one hundred.

As I walked deeper into the woods, the shadows felt over-powering instead of flickering and playful. Giant Bigfoot replicas were staged behind trees and hulked in the background. A rickety bridge, arched in a way that had probably been enchanting at one time, teased of danger in front of us.

As I reached the center of a bridge, a low, rumbling roar sounded from the forest.

I gasped and clutched my heart. Visions of Bigfoot crouched beneath the bridge filled my mind. I scrambled to the other side of the crosswalk.

That was when I heard laughter replace the roar. When I looked up, I saw Nate holding his side.

"Sorry," he muttered through his chuckles. "I couldn't resist."

I let out the breath I held. Nate had made that sound. Of course.

So much for being taken seriously by the man.

"Very funny," I mumbled, brushing imaginary dirt from my jeans.

He grinned. "I thought so. There actually are several sound effects that play from speakers in the woods and under the bridge. You know, wood knocking and heavy footsteps and bloodcurdling screams and ferocious roars—"

Okay, so he liked adjectives too. I stored that in the back of my mind. "I get it. So this is like a giant haunted house combined with an amusement park."

"Exactly."

I hadn't wanted to admit it, but Nate was changing my mind. People loved thrills—from rollercoasters to scary movies to adrenaline-spiking sports. People just might head here to get a rush, to experience a piece of pop-culture history, and have an "experience."

"I'm surprised these Bigfoot replicas have lasted out here this long," I said, glancing at one as we passed. The creature's fur was matted and gross, he was missing an eye, and one of his teeth was broken. "They're in pretty good shape, all things considered."

"They're made of cement and covered with hair. Vandals weren't able to steal them. Believe me—they would have otherwise. I plan on leaving the replicas there. People will be majorly stoked about it. It will be off the chain."

"Totally." I tried to keep the surfer girl inflection from my voice but failed. I loved people and their quirks and idiosyncrasies. People's unique attributes were what made life interesting.

I pointed in the distance to another one of the themed areas.

"You even left replicas of Bigfoot's victims in the woods? That's so . . . tubular. Makes it seem more realistic yet unsettling and frightening."

Chad shot me a dirty look, and I grinned. I was just having a little fun, and Nate didn't seem to notice or mind.

"Dead bodies?" Nate laughed, but this time a tinge of anxiety curled the edges of the sound. "What are you talking about?"

I pointed to the body in the distance. "One of Bigfoot's victims. Right over there."

When Nate's eyes widened, I realized something was wrong. I was trying to get into the spirit of the macabre and twisted. But I could clearly see now that it was a mistake.

"There are no victims out here. That would be . . . sick." Nate looked at me like I had no moral compass, which slightly offended me.

"Then who is that?" Even as I said the words, the truth pounded in my heart. I knew the answer, whether I wanted to admit it or not.

There was a dead body here. A real one, not a fake one.

"Looks like our crime-scene cleaning services will come in handy here after all," I muttered.

CHAPTER
TWO

THIRTY MINUTES LATER, the police showed up and surrounded the body of the dead man in the woods. I'd forced myself to step back and let Nate take the lead as the police chief shot off questions about the discovery. I was getting paid to do a job here, one that didn't include investigating, I reminded myself.

Before I'd told Chad I could come, he'd emphasized several times the importance of this paycheck. He wasn't one to normally stress about money, but obviously something had changed. My guess? Fatherhood.

For that reason, it was better if I kept my distance from this investigation and remained quiet and unassuming.

I might have—just maybe— taken a quick gander at the scene before the police arrived. I hadn't been able to resist. The familiar urge of being able to officially solve crimes had gotten the best of me.

In my past life, I'd been a medical legal death investigator. When I'd lost that job because of budget cuts, I'd floundered for a while. But just recently, I'd been hired by one of the leading producers of crime-scene and forensic equipment. Now I worked part-time for Grayson Technologies, traveling to various police departments in my region in order to train officers and techs how to use the equipment and supplies.

Without disturbing the body, I'd observed that the dead man was probably in his early twenties. Based on the way he looked —name-brand clothing, expensive watch, neat hair—I'd guessed he was from a fairly wealthy family. I didn't see any blood, slashes, or bullet holes, which would indicate a violent death. In fact, his face looked relatively peaceful and serene.

But, somehow, the man had died.

Had it been from natural causes? I didn't know. I guessed that the police wouldn't know either until the medical examiner did an autopsy.

The only thing that had stirred any interest at the scene was a black leather glove I'd seen lying beside the body. Criminals used gloves like that when they wanted to conceal their prints. Okay, okay—so did businessmen on cold winter days, but criminals were so much more fitting at this moment.

"What do you think?" Chad asked as we watched the police work.

We stood away from the scene, near the woods on the opposite side of the path. The trees behind us were entirely too close, and I kept feeling like a branch would reach out at any minute and grab me. Or that a Bigfoot replica would come to life. Or that a killer would nab me, and no one would notice.

All of this was totally irrational, and I knew this. But that didn't change my jumpiness or fears. It didn't help that the sun was already beginning to sink low, casting even more shadows around us. Birds continued to squawk and soar overhead. An occasional small animal scampered over crisp leaves. Even the breeze suddenly felt sharp and angry.

I shrugged as I continued to stare at the scene in front of me. Chad and I both had enough experience to make educated guesses about what had happened, and Chad was entirely too aware that I was, at any given moment, more than happy to share my opinion.

I rubbed my lips together before diving into my theories. "He's not dressed like someone who came out here hiking or hunting. It almost looks like he stopped by in-between things on his work schedule, you know? I mean, who wears khakis and loafers into the woods? Maybe he was applying to be one of your subs?"

"Most of the subs have a background in the coal industry. When the mines shut down around here several years ago, a lot of the unemployed decided to start up businesses."

"Why'd the mines close?"

"Something about the weak coal market and dried up reserves," Chad said. "I'm not sure that has anything to do with this. But I do know that most miners don't generally wear khakis and loafers."

"Nate said there's a college around here and that fraternities sneak onto the grounds?"

Chad nodded. "Yeah, there's one in Whitehurst."

"My guess is that's where he's from then. Maybe he's one of those frat boys."

"Good deduction." Chad shifted, continuing to stare at the scene. "Maybe an animal got to him."

I frowned as I thought about his theory. "There's no blood. Attacks by wild animals are usually messy."

"That's true. There's really no sign of struggle at all, is there?" He paused and rubbed his chin in thought.

"Based on rigor, I'd guess he's been dead less than a day. Besides, any longer than that and wild animals would have gotten to him."

"I was thinking the same thing."

I frowned as my thoughts went to places I didn't intend for them to go—places where they could get in trouble. Places where a yearning to investigate would grow in me until it was too big to contain. It had happened before, and I recognized the signs as easily as most people recognized a sneeze coming on.

"It's strange." I rubbed my throat in contemplation. "I didn't see any other cars out there by the gate when we pulled up. I wonder how he got here and where he got in. Is there a fence around the whole place?"

"There *was* a fence around the whole place. Who knows if it's all still standing? That will have to be addressed at some point."

"Probably a good idea." But that was probably a weeklong task within itself. This would be a challenging job—even more so now.

Chad crossed his arms and cast a glance at me. "Figures this would happen when you're here."

I shoved my eyebrows together. "What do you mean?"

"You seem to attract stuff like this."

I couldn't even argue. I had a knack for finding mysteries. "I do, don't I?"

"Maybe God really does put you in the right place at the right time."

"Some might say the opposite: it's the wrong place at the wrong time."

"All the good you've done helping people, I'm going with my original theory." He sighed. "I wonder how this will change things. Don't get me wrong—I know our priorities have just shifted here. But we won't be able to wait around indefinitely before starting to work. I do have to get back to Virginia and other jobs I've committed to there."

"The police will probably rope off this area, but we'll be able to conquer the rest of the park. And when I say conquer, I'm not exaggerating. This is one big task."

Chad nodded. "But isn't Nate brilliant? I love this idea. There's nothing else out there like it."

I shrugged, not sure I'd take it that far. I didn't know what to say. There wasn't anything out there like this. But this place defined biting off more than you could chew. "I just hope this dead body doesn't put a damper on his plans."

Chad started talking about a game plan for knocking everything out, but my mind kept going back to the body I'd found.

All these years of cleaning up after crime scenes, yet dead bodies still affected me. Sure, I'd learned to compartmentalize. Some death scenes affected me more than others. But death was no laughing matter.

Questions filled my mind. Who was the victim? How had he gotten here? What had his dreams for the future been? Were his loved ones worried right now? Did they even know he was missing? In their guts, did they sense something was wrong?

Two officers stood near the body while another took pictures. I glanced over as I saw movement in the distance and spotted a middle-aged woman walking toward the scene.

"Marion Edwards?" I muttered as I soaked in the woman's short, dark hair and stout build.

I thought I'd said the name in my head, but I must have voiced it out loud because the woman stopped and turned toward me. Her eyes widened with familiarity.

"Gabby St. Claire?"

I mumbled an apology to Chad, who was still yammering about the job, before walking toward Marion. I'd always liked Marion in the few short months I'd worked with her. She'd seemed down-to-earth and friendly.

I wasn't sure how to greet her—we weren't exactly friends, more like acquaintances. But when I saw her outstretched arms, I figured a hug was in order. I was quick on reading body language like that. Yes—that was sarcastic.

"I never in a million years thought I'd see you here." She pulled back and stared at me like an aunt might stare at a long-lost niece. "Are you working for the state police now?"

I shook my head. "I actually work part-time for Grayson Technologies, but I'm not here in an official capacity of any sort. I'm freelancing a construction job."

Her eyebrows shot up. "Grayson Tech? I love their products. Top of the line. Well-respected. Innovative."

I smiled and nodded. "I agree."

"Walk with me," she instructed.

Of course, I obeyed. She limped slightly as she traveled down the rickety path. She'd had a bad knee ever since I'd known her and had been through at least two knee replacements, if I remembered correctly.

"Have you seen the body?" She glanced back at me.

"I was the one who found him."

"Sorry to hear that. At least you had experience enough to know not to touch anything or disturb the scene. That's half the battle sometimes." Her breathing was labored as she walked, leaning heavily on her cane.

"We don't have very many cases like this around here," Marion continued. "We have a few hunting accidents every year. Maybe some car crashes and a domestic dispute every now and then."

"I didn't realize you'd moved here."

She nodded. "I actually met a man online. We dated long distance for several months, and then I decided to take the plunge." She shrugged and cast me a lovelorn look. "I've been single for fifty years. When you meet a nice man, it causes you to reevaluate where you are in your life."

"I had no idea." I liked hearing about this human side of her. I'd known she was single, but I had no idea that she'd even been looking for love. I'd just assumed she was career oriented and content.

"I work part-time in private practice and as medical examiner on the side," she continued. "Truth be told, I like working with the dead best. They're easier to deal with than the living."

"I hear you." The dead didn't talk back or argue or trust Dr. Google's opinion over a medical professional's. I was not a medical professional, but I'd been around enough to know how it all worked.

When we reached the body, Marion put a hand on her hip and sighed. "What have we got here, boys?"

The police chief began filling her in, not sharing anything I didn't already know. Marion gently pulled back the top of the white sheet draped over the body. She frowned as she stared at the victim's face.

"He's a young one," she muttered. "Give me a few minutes, and I'll tell you the approximate time of death."

Nate called me over to the walkway as Marion examined the body further. I bypassed the officers and ducked under the yellow crime scene tape to reach him and Chad. The once-exuberant man now seemed pale and jittery instead of carefree and energetic. Anyone would have that reaction after what we'd seen.

"This might change things, guys," he whispered. "This isn't good."

I stole a glance at Chad as I braced myself for what he might say next. "What do you mean?"

"This place was shut down twenty years ago because three people died here," Nate confessed. "What if that happens again?"

CHAPTER
THREE

BY THE TIME the police left, darkness had arrived, and Mythical Falls felt spookier than ever.

I drove my car down an old service road in order to reach my cabin in Bigfoot Woods.

Apparently, Nate had already restored two cabins, and we were all staying in one of those tonight. It would be our temporary residence for the evening. Nate had been sure to mention that the one we were staying in didn't have any raccoons or other rodents like most of the other buildings here.

Comforting.

I pulled my suitcase from my trunk and turned to scan the area. The cabins looked like a row of old prospectors' residences. Six structures lined the stream behind it, each two stories high and narrow, with rustic-looking wooden porches. Behind the houses, there was supposedly an old mill, complete with a water wheel. From where I stood, I could hear the slight trickle of the stream.

My gaze traveled across the street to buildings constructed to look like an old town. Chad had mentioned that old carnival games used to be there—everything from the Bottle Ring Toss to Pop the Balloon and Skee Ball.

As I stood by my car, nature was alive and well around me. In the nearby woods, woodland creatures—I assumed—scampered through the dry underbrush. An owl hooted. Crickets chirped.

Ordinarily the sounds might be comforting or even intriguing. But, tonight, each noise just reminded me of how alone I was out here.

I couldn't wait to get inside. This was not the way I'd intended on starting my stay. I had no idea I'd just accepted a job at the Little Amusement Park of Horrors.

Nate, Chad, and I hadn't had time to talk since earlier. No sooner had Nate mentioned that there had been other murders here, the police chief grabbed him to ask some additional questions. Convenient.

I followed the sound of Nate and Chad's voices and walked into an old, dusty-looking cabin.

"You found us!" Chad looked up from the kitchen table, where he had papers sprawled and a pencil stuck behind his ear.

I set my suitcase on the floor. "Here I am."

"Your room is down the hall," Nate said. "Make yourself at home."

I did just that before hurrying back to the kitchen, anxious to talk about what was going on here. Nate stirred a pot on the stove, and Chad yammered on about his schedule over the next few days and his plan for completing everything on time. The scent of something savory wafted through the air.

I tried to find a good opening, but the two men were focused on the workload for the week. I had no choice but to listen and wait. Apparently, Nate wanted to eventually open a restaurant on the Mythical Falls grounds. He planned on opening the cabins only here and in Area 51. But he'd do one area at a time.

Braxton, another of Chad's employees, was working on electricity, but he was staying with a friend who lived forty minutes away and driving in every day. Braxton was a know-it-all who didn't particularly like me. That meant I'd not only be dealing with the legend of Bigfoot while I was here, but also with the real life drama of Bigmouth. Yay for me.

As the conversation went on and on, I looked around the cabin. It had a great room with a small kitchen, a dining bar, a living-room area with a fireplace, and one bathroom. The whole building was probably less than eight hundred square feet, and it retained a rustic feel—except for the kitchen, which had new stainless steel appliances and granite countertops. Nate had already brought in some contractors to work on the bathrooms and kitchens, if I remembered correctly.

I sat on the typical lodge-style couch, trying to be patient. The mauve cushions under me expelled dust every time I moved. At least the fire in front of me was warm and soothing—very welcoming after our earlier shock.

I didn't have a chance to squeeze a word into the conversation until we were all seated at a rickety card table with sliced venison, microwaved mac and cheese, and canned green beans.

"So," I started, my appetite waning from both the impending conversation and the unappetizing meal. "There have been other murders here?"

Nate paused from heartily slicing his meat and glanced at Chad. "I never said *murders*. I said deaths. *Deaths*. Not everyone died at the hands of someone else. That's kind of a weird assumption."

I scowled.

"Please, tell me more." I kept my words even and calm even though irritation pooled in my gut.

"Well, the first one was a total accident." Nate shoveled a forkful of meat into his mouth and pushed it into his cheek so he could keep talking. "A woman fell off the Ferris wheel. From the tippy-top." His eyes widened as he revealed that fact. He made a whistling sound and then a splat—which wasn't pretty considering he had a mouthful of food.

I swallowed hard. That would be a terrible way to go and a terrible death to witness. I imagined families with kids being nearby, enjoying a day at the park, when the horror occurred in front of them. It would be enough to scar someone for life.

"This woman . . ." I started. "She randomly fell off the ride?"

Nate swallowed his food with a flourish. "That's right. There was an investigation. Law enforcement thinks the safety bar came loose. She and her friend leaned down for a better view. The next thing, the latch opened and down she went."

I frowned. "That's terrible."

"Yeah, isn't it? The next guy who died was an employee. He was walking beneath the Flight of the Flying Saucer—"

"The what?" I asked.

"Oh, that's the old rollercoaster," Nate said. "Most people around here called it the Vomit Comet. Anyway, he was looking for some money that someone dropped or something. Maybe it was a car key. Minor detail, right?" Nate scratched his head. "Anyway, he was down there at the wrong time because the coaster whacked him."

"That's also terrible." I frowned again. What horrible ways to die.

Nate nodded, reminding me a bit of an innocent puppy who didn't know any better but to enjoy his food and play fetch. He, at least, had the courtesy to lower his voice slightly before finishing. "The third is a little more grisly."

My muscles tensed, unsure how it could get worse—and that meant a lot coming from a crime-scene cleaner. "Okay."

"A man sneaked into the park at night and went down to Mythical Falls."

"This *is* Mythical Falls." What was I missing here? I thought all of the deaths had taken place here.

Nate put his fork down and stared at me. "This *is* Mythical Falls, but there's also a *real-life* Mythical Falls down by Loch Ness Lake. We didn't get to finish our tour earlier, or I would have shown you. There's a path that takes you down there. It's a beautiful place. Beautiful."

"I bet." I narrowed my eyes again. "And you have Bambi stuck in your beard."

"Oh, thanks." He plucked out a piece of venison and, to my horror, stuck it in his mouth.

Gross.

"So, a man sneaked down there. Or is it snuck? I dunno. Anyway, he was found the next morning. And he was—" Nate wobbled his head back and forth as if he was having a hard time saying murdered, which was strange considering the ease he'd talked about the other two deaths. He ran a finger across his neck.

"His throat was slit?" I questioned.

Nate shook his head and looked at me dumbfounded. "No, he was dead. Isn't that a universal sign for dead?"

I tried not to scowl again. "What happened to him?"

Nate leaned closer and lowered his voice. "He was murdered."

"Murdered?" I muttered.

Nate picked up his fork again. "It's true."

"Did they ever catch the person responsible?" My throat suddenly felt tight. I'd always been creeped out by the woods and camping and isolated wilderness areas. The only thing that could make this worse was if it started thundering and lightning right now.

As if God himself had read my thoughts, thunder rumbled outside. My fork flew out of my hand and landed on the filthy floor with a clank.

I'd just walked into the middle of *Friday the 13th*.

As I picked my fork up, I noticed my hand was trembling. I had to get focused here and act like the grown woman I was. I also had to remind myself to keep this fork away from my mouth in my preoccupation. "So the park closed after the murder?"

Nate nodded, already back to eating his venison. "Yeah, everyone said it was cursed and all of this junk that freaked people out. It was really just a run of bad luck, though. It was a shame. There's not much to do out here in this area unless you like hiking and hunting, maybe some rock climbing or mountain biking or whitewater rafting or skiing—"

"That sounds like plenty to do," I interjected.

"Well, only if you're the outdoor type. Some people want options, and Mythical Falls was a great one. People still talk about their memories here—getting engaged, their first kiss, childhood vacations. I want to bring that back. This area needs this, especially since the mines closed down. Morale has taken a serious dip."

"I see." I hoped finding another dead body here didn't put a damper on his plans. There was a good chance it would.

"I desperately need your help, though. We have paths to clear, cabins to paint, and walls to repair. We've got to secure some hazardous structures. It's a big job, but I knew there was no one else I wanted to ask but my old buddy Chad."

His old buddy Chad.

Strange. Certainly there were other contractors in this area he could use. Why bring in a crew from Virginia? And where had this man gotten the money it was going to take to restore the place? I kept coming back to that question.

I knew what Nate was paying us, and it was a hefty sum. That wasn't to mention the fact that he'd bought this property in the first place. How much had that been?

My suspicions started to rise, which was ridiculous. I needed to nip this in the proverbial bud.

"What do you do for a living, Nate?" I asked, trying to ease into the questions. I'd learned—the hard way—that tact usually got me a lot farther than bluntness. However, push me hard enough or stress me out and that bluntness came out again.

"I'm a financial planner."

I blinked, certain I'd heard him wrong. I'd expected him to say adventure guide or backpack expedition leader. "Come again?"

He did the woodpecker laugh. "Yeah, that's right. I'm in finance. I'm sure you're wondering how someone my age can afford to do this. It's a natural question, I assure you."

"Since you brought it up, do you mind if I ask how? I am curious. I can't imagine how much all of this cost." Believe me—I'd already tried to several times.

"No, I totally understand." He shoved another piece of meat in his mouth. "Let's just say I got an inheritance and leave it at that. Intriguing, right?"

"Totally." I had to work on sounding more sincere—*being* more sincere. Actually, I was a pretty sincere person, but Nate was bringing out a sugary sweet kind of sarcasm that I hadn't indulged in for a long time.

I'm going to do better, Lord.

"As you can see, restoring Mythical Falls wasn't a natural choice," Nate continued, not the least bit fazed. "But, then, I decided to take the leap. Life is too short not to, right?"

"Reasonable risks can be good," I conceded.

"I just don't want to always live safe. I want to make an impact. This is going to be my impact."

I just don't want to always live safe. I want to make an impact.

His words echoed in my head. I was moving in the opposite direction. I wanted life to be stable. I'd never had that, and I yearned for consistency.

I shoved my plate away, realizing I would be eating some crackers I'd packed when I got to my room. "I think I should get some sleep tonight if we're going to get started in the morning. I'll help clean up first."

"No, don't worry about it. I've got it," Nate said.

"If you're sure. I do want to call Riley and check on him."

Nate gave me a look of pity. "Good luck finding a signal around here. If you haven't figured it out yet, phone service is spotty in this area, to say the least."

"I was hoping I was just in a dead spot earlier." As I said the words "dead spot," my stomach dropped. It seemed a little too appropriate for this place.

I stepped outside onto the ramshackle porch and pulled out my cell phone. Sure enough, there was no service. I raised it higher, hoping that I might pick up on something. But no, no bars showed. Nate had been telling the truth.

Chad followed me, his phone also raised. "There's a magic spot around here, if you can find it. There's an art form to it, and if you move just a centimeter, you'll lose your connection."

"Good to know."

He sighed and lowered his phone after several moments of walking with it in the air. "I really wanted to check on Sierra and Reef. I can't wait until they get here."

Riley, Sierra, Reef, and another worker named Clarice were supposed to come tomorrow to help out. I was looking forward to the rest of the gang arriving also. "This is going to be fun."

We'd all talked about it being a mini-retreat or a friend weekend of sorts. All of us hadn't had much time to spend together lately.

Chad shook his head. "I said I can't wait, yet there's another part of me that can. I mean, if there is something going on here, maybe the rest of the gang shouldn't come."

"You think that man was murdered?"

Chad shrugged. "Until I know for sure . . . it's pretty desolate out here. There aren't many people to hear you scream for help."

I shivered. "Now that you put it that way . . ."

He shrugged. "I just don't want to put them in harm's way."

"That's noble of you."

He cut a sharp glance at me. "I mean, I don't want you in harm's way either. But you always put yourself there and no one can usually stop you."

"I resemble that comment."

Chad grinned. "Exactly."

I sighed, the chilly air around me feeling especially frigid as goose bumps popped out on my arms. That was my cue to call it a night.

Just as I turned to go inside, I heard something in the distance. My skin crawled.

My gaze met Chad's.

Wood knocking.

It was classic Bigfoot 101: The creatures supposedly hit two sticks together or against a tree to create a noise as a means of communicating.

And, as if that wasn't scary enough, it was followed by the sound of someone—or something—extremely heavy and large rushing through the forest.

"SOMETHING WAS OUT THERE," I said as soon as I was safely inside the cabin. My heart still raced as my adrenaline pumped out of control.

In my head, I could hear the British band AllSTARS singing "Things That Go Bump in the Night." Yes, that song may have even made it onto a Scooby-Doo soundtrack. But both the tune and the TV show seemed more than appropriate for this park at the moment.

"Something was definitely out there," Chad agreed.

I paced in front of the fire, trying to even out my thoughts so I wouldn't sound like an idiot who jumped to conclusions too quickly. "I'm trying to keep a level head. But what could have made that noise?"

Ripples of excitement rushed through Nate's gaze as he listened to our recap. "Oh my gooey goodness. You really heard wood knocking? Wood knocking? What if he's out there?" He made quote marks around the word "he" before humming the theme song from *The Twilight Zone*.

"You mean Bigfoot?"

"Of course." Nate gave me a "duh" expression.

Was Nate serious? Or had Chad and Nate teamed up to scare

me? If this was all one giant prank then I was going to feel foolish . . . and get some serious revenge. I was talking plastic-wrap-over-the-toilet-seat revenge.

Okay that might be kind of lame. But I'd think of something better or my name wasn't Gabby St. Claire.

"He has been spotted in this area." Nate wiped his damp hands on a dishtowel. "My father's friend's uncle's cousin saw him while he was hunting one time. Scary stuff. He said the creature was gentle, though. Bigfoot just looked at him in the woods then ran away as if the hairy dude wanted his privacy."

I shook my head at the unexpected turn in conversation. "You guys! This is crazy. It wasn't Bigfoot. But it was something —or someone." I turned to Nate and narrowed my eyes. "Unless you accidentally turned on one of those old background tracks you were telling us about earlier."

"No way, man—woman. Pardon me." He raised his hands. "I don't want to offend anyone's sensitive sensitivities. Those speakers aren't even hooked up."

He offended me in so many ways that he didn't even realize, but that was beside the point right now. I crossed my arms and eyed Nate. "So maybe someone is trying to scare us off."

He pulled his chin back and squinted. "Why would they do that?"

Wasn't it obvious? "Maybe someone doesn't want this place to open back up."

"Who wouldn't want it to open? No one would have a reason for that. No one." Nate shook his head and looked at me like I was the insanely crazy one.

Chad, who had been relatively quiet, joined the conversation. "Maybe it's the family of one of the people who died here," he suggested. "Maybe this goes back to the dead body we found earlier today. Maybe Bigfoot killed that man. The possibilities are endless."

Before I could stop myself, I scowled at Chad. I thought my

friend was more sensible than this. Apparently, I was wrong. But I needed to say that more diplomatically.

"I think we're reading too much into this." I was careful to keep my voice even and, hopefully, inoffensive. "Maybe that noise was a coincidence. Maybe it was another animal making that sound, and, since none of us are nature experts, maybe we're just ignorant about what it really was. We've got to keep cool heads."

"Did you just call us ignorant?" Nate's bottom lip dropped open.

People seriously trusted this guy with their money? With their life savings, for that matter?

"It just means uninformed. It doesn't mean stupid."

Nate's mouth dropped even wider. "You just called me uninformed? I'll have you know that my father was an avid outdoorsman. I've camped my entire life. I know animals, and none of them make that sound. None. Zip. Zero. Nada. None-ya."

I stepped back, weary of arguing. "I'm done. I was just trying to offer an alternate point of view, but I can see that's not welcome."

"Listen! Both of you." Chad stepped between us, a knot on his forehead seeming to symbolize a possible headache. "It would be easier for all of us to keep a cool head if that dead body hadn't turned up. We all just need to get some rest. That's the best thing we can do right now."

I finally nodded. "I agree. Traipsing through the woods at this hour will only end badly."

"We can all agree then," Nate said. "There are bears out there, not to mention mountain lions and cliffs and yeti. The dangers are . . . well, they're uncountable."

The look he gave me seemed to say, *See? I told you I know the outdoors.*

"Got it."

"No more deaths, okay?" Nate stared at us both.

"Okay," Chad and I said together.

With that, we all escaped to our respective rooms.

But I was halfway tempted to make a run for it first thing in the morning.

I hadn't slept last night. No, I'd been thinking about that wood knocking and the hurried, heavy footsteps. About the dead body. About being in the middle of nowhere where we could die and no one would find us for days.

Okay, maybe that last part was an exaggeration, but, still. I didn't usually freak out over stuff like this, but I felt a tinge of freak-out lingering on the horizon. If one more thing happened here, I wouldn't be able to contain my urges anymore.

I would freak out.

I turned over in bed and let the scent of bacon tease my taste buds. Someone was making breakfast. They were making *bacon* for breakfast.

This day couldn't be all bad. Not when it started with bacon. Besides, Riley would be arriving soon, and I couldn't wait to see him.

My stomach growled, so I climbed out of bed and got dressed. When I walked into the kitchen area, Nate was at the stove, and he looked as cheerful as ever. He was wearing jeans and a red-and-black flannel shirt. His beard was neatly trimmed, and his hair looked damp, like he'd just gotten out of the shower.

What was the word I'd heard used before to describe his look? Ah, yes, I remembered—*lumbersexual*. That word seemed appropriate here since he was essentially a well-groomed lumberjack.

"Good morning!" he called merrily, glancing over his shoulder from the stove.

"Good morning." I glanced around. "Where's Chad?"

"He ran into town to grab some supplies. He said he'll be back in an hour." He flipped the stove off. "Speaking of which, I'm running to the office today. There's some kind of retirement-fund crisis I have to deal with. People get so bent out of shape over stuff like that—it's like their future depends on it."

This guy could not be for real. I lifted up a quick prayer for anyone who had ever invested money with him. They were going to need all the help they could get.

"I figured you and Chad could handle yourselves. Seamus and Braxton are on their way—"

"Who's Seamus?"

"Oh, sorry. He's someone I brought in to help with roofing. He's a local."

"Good to know."

"Anyway, I did fix a diggity doggone good breakfast for you." He handed me a paper plate full of food. "Yes, that's right. For you. No one ever said I didn't treat my employees right. Drop the mic."

I stared at the bacon and eggs, unsure how to interpret his gesture. "That was nice of you. Thank you."

"It's the least I can do after my embarrassing slip-up yesterday. You know?"

I was about to say "thank you," grateful that we could make amends, when Nate continued.

"You know—when I said onward, ho, and you thought I was referring to—"

My jaw flexed. "I did not think that."

He stared at me and then smiled slowly. "Right."

He said the word with that woodpecker cadence, one that made it clear he thought I was not very bright.

I decided to ignore him and instead I began gulping down the breakfast—including plenty of coffee. It was just that kind of morning. I hadn't finished when Nate grabbed his leather jacket and said goodbye.

As soon as I finished eating, I tossed my plate, put the silverware in the sink, and stepped outside to get a look at this place in the daylight. The air outside felt chilly—probably in the fifties, but the brisk wind that swept across the mountainside made it seem at least ten degrees cooler. Nate had mentioned something yesterday about a cold front coming this way that would make it feel more like December than September. At least the sun shone brightly overhead and the sky looked cloudless beyond the canopy of branches above me.

Maybe I expected things to look less overwhelming with the bright sun illuminating the area.

It didn't. In fact, the darkness last night had concealed a lot of the flaws in the buildings across the street. Seeing them reminded me of how much work we had to get done.

While I waited for Chad, I stepped around the side of the cabin. As I rounded the corner toward the woods, I spotted the stream, trickling over gentle rocks. I sucked in a breath at the pure beauty in front of me. The scene looked exquisite and serene.

As I turned to head back to the cabin, something on the ground caught my eye.

It was a gigantic footprint, right outside my bedroom window. Not a normal footprint, though. Gone were any treads from a tennis shoe or boot. No, it was a bare foot. A big, bulky imprint with knobby toe marks topped off with sharp, pointy claws.

I swallowed hard.

It wasn't Bigfoot. It couldn't be.

But what else would have left a footprint that looked like that?

"I SPENT most of the week doing demolition and trash removal on these cabins." Chad rubbed a wall that had been freshly plastered. "The foundations of these buildings seem solid, and Seamus is going to work on the roofs. Meanwhile, Braxton is slowly working cabin-by-cabin on electric. We're keeping the wood floors, but they'll need to be sanded down . . ."

I tried not to tune him out as he talked about floors, and subcontractors, and roofs. I was itching to get started on these floors. What could be a better way to spend my day than sanding them down? I could actually think of a million things I'd rather be doing. But Chad was counting on me.

"There's also a landscaping crew coming in," Chad said. "The walkways have to be safe. Fences have to be put up around certain areas to keep visitors out. A specialized crew will be working on getting rid of the Ferris wheel."

I grabbed some safety goggles from a tub of supplies we'd hauled inside. "This is a big job, Chad. Bigger than a week."

"I'm trying to conquer this place bite by bite." He gave up on his obsession over the plaster and moved on to examine part of the baseboard. "I can stay longer if I have to. Hey—if those renovators on TV can flip a house in a weekend, I can turn this place around in a week, right? The most important thing is: one, it's safe here, and, two, we get as many cabins as possible ready to be rented."

He sounded nearly frantic. I'd never seen my friend like this. I needed to do whatever I could to calm him down. "I've got the floors covered. I should be able to knock out sanding them all today. Then I'll come in and clean them, so they'll be ready to be sealed. After that, we can work on new doors and windows."

"The window crew is coming later next week."

I nodded. "Great. It sounds like everything is on schedule then."

I thought that would wrap up our conversation and allow me to get started, but Chad was pacing now and staring at his clipboard. I was slightly overwhelmed at all of his jabbering, but I didn't mention it to my friend.

"I've got this covered here, Chad. Really. I have five hours until the rest of the gang arrives. I can do it."

He stared at me a moment and then nodded. "I'm going to check on Braxton and see how the electric is coming. I keep telling Nate he needs to think about overhead lights for the outdoors, especially since people will be here at night."

Chad's brain was still shooting all over the place. I grabbed a mask and raised the handle of the orbital sander, ready to get busy. Except I wasn't. I wanted to talk about the murder and this place's history—really, anything but renovating.

"I still don't know how Nate can afford to do this," I said, trying to sound casual and not obsessive compulsive. But curiosity had always gotten the best of me.

Chad shrugged and randomly began measuring the door-frame. "I don't know this for certain, but I heard some locals have invested in the place. That would explain some things."

My stomach sank. "You mean people have invested in this place instead of, let's say, retirement funds? That sounds risky."

He snapped his measuring tape shut. "People trust Nate with

their money. That's his job. He's got a way of influencing people."

"Good for him." I couldn't imagine it was good for his clients, but I could be wrong. Maybe he was a lot smarter than I gave him credit for.

"So you found a big footprint outside your window, huh?"

Ah hah! I was hoping Chad might give his full attention to my earlier discovery. He'd been so preoccupied with talking to some subs that he'd hardly acknowledged me when I first told him.

"It was right outside of my bedroom window." I shuddered. Based on the placement of the footprint, it was almost like someone had been staring inside at me last night while I slept. The thought wasn't comforting.

"Wood knocking, a figure rushing through the underbrush, and a large footprint." He shook his head, lingering in the doorway a moment. "It's not looking good."

I cut a sharp glance at him, trying to read my friend. "You really don't believe in Bigfoot, do you?"

He shrugged, looking as laidback as ever. "I can't say I do. I can't say I don't. We'll see if that changes over the next week." In his spookiest voice, he added, "They live among us."

I scowled. "Very funny. The next thing you're going to tell me is that Bigfoot murdered the man we found yesterday."

"All I can say is this: the truth is out there."

I plugged in the sander. Maybe it was time for this conversation to be over.

Because no one was going to make a believer out of me. Bigfoot was a myth—and that was all.

I stretched my back muscles as I pulled my goggles off. I'd somehow managed to finish three cabins in five hours. I'd used the orbital sander to strip all the finish off the wood floors, and then a hand held sander to get the edges. Since the cabins were empty and little prep work had to be done, I'd breezed through the job.

But right now, I looked like a grungy mess. A mixture of dirt and powder-like sawdust covered every surface of my skin and hair and clothes. I wished I had time to change or freshen up, but it would be an act in futility since I had more work to do.

Everyone was set to arrive any time now, and I knew they'd have trouble reaching both Chad and me on our cells. I needed some fresh air, and I wanted to see how everything was going up in the Bermuda Triangle. Apparently, a crew had arrived this morning to begin demolition on the Ferris wheel.

I started up the solitary path leading to the park's entrance. In the distance, I spotted the yellow crime scene tape from yesterday. My thoughts went back to the dead body. Had the autopsy already been done? What had Marion found?

We'd been in this general area when Nate had called the police yesterday, I realized. Out of curiosity, I pulled out my phone and raised it in the air.

Still no signal.

I continued to hold it high, desperately searching for a sign of life outside of this old graveyard of an amusement park. Having no contact with the outside world was a bit unnerving, and I didn't like it. At least I had the radio now. Chad had dropped one by as he was supervising tasks throughout the park, just in case I needed to get in touch.

Finally, as I crested the hill, one bar appeared on my screen. Immediately, a message popped onto my screen.

Marion had called me.

My curiosity spiked. Why would she be calling?

I paused, afraid to move for fear I'd go out of range again before calling Marion back.

"Gabby, thanks for the callback," Marion said. "I was hoping I'd hear from you. Listen, while you're in town, I wanted to invite you over for dinner one night. It would be nice to catch up."

Catching up with an old colleague? That sounded perfect. "That's nice of you. I'd love to."

"I hoped you would say that. How about Wednesday evening?"

I had to work on Monday and Thursday, and as long as I met Marion after daytime work hours, I couldn't see where it would be a problem. "As far as I know, I have no plans."

"Wonderful. I'll text you my address. Feel free to bring a friend with you, if you'd like."

"I appreciate that." I paused, trying to find my words before the opportunity slipped by. "By the way, did you do the autopsy yet?"

"As a matter of fact, I did. I found it very interesting. The boy —I call him a boy, but he was twenty-one, and his name was Caleb Kidwell—he was strangled."

"Strangled?" My free hand went to my throat as my muscles tightened. "Really? I wouldn't have guessed that simply by looking at him. Of course, he was wearing a high collared puffy vest, so his throat was concealed."

"Not only that, but he was strangled by hand—by very large hands," she said.

My pulse spiked. The large hands were just a coincidence. They had nothing to do with the very large footprint I'd found outside my window. I might have trouble convincing Chad of that, however.

"It gets stranger," Marion continued. "There was a death at the park nearly twenty years ago. I pulled up the records. This other man was murdered the same way—strangled from behind. Even the size of the hands match."

I SUDDENLY DIDN'T LIKE STANDING STILL on this path in the middle of the woods by myself. My skin rose. What if someone was out there watching me? I shivered, my gaze scanning the trees. Bigfoot figures stared back at me, but I didn't see anyone else.

Chills raced up and down my spine. Two nearly identical murders nearly twenty years apart. One ended up closing down the park, and the other occurred right before the park reopened.

"That's . . . eerie," I finally said to Marion.

"You can say that again. It looks like we could have a copycat killer here in the county. That's a first for this area. When people hear . . . well, no one will be sleeping at night."

"Including me. Thanks for sharing that."

"By the way, I told the chief about you and your work. Told him he could trust you. I consider you one of my colleagues still, whether it's official or not."

"I'm honored."

"I mean it, Gabby. You should also keep your eyes open. I don't know what's going on out there at Mythical Falls, but it doesn't sound good. Be careful."

Her warning sent another round of chills up my spine.

Just as I hung up, I spotted three figures at the top of the hill in the distance. My heart leaped with joy. Riley was here!

It was hard to miss his tall, lean frame as well as his dark hair, blue eyes, and easy smile. He carried himself with confidence but also kindness and compassion. We'd been through so many struggles to get to the point where we were now.

I started toward him, a little skip in my step, until I was close enough to throw my arms around his neck. At his familiar scent —leathery and pleasant—I already felt calmer. "You're here."

"Good to see you too." He chuckled before squeezing tighter.

As I reluctantly stepped back, Clarice pulled me into an exuberant hug and squealed, "Gabby!"

I froze in surprise and awkwardly patted her back. "Clarice . . ."

"What? I thought you greeted everyone so enthusiastically." She blinked, appearing totally sincere in her assessment.

Clarice looked like she'd be more comfortable on a runway during fashion week than here helping us with construction. But, for some reason, she liked working with Chad and me. She was blonde and lithe and loved brand-name clothing. At the moment, she was wearing thong sandals, a long cardigan, and layered necklaces. Sometimes she came across as slightly airheaded, but at heart she was an asset to the team.

"Of course. I'm glad to see all of you." I glanced around, noticing not everyone was here. "Speaking of which: where are Sierra and little Reef?"

"Reef has an ear infection." Chad's earlier excitement was obviously gone, and his voice sounded dull. "She's going to try to come later in the week, if he's feeling better."

I frowned. "Poor little thing."

I loved Reef. He stirred some kind of motherly instinct in me and made me yearn for things that I'd never yearned for before. It was a strange thing, an emotion that somehow bridged the gap for me between youth and being an adult. Though I'd been working for years, I'd always felt like, at heart, I was a teenager.

But the longing for family and stability made me feel like I was ready for the next step in my life—a feeling foreign to me until recently.

Riley rested an arm around my waist and glanced around. "It looks like we have our work cut out for us."

"You don't even know the half of it," I mumbled.

"Listen, I need to check on the Ferris wheel crew. Walk with me." Chad snapped back to the task at hand. "Plus, it will give you all a chance to see more of the place. Gabby and I were cut off yesterday before we finished."

"Cut off by what?" Clarice asked, her eyes widening.

Chad and I exchanged a glance.

"We'll tell you about it later," I finally said. "For now, let's take a tour. We're in for an experience we'll never forget."

We walked toward the Bermuda Triangle. Though I'd seen part of this area, I hadn't gone beyond the entrance, and I wasn't sure what I expected to see here. Lost things, I supposed. Amelia Earhart? Maybe. Ships that had disappeared? Sure. Gold treasure? In my dreams.

What I saw horrified me even more.

There were clowns. Everywhere.

"Gabby?" Riley asked.

He grabbed me before I could run away.

Clowns—creepy clowns—probably made with cement just like the Bigfoots were—had been placed strategically around the area. Behind light poles. Peering around buildings. Sitting on benches.

Their macabre faces also had missing eyes and ears. Wherever I looked, they were watching me. Even the one-eyed ones.

I forced my gaze away. In the distance, I spotted a half-sunken ship, a crashed jet, and a unicorn. Bronze plates around the area shared "facts" about the Bermuda Triangle.

"I hate clowns," I whispered, unable to pull my eyes away from them.

"You do?" Riley said.

I nodded, sweat sprinkled over my forehead. "I always have. I try not to share that with many people. But it's true. I went to a circus one time as a child, and that was all it took. I never wanted to see another clown again for the rest of my life."

"We've known each other all this time, and I had no idea. I guess there's always something new to learn. That's one more thing to love about you. I know you'll surprise me for the rest of my life."

My stomach sloshed with unease. *The rest of my life.*

The fact that Riley and I were planning to spend forever together should make me the happiest person alive. So why did a feeling of impending doom linger in the back of my mind? Ignoring the feeling was easier than facing it head on so, as always, I shoved the thought to the back of my mind.

He took my hand into his and squeezed it. "The clowns won't hurt you. I won't let them."

I smiled, realizing how foolish I sounded. I was nearly thirty years old. I'd seen a million and one crime scenes—most of them gruesome. And clowns creeped me out. *Clowns.*

Seriously, I was above all of this. I had to get a grip and stop letting this place get to me.

I pulled myself together as I noticed everyone waiting for us at the top of the hill. This was no time to show weakness. "Okay, let's go."

As I walked, I tried humming circus music to cheer myself up. It didn't work.

"This is where they put everything weird that didn't fit other places in the park," Chad said, unfazed by the area. "There were bumper cars, a carousel, and a funhouse in this area also."

"You sound like you've been here before, Chad." I tried to block the grotesque figures from my memory and distract myself by nosing into other people's business. It had been an effective method before.

"That's because I have," Chad said, adjusting the Norfolk Tides baseball hat he wore.

I stopped in my tracks. "What?"

He nodded, like I should have known, and kept walking. "I was only ten years old the last time, but I came here with my family every summer. Bigfoot Woods was my favorite part of the park, followed by the Bermuda Triangle. I don't know . . . Area 51 was pretty cool also."

"You learn something new every day . . ."

I paused by the Ferris wheel, and my gaze traveled upward. I imagined the tragic accident that had occurred on it two decades ago. Seeing someone fall to her death would be horrifying . . . and definitely put the park's reputation on the line.

Thank goodness the crew was taking it down this week. The thing was practically a monument to decay and death.

At that moment, a scream cracked the air.

I jerked my gaze toward the woods as my blood went cold. The sound had come from far away, yet fear still rippled through me. Someone was in trouble. Big trouble.

I took a step closer, ready to spring into action, when a strong wind whipped over the landscape.

Something groaned. Something loud. Close. Unsettling.

I looked up just in time to see one of the cars from the Ferris wheel falling toward me.

CHAPTER
SEVEN

RILEY THREW me out of the way. As we both collided with the dirt, the Ferris-wheel car hit the ground beside us with a sickening crash. A nuclear aftershock of dirt and dust billowed out. The air cleared just in time for the car to let out a moan and collapse into several pieces on the ground.

I sucked in a shaky breath. That had been close. Too close.

Chad and Clarice appeared beside us. Based on their wide eyes and gawking expressions, they were just as shaken as we were.

"Are you okay?" Chad asked as he knelt next to me.

I blinked, trying to figure out the correct answer to that question. I didn't feel any overwhelming pain, other than an achy hip and shoulder. That was a good sign. "I think so."

I glanced at Riley, who stretched beside me, rubbing his elbow while he grimaced. He flinched as he pushed himself up and stared at the mangled metal car only two feet from us.

"I'm okay," he muttered. "But what happened?"

Chad raised his head toward the top of the Ferris wheel. "I guess that wind knocked the car off. Maybe the crew didn't leave it secured when they left for lunch. Speaking of which, maybe we should move away from it. Talk about safety hazards."

Riley stood and then helped me to my feet. We both brushed the dirt from our jeans, and I checked the palm of my hands for scrapes. They appeared okay, but I was going to have some nasty bruises in the morning.

I shivered again. That could have been ugly. Really ugly. I thanked God for Riley's quick reflexes.

I had other things to think about at the moment, however. All the excitement over almost dying had distracted me from my original reason for concern.

"Did you hear that scream?" My gaze traveled from person to person. I hadn't imagined it, had I? Somewhere from deep in the heart of these mountains, someone had shrieked with terror.

I remembered the dead body we'd found yesterday, and I knew the sound was nothing to take lightly. I hoped we wouldn't find another dead body out there.

Please, Lord.

"Yeah, I heard it." Chad stared off into the thick landscape of trees.

"Who else is here?" Riley scrunched his eyebrows together, worry sketching his features.

Chad and I exchanged a glance.

Finally, Chad shrugged. "Only Seamus and Braxton. That scream came from a woman."

"Then who . . . ?" Riley started.

"We should probably go check it out," I said. "Someone must have sneaked onto the grounds again. We should make sure everything's okay. Any more accidents and this place will shut down for good."

"I agree that it's a good idea." Chad nodded. "Why don't we split up? I'll go with Clarice. You and Riley go together."

Riley and I started back down toward Bigfoot Woods. I was so excited to see him, but this wasn't the way I'd anticipated this adventure starting. I hadn't even had the chance to tell him yet about the—

"Is that crime scene tape?" Riley's eyebrows furrowed together as he stared in the distance.

I squeezed his hand and frowned. "As a matter of fact, yes. It is."

I gave him an update on what had happened yesterday, including my resolution to stay out of it and let the authorities do their job.

"Without fail, this always happens when you're around." Riley slid a glance toward me and grinned.

"I'm beginning to realize that. Although, in my defense, the past several times I've been around dead bodies, it's been because I was asked to be there to investigate."

"I can't argue with that." He glanced around at the branches as they formed a canopy over us.

I wondered if he thought the same thing I did: it was almost like those trees were reaching for us, like the forest was alive.

"Think of it like Cemetery Island," I told him. "That was even more isolated than this place. At least you don't need a boat to escape this mountain if it comes down to it."

We'd gone undercover at a couples retreat on a fog-entrenched island in the middle of the Chesapeake Bay. It had been an interesting experience, to say the least.

"That's one way to look on the bright side," Riley mumbled.

"After this trip, I think I'll be ready to stick around Norfolk for a while. No more isolated, spooky places. Agreed?"

"Agreed. You've been quite the traveler over the past twelve months or so. Cincinnati, Oklahoma, Cemetery Island, and now here."

"It's been fun, but I miss my routine. I miss getting coffee every morning across the street at The Grounds and staying in touch with all the interesting and strange residents of our apartment complex."

Please don't ask about a wedding date. Please.

Things were going so well. Why ruin it by firming up our plans?

Thankfully, the question didn't come up.

We kept going down the path, farther into the woods and past the mock town where our cabins were located. I hadn't gone this far into the park yet, and it seemed to get darker and darker as we went deeper into the wilderness and farther away from the main hub of Mythical Falls. I tried to tune out all of the Bigfoot figures that seemed to be watching me every time I turned around, and I comforted myself with the realization that they were better than clowns.

As I remembered the scream, I squeezed Riley's hand. What kind of scream had that been? A scream of fear? For help?

It had been a woman—I felt certain about that. Everything had happened so quickly, I'd gotten distracted. I hoped we weren't too late to help.

As we reached the bottom of the incline, I spotted two people in the distance. Both appeared youngish, probably in their early twenties, and they wore swimsuits. Interesting considering how chilly it felt here—it was probably in the low sixties. I imagined the water would be much chillier.

The good news was that they both also appeared to be okay as they giggled in each other's arms. They didn't seem to hear us approaching.

Riley and I exchanged a look before continuing toward them. We'd come this far. I wasn't walking away now. I had to confirm they were all right.

"Excuse me!" I called. "Is everything okay?"

They turned from canoodling, and their eyes widened when they spotted us. As we got closer, my impressions were confirmed. They were younger—probably college age. And they'd apparently been having a romantic rendezvous here.

"It's . . . all good," the boy answered, water dripping from his eyelashes. "Of course."

We stopped in front of them, and I immediately cringed, unable to deny how awkward I felt. They'd obviously thought they were totally alone. They had a blanket set up on the ground, as well as a picnic basket and two bags—hopefully with real clothes inside—resting at the blanket's edge.

"We heard a scream," Riley said, his hands going to his hips.

The girl blushed and stepped away from the boy. She was painfully thin and had blonde hair that looked stringy with dampness. The way she kept averting her gaze made her appear shy.

"That was me," she started. "I'm sorry. Roy jumped from the waterfall, and he didn't come up for a minute."

I looked at the boy, and he shrugged. A touch of mischief stained his dark-brown eyes. He was almost equally as skinny as the girl. I could probably count his ribs if I looked hard enough. His brown hair was a little too long and he looked like he hadn't shaved in a while, though his facial hair was thin and patchy.

The girl cast a bashful glance his way. "It turns out Roy came up behind the waterfall, he ran through the woods and surprised me from behind. I thought it was the Bigfoot Strangler."

"The who?" Riley and I asked at the same time.

"The Bigfoot Strangler. He's a legend around here," Roy jumped in, more mischief flashing in his eyes. "You haven't heard of him?"

"We're not from around here," I said, curious about what Roy would say. I loved a good story . . . usually. However, I had to live here for the next week, so I needed to be careful what kind of thoughts I allowed into my head.

"He's like a phantom, and he wreaks havoc in these woods," Roy said. "He's the reason this place closed so many years ago. He doesn't like people being on his property. These woods were his long before humans came and took over. I heard he even arranged that Ferris wheel accident where the girl died."

I let out a small sigh. I didn't believe in phantoms or ghosts or even Bigfoot. But I could understand why people got freaked out, especially with so many deaths in such a short amount of time. Plus, local folklore had a way of being passed down through generations. Throw in a few supposed "eye witness" accounts, and new family stories were launched.

"I'm surprised you're here if this phantom frightens you so much," I finally said, watching their reactions carefully.

"This place is a locals' favorite . . ." Roy snaked his arm around his girlfriend's waist.

Make-Out Point was more like it. But, at his words, I glanced around. There was something halfway magical about the area. A gentle waterfall trickled down the mountainside in the background. Mist rose up all around, creating the illusion of enchantment. This must be Mythical Falls. In the distance, I saw a weathered Nessie's head rising from the placid waters farther away from the rapids.

Several wooden cutouts remained, the kinds with face holes where people could pose as their favorite mythical creature.

The signs were faded now, but I easily imagined families posing there in days of late. I imagined cotton candy and popcorn and old Polaroid photos. I pictured lifelong memories.

The kind I'd longed for as a child. My dad had been an alcoholic, though, and my upbringing had been anything but ideal.

Just then my radio crackled.

"Everything okay down there?" Chad asked.

"Yes, it's fine. Just a misunderstanding."

"Then come back up here. I found something you'll want to see!"

Riley and I glanced at each other. What now?

CHAPTER
EIGHT

WE FOUND Chad in the crossroads of the Pharaoh's Tomb and Area 51. I quickly scanned the area as I approached and spotted several old rides. None of them seemed as hazardous as the Ferris wheel.

Thank goodness.

One looked like a spider, but all of the cars were gone. Another was shaped like a flattened pinwheel. Names like "Alien Encounter" and "Space Sensations" welcomed us.

Chad stood at the edge of the area, near the woods that separated each "land." He called us over with a wave offset by tense shoulders and a rigid jaw line. Something was wrong.

Again.

"What's going on?" I braced myself for the worst.

"Look what I found." Chad nodded toward the ground.

Cans of gasoline had been stashed behind a huge, gray boulder. The cans were metal and appeared new, not like something that had been left here two decades ago. They showed no rust or any other signs of age.

"Are they full?" I asked.

"They are. I'm wondering if someone abandoned them here."

Chad locked gazes with me. "If they got interrupted before they could do some damage."

"You think someone was going to burn this place down?" I clarified. I was usually the one coming up with the outlandish theories. Instead Chad had gone from zero to sixty in 5.2.

He wobbled his head back and forth a moment, as if contemplating his answer. "I suppose that's what I'm saying. More directly: What if the guy we found dead yesterday was about to light this place on fire but someone killed him before he could do it?"

My eyes widened at his theory. "Who would do that?"

Chad shrugged again. "Someone who didn't want this place to be destroyed."

I'd have to chew on that theory for a moment. "You really think Caleb Kidwell left this here?"

"Caleb Kidwell?"

"He's the boy who died."

Chad shot me a confused glance, but he didn't ask how I knew his name. Instead, he nodded toward the ground. "There was a leather glove beside him. That one looks like a match."

I glanced down and examined it more closely. "You're right. That appears to match the one found at the death scene."

"And, if this kid—Caleb, you said—parked on the other side of the gate, the area where his body was found would be dead center between the fence and these gasoline cans. I wonder if he was walking back to his vehicle when someone caught him."

I frowned as I thought it all through. "It just doesn't make sense why someone would kill him, though. The only person who might kill him in order to save the park would be—" I stopped myself before I said Nate's name.

Chad sensed exactly where I was going with my train of thoughts, though. "Nate would never do this."

I raised my hands. "I didn't say he would."

He gave me a pointed look. "You almost did."

"I'm just saying that if your theory is right, then Nate is the only one with motive—albeit it would be the *extreme* motive of trying to protect his land from further vandalism. Though that seems like a stretch, I can't think of anyone else who fits the bill."

"I don't know if I'd take it that far. Besides, he would have done a better job hiding the body."

"I suppose."

"I'm sure there are other people out there who have motive, but there's so little we know at this point. Finding out that information will take a lot of time and effort, and we didn't come here to figure out a murder. We came here to restore this place."

I straightened and nodded. He was right. I had to stay focused. "Aye aye, sir. We should call the police and then get back to work."

That night, after working our rears off all day, we went to meet Nate for dinner at a place called Yuck Yuck's. The restaurant's name itself was enough to want to keep me away, but I had to admit that I was thrilled to be off the Mythical Falls property for a little while.

The other part of me was thrilled to go into town because, as much as I told myself that I was staying out of this investigation, I secretly wanted answers. The need was a part of the fiber of my being, if you wanted to be dramatic about it.

I liked answers. I didn't like for things to be unfinished. The hectic schedule we had to get everything done at the up-and-coming resort left me little time to indulge in my normal nosiness. Since we'd arrived, my curiosity had been exploding like a volcano.

Today's events had only added to my nosiness. After I'd nearly been killed, Chad had contacted the Ferris wheel demolition crew, and the supervisor had claimed they hadn't left the contraption—their words, not mine—unsecured, and the old theme park was cursed.

Comforting.

At the moment, I glanced around Yuck Yuck's. The inside of the place was just like someone might imagine: dirty floors, aged tables, walls crammed full of local nostalgia; and blinking signs in the window. The smell of fried foods and cigarettes stained the air—even though no one was smoking inside. All the patrons seemed to be locals, based on the looks they shot us—curiosity, distrust, wariness of outsiders. Many of them appeared to be hunters, I guessed, looking at their camo and listening to the stories they told about bucks and tree stands.

Yuck Yuck's was the only eating establishment I'd seen within ten miles of Mythical Falls. There were also gas pumps out front, and, in a separate but attached building, one could pick up beer, hand soap, or greeting cards. The joint was located on the outskirts of Whitehurst, a small college town.

My crew sat away from the bar area, in a corner where we ordered some pizzas and soda. Seamus had joined us. He was probably in his late twenties. He'd grown up around here and had been one of the people laid off from the mines when they closed. He was on the shorter side with a prematurely receding hairline, crooked teeth, and a quiet demeanor.

Several people called hello to Nate when he walked inside, and he gave a few people high fives as he made his way from the bar toward our table. He wore a loose tie, which made it appear he'd just come from work. His office was in Whitehurst, from what I'd gathered. He must have stopped by his house and changed clothes after leaving Mythical Falls this morning.

"So I heard we had some more excitement today." Nate's eyes looked animated with life as he squeezed around the table. "What's going on?"

Chad filled him in on everything that happened up until the point the police arrived—including the Ferris wheel incident, the scream, and the glove. Nate's eyes widened with each new detail.

"Creepy," he muttered, all surfer/skier like.

"The police confirmed that the glove matched the one found by Caleb," I filled in. "They're looking into the theory that he was trying to put the whole place up in flames before he was murdered."

"No way. I can't believe someone would do that. Maybe he was a pyro." Nate's eyes widened as he made the motion of lighting a lighter.

I shifted as I remembered my earlier theory. "You didn't know him, did you?"

His eyes got wider—maybe a little too wide. "Me? The dead guy? No way. Why would I know him?"

"Just wondered if he had a personal vendetta against you."

"Personal vendetta." He did the trademark laugh. "That's crazy. Why would anyone hate me?"

Why would anyone hate him? *Let me count the ways.* 1. His laugh. 2. His overuse of adjectives. 3. Because he looked at women like they were meat.

The list could go on and on.

"No, this is random," Nate said. "I sure hope the police figure things out."

"Me too."

Nate wouldn't do something like this in order to stop someone from destroying the park . . . right? In a fit of rage and panic, he wouldn't have strangled someone who threatened his future . . . would he? He didn't appear to have abnormally large hands.

No, I couldn't think like that. Nate would have to be seriously mentally off to do something like that.

Chad gave me another pointed look, and before I could try to deny assumptions, our pizza came. A waitress named Bertha— no joke—brought it. She looked nothing like a Bertha, though. She was thin, pretty, and blonde—and she gave a special wink to Nate. He winked back. "Thanks, Sweetheart."

I cleared my throat, unable to get the thought of Nate as the killer out of my mind. I had to mix things up before I said something I shouldn't. "You know, I'm going to run to the restroom before we eat."

"Sure thing." Nate slid out so I could escape for a moment.

A woman wearing a tight outfit was leaning over a mirror when I stepped inside. She was probably my age, a brunette, and she gave off the "single" vibe. She did a double take when she spotted me.

"Now there's a new face," she muttered.

I could only assume she was talking about me. "Where I'm from, it's unusual to run into someone I know while I'm out and about. It sounds like it's unusual to run into someone you don't know around here."

She chuckled. "You got that right, Sweetie. Name's Mavis Wells."

"Gabby St. Claire." I took a place beside her at the mirror. Going into the dingy stall at this point seemed too awkward, because I was certain she would keep talking to me, even if I did.

"You part of Nate's crew?" She reapplied some bright-pink lipstick.

"How'd you know?"

"Who else would you be?" She chuckled, as if the answer had been a given. "How are things going out there at Mythical Falls?"

I contemplated my answer and decided it was better not to say too much. "Okay. We're just getting started."

"I see."

I shifted, realizing this would be a good opportunity to get more information on Mythical Falls and everything happening there. Small town local with a gift for gab and prior knowledge of what was going on? Check, check, and check.

"You ever been out there?" I asked.

She put the top back on her lipstick and puckered her lips together. "Many times. It was a great place back in the day. I hope Nate makes something of it again. It's a shame to see it just sitting there for all these years. I didn't think Nate would ever actually do something with the land. I figured he'd sell it to Scotty Stephens."

"Scotty Stephens?" I made myself busy by examining a curly red hair.

She nodded. "He's been wanting to buy the place for years. He wanted to start a retirement community, kind of like the ones they have down in Florida."

That was unexpected. "I'm sure there are plenty of other pieces of property in this area, right? I mean, I drove past miles and miles of nothing to get here."

She shrugged, puckering her glossy lips for the mirror. "I suppose. But he wants Mythical Falls."

"Nate wouldn't sell, huh?"

"Nope. The place was his great uncle's. He couldn't let it go. His great uncle Jebidiah was like a dad to him, so I guess the land has sentimental value."

"I see." I hadn't realized that aspect of this. Why hadn't anyone mentioned it? Why hadn't *Nate* brought Scotty Stephens up?

"When Scotty heard that Nate was trying to fix the place up, he was madder than a hornet. Apparently he'd offered millions of dollars, but Nate always said no."

"Isn't that interesting. Does this Scotty Stephens live around here?"

"Oh, yes. He has a home here but also in Beckley. He made a fortune in the mining industry before it went bust."

Could this Scotty Stephens be the first real person I'd heard about who had a real motive? Quite possibly. Well, other than Nate.

What if this Scotty guy was willing to kill to get his hands on this property?

It was something worth looking into . . . if I wanted to get involved. Which, of course, I didn't.

In theory, at least.

CHAPTER
NINE

RILEY and I rode back to Mythical Falls together. I hadn't had a chance to talk to Nate yet about Scotty Stephens, but I hoped that opportunity would come up soon. I didn't like being kept in the dark by someone I was supposed to be helping. Trust was a delicate thing, easily damaged and slowly repaired.

My life was living proof of that.

We climbed into my Honda, but I let Riley drive. I'd saved a long time to buy this car, and I couldn't be more thrilled. It felt good when my hard work paid off and I could buy the vehicle debt-free.

Before I could even clip my seatbelt in place, my phone rang.

"Who could this be?" I glanced at the screen, pleasantly surprised when I recognized the number. "It's Marion."

"Marion?"

"I'll explain in a moment." I put the phone to my ear and answered.

"Gabby, I'm so glad I caught you. I was afraid you'd be out of range. Is this a bad time?"

I stared at the small town of Whitehurst as we breezed past. The whole place was only one block so by the time I looked, it was gone, and woods surrounded us instead. "We're just leaving Yuck Yuck's."

Marion chuckled. "That place is a fixture around here. You've got to go there at least once for a slice of pizza and a slice of life. Did you try the Appalachian Oysters?"

"Are they anything like Rocky Mountain Oysters?"

"Similar."

"Then no. And I won't."

She chuckled again. "Of course, that's not why I called. I had something to run past you."

"Go for it."

Riley grabbed my hand. It was our routine when we rode together, and if he hadn't done it, I would have been worried. It was such a simple gesture yet it seemed to speak volumes.

"I was talking with Caleb Kidwell's family," Marion said. "His parents want to hire someone to look into what happened, to be a second set of eyes and corroborate what the police find out. The family has money, and they're willing to pay. I wondered if you'd be interested."

"Me? Interested in an investigation?" I nibbled on my bottom lip. Everything in me wanted to scream, "Yes! Yes, of course I'm interested!" But I did have other obligations while I was here, and I needed to be wise and keep that in mind.

Riley shot me a look, which seemed to reaffirm my priorities. I'd promised Chad I'd help. I couldn't back out on him now.

"I understand they'd pay you—probably pretty well," Marion continued.

I frowned and looked away from Riley, out the window at the darkness outside. "I want to help. I do. But I'm not sure if I'll have time. My schedule is pretty packed."

"Would you at least think about it? It would mean a lot to the family."

Think about it? Great idea. There was no harm in *thinking* about something. "I'll do that. You can give them my number. You know—just in case."

"Wonderful. I'll do that. And I'll see you on Wednesday."

I hung up and sat in silence a moment, my thoughts turning over in my head. The desire to investigate clashed with the desire to help Chad. Fix up an old theme park? Or find a murderer and help a family get closure?

I obviously knew what my first choice was. But my mom used to tell me that I was only as good as my word. And as someone who had trust issues, it was important to me that people knew I was responsible.

"So . . . ?" Riley asked.

I gave him a quick update on everything, ending with the bathroom conversation and my phone call with Marion. I finished just as we pulled into Mythical Falls. Riley put the car in park behind one of the old prospector cabins.

Now that Clarice was here, she and I would have our own place to stay while the guys bunked next door. However, at the moment, the rest of the gang was out at a campfire not far from the cabins.

Over pizza, everyone had decided to have a campfire tonight, which honestly seemed like a terrible plan after everything that had happened. But maybe I was overreacting because no one else thought it was a bad idea, as long as we all stuck close. Who was I to argue?

"Let me grab my jacket before we meet everyone," I told Riley.

I felt his presence behind me as I unlocked my cabin and stepped inside. He lingered by the door as I grabbed a heavier jacket than the parka I had. It was downright cold right now, despite being September.

Riley stayed at the door, facing me, as I approached.

"You want to get involved," Riley said, putting his hands on my waist and pulling me closer. "I know you do."

I closed my eyes for a moment and relished the warmth that radiated from him. I found strength simply in the fact that he was here, and that he was back in my life. I only wished the past didn't constantly batter me and play with my psyche.

"I do. I do want to know what happened," I admitted. "But Chad is counting on me."

"Maybe you can figure out a way to squeeze an investigation in somehow," Riley said. "If anyone can do it, it's you."

"Investigating to me is like breathing for most people."

"I can't argue with that."

"At least that conversation with the woman in the bathroom takes your suspicions off Nate," Riley said. "You could see the hair on Chad's neck standing up when you suggested his friend might be guilty earlier."

I shrugged, clearly remembering the moment. "It wasn't personal. I was being objective, something that Chad is not."

Riley shifted and peered at me with squinted eyes. "You really think Nate could be guilty?"

"There's really so much I don't know. I'm just getting started." I blanched. "I mean, I'm not getting started. But if I *were* just getting started, then I'd really just be scratching the surface of all this. You know what I mean?"

Riley smiled. "I know you. You're going to get involved."

Boy did I ever want to. But . . . "I came here to do a job for Chad, not to investigate."

"Well, if we all continue to be in danger, you may not have any choice but to investigate. Otherwise, all this will be for naught."

"Good point," I told him, another ripple of excitement rushing through me.

"I'm glad we can work on this together," Riley said. "I know we've both been busy over the past couple of months as we've tried to settle into a routine again."

It was true. I'd been getting the hang of my new job with Grayson Technologies. He'd been working for a new branch of his law firm. In between times, I'd been trying to help out with Reef and doing side jobs for Chad. It was a busy, full season. But

Riley and I saw each other as often as possible. It was easy since we lived across the hall from each other.

"It will be fun to work together." I wrapped my arms around his neck. "It will be like old times. We haven't had an adventure together—"

"In a few months. It really hasn't been that long."

I shrugged. He told the truth. And I should be grateful that life had been rather boring lately. But I was programmed to want adventure, and I'd been itching for another mystery to tackle. But boring meant uneventful and without drama or heartache. There was a lot to be said for that. It was like I was being pulled in two different directions.

"Either way, this will be fun," I continued. "The mountains are beautiful, the old theme park is fascinating, and we're together. What more could we ask for?"

"Sounds like famous last words to me."

I grinned. "They very well could be."

Fifteen minutes into our time around the campfire, I found a moment to chat with Nate. Chad and Riley were conducting a snipe hunt with Clarice—remaining close, of course. It was only smart with everything that had happened around here in the past couple of days.

Nate had decided to stay by the fire, and he looked particularly pensive and quiet. Maybe all the alcohol he'd consumed at Yuck Yuck's had finally worn off. Maybe he had something on his mind. I had no idea.

I moved in for the kill—um . . . . bad thought choice. I approached him with my questions. "So, I wasn't aware that this place used to be your great uncle's," I started, trying to sound casual.

"Really? I didn't mention it? That's weird. I just assumed I'd mentioned it. Or that Chad had mentioned it. How do you think I afforded this place? Easy. I didn't. He left it to me."

"When did he do that?" I plunged my stick into the fire and tousled the flames.

"Three years ago. I wasn't ready to take the plunge at that time, though."

"I see." I continued to twirl my stick, watching flecks of fire race through the air. "Were there other people who wanted to buy the land?"

"Oh yeah. One in particular. Scotty Stephens." He rolled his eyes.

"Did you mention him to the police?"

Nate drew his thick eyebrows together and looked hopelessly confused. "Why would I do that?"

"There was a murder here. He might be the prime suspect."

"Nooooo . . ." He said the word with the same cadence as his woodpecker laugh. "He might be a shark, but why would he kill?"

"To shut this place down? To prevent you from opening so you'll sell to him?" Wasn't it obvious?

"He wouldn't do that."

"I heard he was pretty nasty. You might be surprised at what some people might do. People you least suspect."

He shrugged. "I guess I'll mention him to the police then. But I don't think he did any of this. Someone with that much money doesn't need to kill."

Before I could dwell on the thought too much, I heard the sound of someone—multiple someones—rushing through the woods. Quick footsteps, rustling underbrush, frantic words.

Fear clutched my heart. What had happened out there in those woods?

The next instant, Chad, Riley and Clarice appeared through the woods. Chad was laughing hysterically while Clarice scowled.

"Snipe hunting is so stupid," she muttered before looking at me. "You could have told me."

I shrugged. "It's a rite of passage. I'm sorry."

Clarice scowled again. "I'll get you all back. If it's the last thing I do."

Her words were supposed to be funny. But something about them caused me to stiffen.

What if this all was just one big prank? Or what if it was revenge?

There were so many possibilities that my head wanted to explode.

RILEY and I met the next morning to read our Bibles and pray together. It was Sunday, and normally we'd go to church. Since we were here, we'd decided to have a little mini service of our own. We'd invited Chad and Clarice, but both had declined.

After breakfast, Chad handed out orders. I was in charge of sealing the floors, Riley was helping Braxton with electricity, and Nate and Clarice would be working together on plastering and sanding the walls.

I worked steadily applying sealant, and the cabins looked amazingly better by the time I finished them. Despite my progress, I was more than happy when Chad called me on the walkie-talkie at lunchtime.

"Gabby, you need a break?"

I paused. "Sure. I'm almost done."

"Great. Could you go check on the landscaping crew? I'm tied up here at the other cabins helping Brax with electrical. Just make sure the crew is running on schedule. I have to stay on top of people if I want this job done on time."

"Sure thing." I put down the long-handled brush and arched my back. I was still sore from my near collision with the Ferris-wheel car yesterday. Every inch of my body seemed to remind me of my brush with death.

"Feel free to take the ATV."

Nate had brought the vehicle this morning to help us get around. But I decided to walk.

I wandered up the path, past the creepy Bermuda Triangle, and found a crew of four workers removing random pieces of wood and siding and any other litter in the area. Another three people worked on cutting back the branches and underbrush from around the buildings.

I had to admit that in just the short amount of time we'd been here, the differences were pretty dramatic. A lot of the rubble was gone. Random vegetation had been wacked. It was amazing what teamwork could do.

One of the crew members looked up as I approached. The man was tall, thin, and had a brittle-looking, brown-and-gray beard that came all the way down to his chest.

"I'm Gabby. Are you in charge of this crew?"

He nodded. "I'm Bill, part owner of the Brilliant Brunke Brothers Landscaping."

"The Brilliant Brunke Brothers?" I repeated, intrigued by the name.

He nodded, all business. "That's right. I'm Bill, and these are my brothers Phil, Will, Gill, Hill, Dill, and Quill."

There was so much I wanted to say about their names. Like, *so*, so much. But I remained quiet.

"My mom had quite the sense of humor," Bill said, resting his hand on the hammer at his tool belt. "Or she wanted to make us miserable for the rest of our lives."

I chuckled. "It sounds like it."

I surveyed the group quickly, and it hit me that this merry unit was a little like the seven dwarfs—only they weren't all short and instead appeared to be in various shapes and sizes. However, they did whistle as they worked, and they each had beards.

I decided that Bill must have taken on the role of Doc, the fearless leader of the group. I wondered which ones were Grumpy, Happy, and Sleepy. Sneezy, however, had always been my favorite.

As if right on cue, one of the brothers sneezed—a loud, juicy-sounding sneeze.

Another brother scowled. "Turn your head. Didn't Mama teach you anything?"

That brother was Grumpy, I decided.

"He just made my job easier," another brother said. "He blew half of my leaves right into the pile."

Happy, I realized.

This crew was going to be a lot of fun. And I needed some fun.

"Chad sent me here to check on your progress," I said. "How are things going?"

"Can't complain. We're making good time, and things weren't in as bad of shape as I thought they might be. Really, it's mostly surface stuff that we're working on here. I think we can finish up by the end of the week."

"Great news. Anything you need?"

"I think we're good, as long as Nate agrees to stick with only a few areas of the park," Bill said. "I had to convince him not to touch the Pharaoh's Tomb area yet. It's just too much for our skeleton crew here. It's best to focus on one section at a time."

"I'm prone to agree." Thank goodness, Nate was listening to someone.

He stepped back and rubbed his beard. "It's hard to believe this place is opening again."

I bobbed my head up and down, trying to get my mind to slow down. It churned with everything that needed to be done, telling me I didn't have time to talk or chat. However, how would I ever get any answers to the questions that haunted me if I didn't ask any questions? "You're not the first person who's said that."

He continued rubbing his beard. "I can imagine. I'm glad it's opening, though. This area needs something like this. I think it will be good for morale."

"You're one of the first people I've heard say that. Did you come here as a child also? It seems like everyone in this area did."

He nodded. "Yup. As a matter of fact I did. My wife was actually here on the day they found the dead body. The one that closed the park down."

I frowned. "I can't imagine what that would have been like."

"She said it was pandemonium, that's for sure. It started as a whisper among the crowds about another possible death. But when the police came, everyone knew that something had happened. Something bad. Eventually rumors began to surface. Everyone was too scared to come back after that."

I licked my lips, the questions charging out of my mouth like they had a mind of their own. "Were there ever any theories about what happened? Who the so-called Bigfoot Strangler was?"

He shrugged before picking up a stray brick at his feet and tossing it into a wheelbarrow. "There were all kinds of theories and ideas that were thrown out. Most of them didn't make any sense. Some people honestly believed that Bigfoot had gotten them. Lots of locals think he's real. Some people even claim to have seen him here in these woods."

I studied the man carefully. He seemed like he was down-to-earth enough to give a reasonable answer. "What did you think?"

He kicked his feet through the thick weeds, trying to find more trash. "I think someone got revenge on Henry."

"Henry? Was that the name of the man who was strangled?"

He nodded, pausing from his search. "Yes. Henry McClain. This is a small town. Most of the locals know each other. But yeah, I went to church with Henry."

Henry McClain. I stored the name in the back of my mind.

"What a tragic loss."

"Yup. It really was. Henry was a super-nice guy. I don't think he had any enemies, for that matter. The thought that someone would do something like this to him . . ." He shook his head as if he still couldn't believe it twenty years later.

I shifted, not ready to get back to work yet. "Certainly people around town talk. They had to have ideas about what happened —theories that didn't involve a Sasquatch."

He shrugged, grabbed the hammer from his tool belt, and began pounding away at a large, rosebush-sized weed from a crack in the sidewalk. His brothers did the same around him, all working together with ease.

"I suppose they did," he said, his breathing coming heavier. "Some people thought it was Scotty Stephens."

Scotty Stephens. That was the second time the man's name had come up.

"I thought Mr. Stephens only surfaced over the past couple of years," I mused aloud.

Bill shook his head. "No. He's been around these here parts for a long time, wanting to buy this property. He's a powerful man, though. Not many people want to ruffle his feathers. He funds a lot of things in this town."

"Why would he have killed Henry, though?"

His eyes darkened. "Well, there was this other rumor too . . ."

My ears perked. "What kind of rumor?"

"Some people believe that Scotty hired Henry to sabotage the park and close it down. He thought the owner would sell if the park had enough problems."

"So people believe that Henry sabotaged the Ferris wheel and perhaps did other things around the park. That he was paid to do the job, but then something went terribly wrong?"

Bill nodded. "That's the rumor. Some people think that Henry started feeling guilty and threatened to talk. That's why Scotty Stephens had to kill him."

"Was there any evidence to back any of this up?"

"I can't confirm this, but I heard that ten thousand dollars showed up in Henry's account two weeks before he died. Sounds like motive to me."

CHAPTER
ELEVEN

"I NEED you to start working on the old shops across from our cabins," Chad told me after lunch.

"I thought they were a part of the long-range plan," I said.

"They were, but Nate changed his mind. He thinks they could be a safety hazard since their location is so close to the rentals. He wants them cleared out."

I stared at Chad, not saying anything but wanting to argue the merits against this.

Chad raised his hands, obviously reading my thoughts. "I know. I think the same thing—we don't have time for this. But Nate is the one paying us to get the job done, so I have to let him call the shots. Clarice is going to help you."

The task would be much more pleasant if I had a good attitude, so I needed to suck it up. With that thought, I nodded like a good, little employee. "Great. I'll get to work then."

"I'll send Clarice over." Chad gave me a rundown on everything that needed to be done.

I tried to focus on his instructions instead of dwelling on the bombshell that the Brunke brothers had dropped on me. Why wasn't Nate telling me any of this? About Henry? About the mysterious money he'd come into? About Scotty Stephens' million-dollar offer?

Those were my questions. This seemed like information he might want to share, but he had a knack for leaving out important details.

Was that because Nate was somehow guilty?

I doubted it. He probably just didn't want to scare us off. But I stored that information in the back of my mind, just in case it was useful later.

The mystery and intrigue around this whole situation deepened.

After Chad left, I stared at the old ghost town and frowned. I remembered what Nate said about raccoons. And mice.

I'd seen worse. I'd cleaned worse. But that didn't mean I was looking forward to this.

I grabbed the supplies I needed from Chad's van—formerly my van—and started across the street. I opened a lopsided wooden door and stepped into what probably used to be an arcade. Old video games were turned sideways on the floor, like defeated toy soldiers after a battle. Abandoned prizes—stuffed animals and dolls mostly—lay in piles like a mass grave.

A chill ran up my spine.

Thankfully, huge windows at the front of the place allowed plenty of sunlight to get in. That was my only comfort at the moment.

I pulled on my safety gear—the place was full of dust and probably animal waste, so I needed to protect my lungs and eyes. Then I grabbed my work gloves and a whole box of industrial strength garbage bags. I had a feeling I'd fill all of them.

"I'm here!" Clarice announced, entering the room with a flair. She raised one hand above her head and held the other one down low, like an ice skater might do at the end of a sequence.

"Don't you look cheerful," I muttered.

She bounced toward me. "I am. I just had the best morning. Nate is incredible, isn't he?"

I thought about everything he'd neglected to tell me and had trouble agreeing. Instead, I said, "I'm glad you like him."

"And he's so handsome also," she continued, pulling on her own gloves with a dreamy look in her eyes.

I picked up a pile of stuffed animals, stifling a scream as a spider darted across the floor. "It sounds like you're hitting it off."

"I just can't believe he's single."

I did my best not to roll my eyes. Just because I thought Nate was a sexist pig didn't mean that some women wouldn't find that attractive. Clarice had bad taste in men. That had been clear since I first met her.

But I had no room to talk. At one time, I'd also had terrible taste in men. Thankfully I'd come to my senses.

"So, what do you want me to do?" Clarice pulled her goggles down over her perfectly painted eyelids. If you wanted your makeup done, Clarice was just the person to go to. Ms. Priss. That's what I'd thought of her as at one time.

I stared at the carnage before me. "We've got to dispose of all these prizes. Once all of this is cleared, I'll find out what Nate wants to do with these games. He could probably sell them at auction for a pretty penny."

She stopped by Pac-Man and jiggled one of the controls. "This is so rad. I mean, can you imagine the fun that people had here at one time?"

I'd actually imagined that several times. "I'm sure it was quite the place to be."

"I think restoring things is so cool. I mean, not only is it good for the environment, but to see something that was dead come back to life? That's awesome!"

Her words struck a chord with me. *Seeing something dead come back to life.* There was something beautiful about that, and I wasn't just referring to old amusement parks, but also relationships and . . . lives. I'd gone through a period of feeling dead, but God had worked me through it.

Now I just needed to work through my fears about my future with Riley, and maybe I'd be back on track.

As if Clarice could read my thoughts, she asked, "So when are you and Riley going to set a date? We're all anxiously waiting for the announcement. I'm trying to be patient, but it's not one of my strong suits."

She billowed open a black bag and began shoving old balls into it.

That was the question of the hour. "I'm not sure yet."

"What's the hold up?"

She'd never been shy about asking questions. "It's complicated."

"Isn't love always?"

I shrugged. "I don't know. Is it? Or is it supposed to be easy?"

"Most things in life are complicated. They can seem simple at first, but—it's like Nate said—things have layers to them. Kind of like an onion." Her voice sounded airy and dramatic, like she was sharing an ancient secret of the earth that no one else knew.

Nate had been waxing philosophical with Clarice? Interesting. "You're right. Life has layers. This place has layers. Layers of dust, dolls, mouse poop, and rotting wood."

"You're changing the subject. So, really—what's holding you back?"

I narrowed my eyes, though she probably couldn't see them beneath my glasses. Instead, I stuffed some dolls into the bag with more force than necessary. "I don't know. Life has been busy."

"Not that busy."

She didn't give up, did she? "Good things in my life have a tendency to get taken away," I finally said, surprised at my honesty. "Every time I get my hopes up, that seems to signal to something in the cosmos that it's time for another tragedy in my life. I don't want that to happen again."

"You're superstitious? I never took you for the type."

I grunted before realizing I was squeezing a doll's neck as if recreating the Bigfoot Strangler's first murder. "I'm not superstitious."

"You sure sound like it. What happened to all that trust in God you're always talking about?"

Ouch! "I do trust in God."

"Doesn't sound like it to me. Doesn't trust mean having faith that, whatever happens, God is in control?"

"Well . . . yes." Was Clarice doing a Bible lesson with me? What was the world coming to? She didn't even go to church except when I begged her to come with me. And this morning when I'd invited her to read Scripture with Riley and me . . . she'd looked at me like one of those clowns in the Bermuda Triangle.

"Then you have to trust God that He's not out to get you."

"I never said that." However, I *had* thought it. Was Clarice way more insightful than I'd given her credit for?

Clarice frowned at the ratty teddy bear in her hands. "It's an easy assumption to make, especially when things have happened to you . . . like things have happened to us."

Both Clarice and I had been abducted by Scum, a notorious serial killer. Nothing bonded two people like facing death together. We'd always have that connection.

"Enough about Riley and me. I want to hear more about you and Nate."

"You're changing the subject," Clarice said in a singsongy voice.

I shrugged. "Maybe I am."

"Gabby, I know you love Riley. That was obvious when Scum . . ."

I grimaced as memories of the ordeal came back to me. At that time, I wasn't sure I would ever have Riley back or if he'd ever wake up from the coma he was in after being shot in the head. He had woken up, but that had only been the beginning of a very long journey that included us breaking up. I'd briefly dated someone else. I'd gotten a new job and given up control of my company. Riley had moved away. He'd come back. We'd accidentally gotten married.

Life was a rollercoaster sometimes.

"Of course, I love Riley," I finally said.

"Well, isn't that all that matters?"

She spoke with more wisdom than I'd given her credit for. "When it comes down to it, then, I suppose, yes. But it's like being burned when you're cooking. It happens once—you say oops. It happens twice—it seems like bad luck. It happens three times—you expect it the next time."

"I get what you're saying." She nodded, moving on to picking up some plastic army figures. "I just want to see you happy."

"I'm happy—and I just don't want to ruin that happiness."

She frowned at me from beneath her mask. I didn't have to see her lips. I knew Clarice well enough. "You're confusing."

"Tell me about it."

"Well, I'm glad Riley has been patient."

I couldn't argue that point. I was sure it would be easy for him to walk away. We'd had about three weeks of bliss after we'd gotten back together. What had triggered these feelings of fear since then?

I thought back on it. Was it the fact that he was settling in at another law office? His practice was where he'd been shot, after all.

Maybe.

Or maybe it was because two of my friends from church— friends I'd thought were solid—had ended up announcing they were getting divorced.

If divorce and breakups could happen to them, they could happen to anyone, right? Who was I to think I was above all of it.

We stuffed the last of the prizes into the bags, carried them to a dumpster outside, and then stepped back into the building.

The change was remarkable, and I could actually see the room as it used to be.

There was a desk in the corner where a clerk had worked at one time. I walked over and stood behind it. With some work, this could be a great cabin one day or maybe an activity center, depending on how Nate wanted to proceed with things.

"I can totally see myself coming here." Clarice pulled her mask down and did a little twirl. "It would be so much fun with my college girlfriends."

"I'm glad you like it."

I glanced over to an old tube TV that sat in the corner. Was that where the clerk watched security cameras? I would need to take that to a special recycling center to dispose of it.

I put my hands on the wood countertop and nodded. "I think we're done in here, for the most part. Chad wants us to clear this area out and then scrub it down. If I remember correctly, next door was the area where kids could mine for gold and gemstones. I can only imagine what it will look like."

"Gemstones?" Clarice raised her eyebrows. "Maybe we'll find something. A nice big rock we can put on our fingers."

"Good luck with that. I did read some of the signs out front. Apparently, a man did find a huge diamond in West Virginia once. I think it's called the Punch Jones Diamond. I can't remember the details, but it was something like thirty-four carats. At first he thought it was quartz, and he put it in a cigar box for fourteen years."

She reached into her pocket. "Kind of like this one?"

She threw a rock toward me. I caught it and looked at it a moment. "Looks like quartz."

"Well, it's all yours. Tell Riley to make you a pretty ring out of it. I found it while we were snipe hunting, and I thought it looked interesting."

I gave her a half-dirty, half-silly look and shoved the stone in my pocket. It would be a good keepsake, if nothing else. "We better get busy then. I'd hate to put Natey the Greaty behind schedule."

Natey the Greaty? I resisted the urge to make a gagging sound.

As I took a step away, a noise caught my ear and I froze. A bleep. Then static. Then voices.

I swerved my head behind me.

The TV came on.

And there on the screen was an old black-and-white commercial for Mythical Falls. Playing on its own. In a building without electricity.

I glanced at Clarice.

Her eyes widened and she screamed.

"MYTHICAL FALLS—A place for fun, scares, and thrills!" an announcer said. "Families come from miles around to experience this unique theme park, deep in the heart of the West Virginia mountains."

Riley hovered behind me, staring at the TV screen and the commercial that played there. The announcer's voice had just the right depth to make him sound ominous and ancient. The smiling faces on the screen seemed a stark contrast to the park's history.

"I would have probably run out of here screaming like a girl too," Riley said.

I rubbed my arms. "I almost did, but I figured someone had to be the adult."

Nate talked in quiet tones to Clarice right outside the window. Was Clarice milking this for all it was worth? Quite possibly. And Nate had fallen for it hook, line, and sinker. He was acting devoted and concerned.

Maybe the two would make a great match.

I leaned against the counter to face Riley. "If I didn't know better, I'd think someone was messing with my head."

"I assure you—Braxton is messing with the electrical here at the park. He must have activated the circuit that's connected with these buildings instead of the cabins. It's the only thing that makes sense."

I nodded. "It's better than Clarice's theory—poltergeist."

Sure enough, some of the video games that had been plugged in had surged to life also. The timing couldn't have been more providential.

Nate's friend Seamus walked into the room at that moment, and Riley and I moved away from each other. I hadn't realized how close we were standing until someone else entered the room.

Later, I needed to think about Clarice's words. The girl may have had some good points. But realizing the truth of the matter and bending your emotions to match wasn't always a quick process.

"Nate wants me to check out these video games," Seamus said.

"I think you guys could get some money from them," I said. "They're definitely vintage."

He stopped by Pac-Man. It appeared to be a favorite here among our crew. "I remember playing this as a child."

"Don't we all?"

"No, I remember playing this here."

Ah, yes. Another person who'd once utilized the theme park. Everyone around here had. Did that mean everyone around here also had a motive of some sort?

"I heard it was quite the place." I crossed my arms and leaned against the counter, waiting to hear his stories.

Seamus nodded, still staring at the Pac-Man screen. "It was. I loved it. My mom used to love it too."

"I can see why," Riley said. "This place had to be a kid's dream. Especially us boys. We have a tendency to love legends, don't we? Pirates, Bigfoot, Atlantis, the Bermuda Triangle. Who doesn't love a good mystery?"

"Exactly. Mythical Falls was ripe with mysteries." Seamus

seemed to stare beyond us. "I hope Nate's dreams are realized. Because, as many people who have good memories of this place there are an equal number who have bad memories. Some people have a hard time getting past them."

"Exactly!" Those had been my thoughts earlier. Bad memories were hard to get past, whether they were memories of theme park murders . . . or memories of bad luck.

Riley threw me a strange glance.

I shrugged, realizing how out-of-the-blue my outburst had been. "I mean, that makes sense."

Riley nodded, seeming to accept my explanation.

Seamus stepped back from the arcade game. "Okay, I have a few people I can call about these. I think I've done what I can on the roofs of those cabins. Now, Nate wants me to examine the fence surrounding the property. That's going to take a while."

We nodded and watched him leave. As soon as he exited the building, Nate and Clarice came inside. I noted how Nate's arm remained around Clarice, and Clarice didn't seem to mind. In fact, she was eating it up, based on the way her face glowed.

Nate stared at the TV screen where the commercial repeated over and over. *Mythical Falls—a place for fun, scares, and thrills! Families come from miles around to experience this unique theme park, deep in the heart of the West Virginia mountains.*

Then, to make matters worse, a clown act appeared on the screen. A small clown jumped on the back of a larger clown, and they juggled balls in the air together with precision.

Weird. It was just weird.

"Yeah, those used to be in the corners and commercials of this place played on repeat," Nate said. "I haven't seen that commercial in years. Years. It's so cool."

"You should use it somehow," Clarice said. "If you do a new ad for this place, you've got to incorporate some of the old stuff. People will eat it up."

"You're a pretty smart chick, Clarice. You know that?"

She glowed. "Thanks."

"I'm looking for someone to help me with marketing around here, someone with good ideas and a bubbly personality . . ."

Her eyes lit. "Really? I could totally see myself doing something like that."

"Me too!"

They stared at each other a moment.

It looked like Chad would be losing one of his employees soon. At least, he would if Nate had his way.

And that, at the moment, was the least of my concerns.

Just then my phone rang. My eyebrows shot up in surprise.

Reception! I had reception here!

I wanted to excuse myself before answering, but I knew if I did that, I'd risk losing the call. I looked at the screen.

It was a number I didn't recognize, but the area code was West Virginia. I made the executive decision to answer.

"Is this Gabby St. Claire?" a woman asked.

"Speaking."

"Gabby, this is Gardenia. I'm Caleb Kidwell's mother. I was hoping I might have a moment of your time." Her voice sounded soft and wrought with tension.

I turned my back on the rest of the gang. They didn't seem to notice. They'd moved on to talking about video games. Riley squeezed my elbow before joining them, affording me some privacy.

"Of course, you can have a moment. More than that. I'm so sorry for your loss."

She sniffled. "Thank you. As you can imagine, this has turned our lives upside down in more than one way. Caleb was our only son."

My heart panged with compassion for the woman. I couldn't imagine. No one should have to go through that.

I didn't know what to say that wouldn't sound trite or clichéd, so thankfully Gardenia continued.

"I understand you're good at solving mysteries."

I shrugged, as if she could see me. "Some people might say that."

"I think you're being modest. Gabby, I'll get right to the point. I'd like to hire you to look into what happened. I understand you're staying on the property, which will afford you a prime opportunity."

"I am staying here . . . but it's because I've been hired to help out a friend."

"I understand that. I know you have other priorities. But, Gabby, would you look into what happened?" A sob broke her voice. "It's not that I don't trust the chief. It's just that he has so little experience with any of this. I really need a second set of eyes."

"I'm not sure how much luck I'll have here, especially since I'm not privy to the information the police department has collected." I glanced behind me to see if anyone was listening. How could I tell a grieving mother no? Easy—I couldn't. "I'll tell you what, though. I'll do my best to find some answers. I'll ask some questions, look around, and see what I can find out."

"Oh, Gabby. That's wonderful. Thank you so much. You can't even realize how much better this makes me feel. I need justice for my son."

"I'll do my best." I glanced behind me again. Chad and Nate were now talking. My heart panged.

I had a lot of obligations, and I felt like I was stretching myself too thin. Would I end up letting everyone down?

I prayed that wouldn't be the case.

That night, after we finished working and darkness had fallen, we all roasted hot dogs over the fire. Nate and Clarice talked in low tones beside each other on the small wooden bench near the campfire. All I heard was something along the lines of, "I'm Daphne, Gabby's Velma, Chad's Shaggy, and Riley's Fred."

I'm Velma? I refrained from comment.

Chad continued to look at his list—the same thing he'd been doing since he arrived. He'd apparently called Sierra earlier and little Reef still wasn't feeling well. She wasn't sure when they'd get here. Braxton and Seamus had departed for the evening.

With everyone else occupied, that left Riley and me some semi-private alone time.

He slid his hand over my back, gently rubbing my tight muscles. "We worked hard today."

"Yes, we did."

"I was hoping that sometime while we were here, we might have time to talk. Just you and me. We've both been so busy lately. We haven't had any good quality time. Not since . . ."

"Since we went undercover at that couples' retreat?" I finished for him.

He nodded. "So much happened there. I know we talked to Pastor Randy afterward about the ceremony—"

"You mean our marriage?" I flashed a sad smile.

"Yes, our wedding." He let out a soft laugh and looked down. The firelight danced across his face, bathing it in an orange glow. The air smelled wonderful—a mix of smoke and burning cedar logs and Riley's leathery cologne.

He was so handsome. Love clutched my heart as I looked at him. I wanted to spend forever with him, but I was so afraid of hoping sometimes. Life had conditioned me to expect the worst. I just need to enjoy the moment, to not dream about the future, to be content in the present.

"That was crazy, wasn't it?" I finally said amidst the crackling of the fire. "I still think about our supposed wedding ceremony, and it just makes me shake my head."

We'd posed as a married couple, and, during a vow renewal ceremony, we'd been informed we were legally married. Riley and I had both agreed that in God's eyes we hadn't committed to each other.

For a while after that, I'd lain in bed at night and dreamed about what it might be like if Riley and I were really married. And, even though Riley had said he wanted to wait and do it right, I feared he would change his mind.

It had happened before.

Our whole relationship had been both simple and complicated at the same time. And I was the queen of ruining these kinds of things. In reality, I was adept at ruining almost anything good in my life. It was a shame.

My conversation with Clarice fluttered back into my mind. *What happened to all that trust in God you're always talking about? Doesn't trust mean having faith that whatever happens, God is in control?*

"You've seemed a little distant since then," Riley continued.

"You think so? I thought we were just busy." As soon as the words left my mouth, I regretted them. They weren't the total truth. I mean, we had been busy. On the surface, we had a great relationship.

But I'd stopped myself from dreaming. From hoping. From becoming too attached.

And I hadn't been able to tell him any of that.

"We have been busy. We've had some good times. I mean, we ran that 5k together. We redecorated your apartment. We went to visit my parents."

"I bought a new car," I added.

"That's right. You've been working a lot. I've been establishing myself at this branch of the law office."

"Not to mention everything going on at church: small group, serving at the soup kitchen, distributing clothes at the women's shelter. All those new initiatives have been great." Perfect things also to fill my time. To help me avoid the conversation where I felt like I had to bare my soul. I'd been there before and done that. When the reactions to doing so weren't what you expected, it made you more cautious.

Was I simply justifying my fears? Trying to rationalize my complacency?

"Anyway, maybe before we leave, we'll get some quiet time. Talk about us. About our future."

I nodded, even though my throat felt tight. "That sounds great, Riley."

He kissed my knuckles before narrowing his eyes. "I know I've already asked you this, but is everything okay?"

I nodded again. "Yeah, of course. Why do you ask?"

"You just don't seem quite like yourself lately."

"I'm fine," I insisted.

He squeezed my hand. "Good. I don't mean to keep badgering you. I know you'll talk to me if you need to."

"Of course." Guilt pounded at me, though, because I hadn't talked to him yet.

I knew that eventually, we were going to have to talk. To really talk. And I was going to have to figure out whether or not I really trusted Riley or not. Whether I was going to be able to risk my heart. To have hope for my future. To allow those dreams of a family and a stable life to invade my thoughts and my soul with such a fervent hope that tears could pop into my eyes.

In some ways, that thought was more terrifying than a serial killer.

CHAPTER
THIRTEEN

THE NEXT MORNING, I pulled to a stop in front of a quaint old building in downtown Whitehurst. I put my car in park and stared at the structure beside me, which had obviously been grand at one time with its cement pillars stretching up three stories high.

Today, it was the home of Stephens Incorporated's Whitehurst office. Apparently, when the coal market had gone bust, Scotty Stephens had turned to solar energy. Their corporate office was located here in town.

This was my workday for Grayson Tech, and I had to head to the next county for a training session. It was part of the stipulation I gave Chad when I agreed to help—he'd been desperate and agreed.

I'd pulled out my business clothes—and by business I meant a khaki skirt that came to my knees and a golf shirt with "Grayson Technologies" embroidered on the lapel. I pulled a black trench coat on over it to conceal my company's name. I wasn't sure they'd appreciate being associated with my unofficial investigation.

The timing of this whole trip had worked out perfectly because I'd needed to do some training with a couple of counties up here in West Virginia. I'd get those knocked out while I was in the area. I loved it when things worked out the way I wanted them to.

Which rarely happened.

I'd left early so I had extra time to stop here. I probably wouldn't be lucky enough to catch Scotty Stephens in the office. But I was going to try to at least figure out where the man was.

A woman with curly brown hair piled high atop her head greeted me in the marble-encased reception area. The building was a former bank, I decided.

"How can I help you?"

I offered a winning smile. "I know this is a long shot, but I'm hoping to speak with Scotty Stephens."

She gave me a look that clearly said, *You know so little, don't you?* "He doesn't work out of this office, Sweetheart."

Sweetheart? It sounded like a southern way of saying "idiot."

"How could I get in touch with him then?"

She fluttered her eyelashes in a way that still made me feel daft. "He's hard to get up with unless you have an appointment. Can I ask what this is concerning?"

"The property where Mythical Falls is located."

"Mythical Falls?" Her eyebrows shot up. "I see. Maybe you could talk to his son then . . . ?"

"I'd love to."

"One moment please." She turned away from me, picked up her phone, and mumbled something indiscernible into the mouthpiece. A moment later, she turned around with a wide smile. "Last office down the hallway behind me. Scotty Jr. is waiting for you."

I hoped I didn't end up regretting this. I also hoped I didn't lose track of time and arrive late for my training seminar.

Balancing more than one job was a hard gig sometimes.

As I walked down the hallway, I noted that the place smelled like microwaved meals. The scent, at the moment, wasn't pleasing.

As I reached the end of the hallway, I could see a man who looked fortyish sitting behind a huge desk. He looked slightly awkward. Maybe it was his oversized ears or the way he paused a little too long before speaking. I couldn't exactly put my finger on it, but something was different about the man.

As I glanced around his office, I saw a package of microwavable mac and cheese in the trashcan. Bingo! Stinky smell located.

"Ms. St. Claire. Thanks for coming in. What can I do for you?" He motioned for me to have a seat.

I did, and attempted a pleasant smile. "I'm here about Mythical Falls."

"Mythical Falls. I'm very aware of that property. What about it?"

"I heard you had an interest in it. Your father does, at least. It's a beautiful piece of land."

"Yes, he does. He's been trying to purchase it for years. What's your connection with the property?"

"I'm a . . . consultant for Nate Reynolds. I'm there this week on the property, and I'm trying to convince him to sell also. I thought I would get some more information on the other possibilities out there before I submitted my advice to him."

His eyes brightened with satisfaction. "I've been telling Nate to sell for years."

I shifted, realizing just how many connections there were in this small town. "You know Nate?"

"I do. Our paths have a tendency to cross. I used to always razz him about Mythical Falls. It never did any good. He's always loved the place."

"I think it's a disaster waiting to happen," I said, taking on the role of devil's advocate. "A bad investment for the future, especially for what he's planning."

He scowled. "It's been the talk of the town—how Nate wants to make it a destination resort. We all know it won't succeed. All these people will lose their money, further sinking the economy in the area."

I wanted to argue with the man out of principle, but I didn't want to blow my cover. I mostly just wanted to prove he was wrong. However, he did have some valid points. "There are much better uses for the land. I agree."

"So what can I do for you exactly?"

I had the sense that this guy was desperate to prove to his father that he could follow in his footsteps. There was a certain eagerness in his gaze that was hard to ignore. "I was curious about why your father wanted this property so badly. What's the lure? If I just had more insight, I might be able to convince Nate that this is all a bad idea and it would be more profitable to sell."

"I doubt anything will convince him. But my father has always seen potential in that property. He wants to start a premiere retirement community there."

"In the mountains? Some senior citizens would have a hard time managing the hills."

"He has it all figured out. There are ways to make it accessible for seniors. We need something like this out here. We have an aging population, and an area like this would be much welcomed."

What I didn't understand was: why open something so upscale in an area that seemed so economically deprived? "Certainly there are other plots of land where his plan could work. Why the Mythical Falls property?"

"He said it's special. Folklore has it that the actual spring on the property was once believed to be the fountain of youth."

"How appropriate for a generation of seniors."

"Exactly—plus, it's peaceful. It's quiet. It's beautiful. It's perfect for people who want to slow down."

I shifted. "Speaking of your father, where is he right now?"

"He's out of the country. In Brazil doing some kind of outdoor adventure. That's what happens when you have more money than you know what to do with. He's been there for the past couple of weeks, and he hasn't given me a date when he'll arrive back. I know what that means: it means he'll come home whenever he feels like it."

Out of the country? It was hard to murder someone when you were thousands of miles away. However, a man like Scotty Stephens could have quite possibly hired someone to do his dirty work twenty years ago. Who's to say he wouldn't do that again?

I glanced at my watch and realized I needed to go. "Thanks very much for your information. I'll definitely take that into consideration when I meet with Nate."

"No problem. I hope you're able to convince him."

I forced a tight smile. "Me too."

AS I WALKED BACK to my car some familiar faces caught my eye.

The Brilliant Brunke Brothers. They spruced up the flowerbeds along Main Street, working together like a well-oiled machine. Bill recognized me and waved me over.

"Good morning," I called. I looked at the neat flowerbeds outside the office building, beds that were mulched to near perfect. "You guys work here too? For the Stephens?"

Bill laughed—not gracefully, but like he knew a joke I didn't—and shook his head. "No, I'd never do that. We work for the city. That's who maintains these streets. It's not a full-time job—just once a week or so. But it keeps the paychecks coming in, and that's good enough for us."

"Understood. I'm sure Nate hates not having you at Mythical Falls today, especially with the workload he had."

"Nate will have to learn that the world doesn't revolve around him," Grumpy called out from the flowerbed, grunting under his breath.

"Oh, Phil, who said he thinks that? He's just a go-getter." Happy. That had to be Happy again. "There's nothing wrong with ambition . . . and a few positive thoughts once in a while."

"Maybe I'd actually have some positive thoughts if I got some sleep at night," Grumpy retorted. "But no, we have to stay up and plan—"

He abruptly stopped and looked at me. The rest of the brothers grew quiet also.

"Plan what?" I questioned. Could this merry band of brothers be behind some of the acts going on at Mythical Falls? I didn't want to believe it.

"It's nothing," Bill said, giving his brothers a sharp glance.

I tensed, wondering what I was missing. "Should I be worried?"

Grumpy shrugged. "That depends on whom you ask. We are sworn to secrecy."

"Oh, Phil, you make it sound so evil," Happy said.

Before I could press for more information, someone across the street caught my eye, and I turned my attention from the banter between Cup Half Full and Cup Half Empty. Was that Seamus?

He obviously hadn't seen me. He walked into the bank, talking in low tones with a woman I didn't recognize. His companion was well-dressed, with long brown hair, a gray suit, and heels.

Bill followed my gaze and leaned on his shovel. "You met Seamus?"

I nodded. "Just briefly. He's doing some roofing for Nate."

"Worst contractor ever. I wouldn't trust his work farther than I could spit." To demonstrate, he actually spit across the sidewalk.

I raised my eyebrows, half afraid the Human Camel might turn his sights on me next. "Really?"

"He did some work for Quill. That roof was leaking again two weeks later during the first rainstorm we got."

"That's . . . unfortunate."

"It's shoddy workmanship. That's what it is." He raised his chin as if he dared someone to defy him.

I certainly wasn't going to. "I'm surprised Nate hired him if his work is that bad."

"I think Nate has some kind of weird connection to him, one where he feels obligated to hire him," Grumpy called before shoving a mum into the dirt. "Not sure what's behind it."

Interesting. I nodded toward the bank. "Do you know the woman who was with him?"

Bill squinted, as if he might see through the bank's walls. "Didn't get a good glance at her. Sorry I can't help. But I do know he's not married, so it wasn't his wife."

I glanced at my watch again. I wished I could stay and see if I could catch a glimpse of her again. But I was already close to being late. I couldn't wait any longer.

I jangled my keys. "Good running into you all again. I've got to go, though."

Bill nodded. "We'll see you tomorrow at Mythical Falls. We've got more brush to clear away."

If only finding the answers was as easy as clearing away the clutter in order to see better. On the other hand, maybe it was.

I needed to start by eliminating suspects. With any luck, I'd manage to do that with the same ease as the Brilliant Brunke Brothers cleared this flowerbed of weeds.

I finished up my training session on advanced fingerprints techniques—one of my favorite courses to teach—and packed up my things. The workshop had taken place in the next county over from Mythical Falls, which was too bad. I would have loved to pick the brains of the deputies involved in the murder of Caleb Kidwell and find out more information.

I glanced at my watch as I packed everything into the back of my sedan. Did I have time to make one more stop? I twisted my lips together as I thought about it. I figured I just might. After all, by the time I got back to Mythical Falls, it would already be dark, and I wouldn't be able to get much work done. So why rush? While I was out here, I may as well make the most of my time.

With that thought in mind, I headed toward Whitehurst College.

I'd called Gardenia on my way into town, and she'd given me the name of some of Caleb's friends, as well as told me what dorm they lived in. I figured I might be able to ask them some questions. If they were truly his friends, they wouldn't mind answering and helping find their friend's murderer.

Once on campus, I quickly found Bravenhurst Hall, but I not so quickly found parking a good four blocks away. I pulled my jacket closer around me as I started the hike toward the dormitory in the quaint college area. The street was lined with old houses that were now home to fraternities and sororities. A few clubs and cafes and a college bookstore were scattered in between.

By the time I reached the dormitory, I was shivering from the brisk mountain air. A student had let me inside, and I stood in the entryway several minutes, simply rubbing my hands together to regain feeling before proceeding.

I grabbed the first person I saw walking past who didn't have a beer in hand. "Excuse me!"

The boy with spiky hair stopped and his eyes widened. "Yes . . . ?"

Had I officially crossed the threshold into old? That's how I felt. It hadn't been that long ago I was a student and working on getting my degree. Now I felt like I was decades older. The boy looked at me like I was a schoolmarm about to reprimand him.

"I'm looking for Tobin Michaels and Frank Bellary. Could you point me in the right direction?"

His face lit. "The Tobs and the Franz? Of course, I know them. I'm headed that way right now. Follow me . . ." He made a dramatic flare with his hands.

I didn't argue. I followed him up two sets of stairs and down a dormitory hall where guys were hollering out their doors. A few might have even been wearing togas. I made it a point not to look too hard.

I tried not to make eye contact with any of them in an effort to appear professional—like a professional investigator, not a professional . . . well, you know.

We stopped in front of a room halfway down the hall, and the college-aged boy deposited me there. "Have fun!" He wagged his eyebrows up and down.

I straightened my coat before continuing. Before my hand could connect with the wood, the door opened and two beefy looking guys stood there. Both had thick heads and reminded me of football players. In fact, the two guys looked remarkably similar to each other, except one was blond and the other had dark hair.

"Whoa." The blond backed up a step. "Who are you? Did Tommy send you?"

"Tomm—" I stopped myself, decided I shouldn't even go there. I was wearing a black trench coat, and they were fraternity boys with overactive imaginations. "Caleb's mom sent me."

His eyes widened, and in one quick motion he pulled me inside his room and slammed the door. Panic pulsed through me as I realized the precarious situation I may have put myself in. When both guys backed away from me as if I was an unknown creature, I sensed they were harmless.

Don't fail me now, instincts.

I sucked in a deep breath, inhaling the stench of dirty socks, old pizza, and expelled gas. It wasn't pleasant, to say the least. But what did I expect from a guy's dorm room?

The dark-haired beef-head narrowed his eyes as he studied me. "How do you know Caleb's mom?"

I decided to play it straight. "She asked me to look into his murder."

The blond's eyes brightened like a scoreboard at the Super Bowl. "So, you're like a P.I.?"

"Kind of. It's complicated. But I've done this before. More than once."

"So, you're like, covert? Undercover? Secret?" The dark-haired guy wagged his shaggy eyebrows up and down. Maybe the eyebrow wag was a Whitehurst thing, but it was kind of strange.

"Well, Frank—?"

"That's me," the blond interjected. "But everyone calls me the Franz. Besides, no one thinks I look like a Frank."

That meant the dark-haired boy was the Tobs.

If The Tobs was implying something, I had no idea what it was, but I wanted to stay in his good graces. "Okay, Tobs, would you be impressed if I said yes, I was undercover?"

"Totally." His voice sank deeper.

I gave a curt nod. "Then yes, that's what I am."

Franz put his hands on his hips and narrowed his gaze. "What do you need to know? We've already talked to the po po. I'm not sure what else we have to say."

I decided to get right to the point. Besides, if I stayed in his room much longer, my lungs would need to be fumigated. "People are saying that Caleb was about to burn down Mythical Falls when he died. What do you think about that?"

"No way." The Tobs shook his head fervently. "He would never do something like that."

"What was he doing on the property then?" I crossed my arms as I waited for his answer.

"I have no idea. Most people think it was a dare." He leaned back against a dresser littered with beer cans—empty beer cans. Half of them clanked to the floor as he nudged the piece of furniture. A few other things also fell—some papers, rocks, and a bag of chips.

"What do you mean?" I remembered what Nate had told me, but I wanted to hear Caleb's friends' version.

Franz exchanged a glance with Tobs before shrugging. "We're

always doing dares here at the college," Franz continued. "Mythical Falls is a favorite place."

"I've heard about that. Some of the fraternities here are especially fascinated, right?"

"That's right. It was good, safe fun. At least, it was until Caleb . . ." Franz looked away, his words choking in his throat. He appeared to be sincerely grieving.

"You said you didn't think it was a dare. Why?"

Franz sighed, making it obvious that I wasn't getting it. "Dares are public. Part of the adrenaline rush is having everyone knowing what you're doing, so they can see if you succeed or fail. He never mentioned that."

"Do you have any theories about what happened?" I softened my voice.

"You mean, besides the Bigfoot Strangler?" Tobs asked.

I should have figured the subject of the Bigfoot Strangler would come up. "Yes, besides Bigfoot."

The Tobs leaned closer and lowered his voice. His breath smelled like cheese balls. Ew. "He's real, man. And he's out there. For reals." He made some kind of mock gang sign that looked ridiculous.

"Moving along," I prodded. I really hoped all of this wasn't a gigantic waste of time or another lecture of the realities of Bigfoot. "Any other theories? Any viable ones?"

"I have no idea," Franz said. "No one disliked Caleb. He was the all-American boy. Smart, wealthy, handsome. At least, that's what the ladies said. I think he was just in the wrong place at the wrong time. What other reason would there be?"

Tobs shifted. "Well, there was one other thing."

My curiosity spiked along with my adrenaline. "What's that?"

Tobs and Franz exchanged a glance. Finally, Tobs nodded, giving Franz silent permission to share whatever it was he wanted to share.

"Well, there's this rumor . . ." Franz cringed, like he didn't want to say his impending statement. But there was a look in his eyes—a look of concern. Or was it fear? Just what was going on here?

Not only that, but there appeared to be a lot of rumors floating around out in this area. I'd never lived in a small town, but everything I'd heard about them appeared to be true. "Okay . . ."

Franz leaned even closer, also expelling the scent of stinky cheese. "I heard Caleb having some whispered conversations on his phone the week before he died. I couldn't make out everything that was said. But I heard something about money. It sounded intense. He hung up when I came closer, all secretive like." He scrunched his eyebrows and raised his shoulders. "We were bros. I didn't think we had secrets. But I was like, whatever, man."

Who said guys didn't have feelings? Franz was obviously hurt by the fact that Caleb didn't share everything going on his life. At least that was true if I was following his train of thought correctly.

"What do you think Caleb was talking about?" I asked. "Any idea what his secret was?"

He glanced at Tobs one more time. "He seemed to have come into some money right before he died." He clutched his chest in dramatic loyalty and persuasion. "I personally wondered if someone paid him to go on the property."

The fear that had rippled over me turned into a cold, morbid curiosity. Mysterious money? Again? That couldn't be a coincidence. "How do you know he came into money? Why do you think that?"

"I found one of his bank statements on the floor," the Franz said. "I thought, at first, that it was mine, but after I looked at it, I realized it wasn't."

"How much money?"

Franz shrugged. "About ten thousand."

My blood turned even colder as the similarities began to hit me. "So your theory is that someone paid him to go to Mythical Falls for some reason."

Franz shrugged, the cloak of suspense surrounding him seeming to disappear. "Not sure. But I am pretty certain that he went of his own free will."

I stored that away in the back of my mind. "I see."

I wondered if Franz or Tobs knew that Henry McClain had also come into some money before he died.

Anticipation buzzed through my blood.

This case was getting more interesting by the minute.

I CERTAINLY HAD a lot to think about. In my mind, everything pointed back to Scotty Stephens—except for the fact that he was out of the country. Still, he seemed like the type who could pay someone to do his dirty work—dirty work that included hiring someone to sabotage Mythical Falls or to possibly kill someone on the grounds, thus shutting the whole place down.

The challenge would be in finding out who the hit man could be, and also in maneuvering how to do that while still helping out Chad. As usual, I'd bitten off more than I could chew, but I wasn't willing to let any balls drop.

When I arrived back at Mythical Falls, the gang was all gathered in the boys' cabin, playing a rousing game of Hedbanz. Apparently, Clarice had brought the silly children's game with her.

Riley planted a kiss on my cheek when I walked in. "How was your day?"

"Interesting," I whispered.

I didn't want to share what I'd discovered with everyone in this room. There were advantages to keeping details quiet. I'd learned that the hard way. Instead, I deposited my purse on the counter, and Riley helped me slip off my coat. I instantly missed its warmth.

"Did you eat?" Riley asked. "Nate made some kind of venison stew."

I shook my head, not feeling the whole "Let's eat Bambi" thing. "I'll be fine. I grabbed a snack on my way here. Did you guys make a lot of progress today?"

"Two more cabins are almost finished." Chad turned from his steaming bowl of dinner, eyes lit with satisfaction. "The pathway is coming along nicely. Braxton almost has all of the electrical issues worked out in the cabins in this area. Seamus finished the roofs. All in all, I'd say we're right on target."

"And I already have people making reservations," Nate added, flashing a bright smile. *"Reservations."*

My eyebrows shot up and I shoved my hip against the counter. "I didn't realize that was an option yet."

He nodded like a little boy at Christmas. "Yeah, baby—" His cheerful disposition disappeared a moment, and he looked apologetic instead. "I call a lot of people that, not just you."

I sighed and crossed my arms. "You don't have to explain."

He laughed. "I just don't want things to be awkward, you know?"

Could they be any more awkward than right now?

"Oh, Nate. You're so funny!" Clarice crowed, her hand landing on his arm and remaining there.

"So I've been told." Nate's chest puffed out in some kind of primal dating rite.

I wasn't feeling quite as cheerful as those two. "Please continue."

Nate's smile slipped, but only slightly. "I decided to go ahead and take the plunge. I opened up reservations starting at the end of October. Why not?"

I could think of a million reasons, but I kept them quiet.

Maturity. That's what it did for you. However, maturity didn't stop the thoughts from cascading through my brain. There was still so much uncertainty about the safety of this place.

"Do you think all the permits and inspections will be complete by then?" It was a logical question. Non-confrontational. Non-opinionated. Non-complicated.

"Of course. I wouldn't have opened it otherwise." He laughed, glancing around the room as he did so, as if hoping others would catch onto his humor. "Right? Right?"

I imagined myself with a gun, shooting that woodpecker laugh until it was dead.

Don't be so violent, Gabby.

"When exactly is your grand opening going to be?" I asked. Had Chad talked to Nate about this? Had he tried to stop his friend from making a major mistake?

"October 15. Two weeks before Halloween. I might even do a trial run a week or so earlier, just to make sure things go smoothly."

His optimism was driving me to the edge of insanity. "You still have employees to hire and kinks to work out. I mean, that's only a month away. Are you sure you're going to be ready?"

Okay, my restraint that I'd just prided myself in disappeared faster than an investment in a decrepit amusement park. Had Nate really thought all of this through?

"Don't worry—I have insurance." Nate stiffened, obviously not happy that I'd brought up any concerns.

Chad scowled at me while wearing a plastic band on his head with a picture of a pig on it. His pointed look begged me to keep my mouth shut, yet the headband across his forehead made it hard for me to take him seriously.

I was obviously raining on some people's parades here. I supposed it was truly none of my business. But many things had been none of my business, and I'd still dived in. It almost always turned out okay.

"I've got to strike while the iron is hot," Nate said. "While it's *crazy* hot. That time is now. *Now!* Not only that, but I just got approval today to fix up an old alpine slide. It's going to be super sweet."

"Alpine slide?" I'd heard of them, but I was having trouble picturing exactly what they were.

"It's like a ginormous slide that slips and turns down the mountain." Nate's eyes were wide and childlike again. "People can sit either on a mat or a cart and ease on down the road—er, the slide. It's super fun. I think that will be a big draw. I figured the old track would be destroyed, but I checked it out today, and it's not that bad. It was called 'Nessie's Neck: Slip and Slide.' Cool, huh?"

Everyone nodded eagerly in agreement. Maybe I was losing my fun touch, but all I could think about was everything that could go wrong. "Up in Flames" by Coldplay began to sound in the overhead speakers of my mind. It was a neurotic quirk I had —a soundtrack that played in my head at the worst times.

Finally, I stood, not feeling like being the wet blanket of the group. "I think I'm going to turn in for the night. It's been a long day, and I want to be well rested for tomorrow."

"Sure thing," Nate called. "Night then."

Riley walked me out.

"Are you on board with all of that?" I whispered as soon as we stepped outside and away from listening ears.

Riley leaned close enough that I could feel his breath on my cheek. "No, but it's not my call. Nate's going to do what he's going to do. We were hired to do a specific task—giving our opinions wasn't one of them."

I frowned. I supposed he was right, but it sounded so harsh when he worded it like that. I *loved* giving my opinions. Even though I had momentary setbacks, I actually daily thanked God for how far I'd come. I wasn't where I needed to be yet, but I marveled at how much I'd grown over the past three years. God was working on me.

"After this week, we'll be gone and out of here," Riley continued. "Nate will have to deal with any of the headaches that come by being owner and operator of this place."

He was speaking like the lawyer he was. And his words were true. This was Nate's problem, not mine. At least I'd be able to put a good chunk of change into my savings after this. I was taking steps in the right direction.

He stopped at the door to my place. The stream trickled in the background. An owl still hooted. Crickets still chirped.

Nighttime in the mountains was refreshing, and the crisp air felt invigorating. Being here with Riley . . . well, in some ways it seemed perfect.

"Want to come in for a minute?" I leaned against the door.

He stepped closer. "I don't know. Is it appropriate for a virtuous, young woman like yourself and a grumpy, old man like me to be alone out here?"

He grinned, and I realized by the way he hung his hands on his belt he was taking on the role of an old-timey prospector. The thought made me giggle.

I played along and batted my eyelashes sweetly. "People might talk."

He grabbed my hand. "People will always talk. But there's one thing they don't know."

I fanned my face dramatically. "What's that?"

"That you're officially my wife."

At his words, a lump formed in my throat. And I straightened, almost panicked.

"That's right." I attempted to sound light. I failed.

He squinted. "You know I'm joking . . . mostly, at least. Right?"

I nodded a little too quickly. "Of course."

He blinked as he studied my face. "I didn't mean to make you uncomfortable."

"I'm not. Why would you say that?" My voice squeaked higher, a dead giveaway.

"Because you look tight enough to spring."

I tried to brush off his words. "It's just been a long day."

He nodded, his expression grim. He wasn't buying my flimsy explanations, and I couldn't blame him. I wasn't sure where this anxiety was coming from, but as much as I tried to tell myself it wasn't there, the truth remained that apprehension lurked deep inside me. It bubbled up at the worst times. Usually when I was with Riley.

Why was I keeping this from him? I should just tell him about my concerns and fears. Right here. Right now.

"How about if I walk you inside? It's probably a good idea, especially with everything that's been going on here lately." Riley's voice sounded subdued. Disappointed. Maybe even hurt.

But there was one thing he hadn't done. He hadn't run. He hadn't jumped ship. He hadn't given up on me.

I nodded, feeling slightly awful now. Fairytales were supposed to be happily ever after. But I'd found that life was more than about happy moments. Happy moments were usually followed by awful moments. Those two things cycled in and out, creating a rhythm to life.

Unfortunately, the awful moments always seared me and made more of an impression on me than the happy times. Sometimes I felt doomed to always deal with tragedy. Maybe I didn't deserve good things.

That was against everything I'd read in the Bible. It was a lie I held onto. But I was having trouble letting go.

As Riley checked the rooms, I moved toward the other end of the cabin. Eventually Nate wanted to add decks with hot tubs included, but that was a long-range plan. Thank goodness. We'd be lucky to get everything done as it was. Of course, knowing Nate, he might change his mind and add that to our workload this week just for kicks.

I wanted to turn the floodlight on as a safety precaution. Criminals liked to stay in the dark, where they could be concealed. I hoped having a light on would deter any unwanted guests.

Instead, I spotted a figure at the window.

A scream caught in my throat.

It was a face. A hairy face. Half man, half ape.

It was Bigfoot.

"WHAT IS IT?" Riley rushed toward me.

My hand shook as I pulled it in front of me and pointed out the window. I opened my mouth to speak, but nothing came out but a squeak.

He followed my gaze, and his jaw dropped. "Is that . . . ?"

I nodded, finding my voice. "Bigfoot."

The creature sprinted away, quickly retreating into the woods. He bounded over the stream with long strides and finally disappeared into the darkness beyond.

"You saw it too, right?" I asked, still feeling frozen and speechless.

He nodded stoically. "I saw something."

"It looked like Bigfoot."

"It looked like Bigfoot," he confirmed. "But I don't believe in Bigfoot."

I took a step back, desperate to put space between myself and the window. "Okay, I'm totally freaked out right now."

Riley began pacing. "Let's think this through. How close was he when you spotted him?"

"He was practically right at the window. Almost as if he was peering inside."

Riley shook his head before running a hand over his face. He was having trouble coming to terms with this also. "Something's going on here, Gabby."

As the reality of the situation settled on me, I rushed toward the locks and double-checked them. They might not keep Bigfoot out for long, but at least they'd buy us some time . . . I hoped.

"You don't have to convince me that something's going on," I muttered. "In fact, you'll never believe what I found out today. I've been waiting for just the right moment to share it with you —a moment when no one else was around to listen."

I filled him in on my conversations with Scotty Stephens Jr., as well as Tobs and Franz.

"Large sums of money were found in both of the dead men's accounts? That's crazy."

I nodded again. "I know. These two cases are definitely connected, even if they are twenty years apart. I just don't know why. The first happened and closed the park down."

"Sounds like someone wants to close it down again before it has a chance to open."

"Most people around here seemed to have lived in the area from generation to generation. The fact that the killer is still here, living among the people, really isn't that weird."

Or he's living in the woods near the people. I kept that part quiet. For now.

"The question is: Who gave Henry and Caleb money and why?" Riley continued.

I dropped onto the couch. "Rumor has it that Scotty Stephens gave the money to Henry, the first man who died. He paid him off to ensure certain acts of mischief occurred here on the grounds so he could buy the land."

Riley wagged his head, his doubt obvious as he sat beside me. "That's pretty desperate. I mean, why does he want this land for the retirement community? Certainly there are other parcels available that could be just as successful."

I snuggled into the cushions, trying to forget the image of

our hairy Peeping Tom. Riley's thoughts mirrored mine. Something was fishy. "He's hung up on this property for some reason. I wonder what's here that has him obsessed for this long."

Riley shrugged. "We're in a replica of an old prospector's cabin. Does that mean there was really gold in this area at one time?"

My eyebrows drew together as I processed his statement. "You mean, you think there could be gold here that he's trying to lay claim to?"

"Maybe."

"Let's say that was true. Then why not just sneak here at night and mine for it? Or pay Nate for permission?"

"Then Scotty Stephens would be showing his hand. Nate would know there was gold here, and he'd want it for himself."

"It's an interesting theory. But I've never exactly heard of a West Virginia gold rush. Of course, what do I know?"

Riley shook his head, deep in thought. "If not gold, then maybe there's some kind of other valuable resource here. Coal? Limestone? Timber? I have no idea. But I'm telling you—there's some other reason he wants the property. He might be willing to kill to get his hands on it."

I shivered at his words. Then I remembered Bigfoot, and I shivered again.

Something disturbing was going on here. Without officially being a part of the police investigation, it would be hard to get answers. I didn't have access to any of the bank records to try and determine where the money had come from.

Plus, there was the gasoline. Had someone set up Caleb to look like an arsonist? Why? I had so many unanswered questions, so many things that didn't make sense.

Tomorrow, it was going to be hard to get back to work restoring this place. Because all I wanted to do was to dig deeper into the deaths of Caleb and Henry. Whether Nate knew it or not, he needed some answers before this place opened. Otherwise, I feared there would be more Calebs and Henrys out there in those woods.

Suddenly, I straightened as another thought hit me.

"What is it?" Riley asked.

"You know when you took Clarice snipe hunting?"

"Of course. Why?"

"She vowed revenge on you. What if that's what she just got?"

"I promise you—it wasn't me," Clarice insisted. "I wouldn't do something like that."

I looked at Nate and he nodded. "She was with me the whole time."

"Maybe the two of you are in on it together," I suggested.

"Aw . . . look at you." His eyes lit with silly admiration as he had some kind of *ah ha* moment. "You're so smart. That would be clever. But we've been here. Right here."

"They're telling the truth," Chad added. "I don't know what you saw, Gabby, but everyone here is accounted for."

I bit down, having no choice but to believe them. But if it wasn't Chad, Nate, or Clarice, then who had been out there? I wouldn't allow myself to believe it was actually Bigfoot.

That night, I tossed and turned in bed. Clarice and I stayed in one of the bedrooms at the guys' cabin, just to be on the safe side. I wasn't sure if I'd ever feel safe here at Mythical Falls, though.

As soon as morning sunlight lit the sky, Nate rallied the troops outside of the girls' cabin. "You've got to see what I found."

Sleepy-eyed, we all followed him. He stopped by the area outside of my former bedroom window.

"Right here." Nate pointed to the ground.

We all gathered around him. Sure enough, there on the

ground was another footprint. If I had to guess, it was approximately the same size as the first one I'd found. In other words: twice as large as a human footprint.

I shuddered as I looked at it.

"Maybe this is a breeding ground for squatches," Nate said, addressing us all like a great storyteller might. "Maybe the rumors all of these years are true."

"I don't know about that." I pulled out my phone, laid a dollar bill by the footprint, and took another picture. I'd done the same thing for the first footprint I'd found.

"What are you doing?" Nate asked.

"Documenting this, of course."

"Why?"

"Why wouldn't I? If this is Bigfoot, we have some evidence. If not, then at least we have something so we can compare notes. We should take a cast of this also. I have some material in my car."

"You brought stuff to cast Bigfoot's footprints?" Nate sounded uber impressed.

I tilted my head, wondering if he was for real. "No, I brought it because police departments across the country use it for casting footprints at crime scenes. I teach classes on how to use it."

"Excellent. It's a good thing you're here, I guess."

"I guess." I took a couple more photos with my phone.

"Chad told me about your history as an investigator," Nate said. "Impressive, senorita—and that wasn't a come on."

I put my phone away and scowled. "I get it."

"Who said science geeks couldn't be hot?" he continued. Seriously—he was like a clueless puppy dog who didn't know when to stop. He froze and added, "That totally wasn't an insult."

"Of course, it wasn't."

He laughed. "I'm glad you're such a good sport, Gabby. All right, Chad, I'll let you take over from here. I actually have today off. What would you like for me to do?"

"We're going to start working on the cabins in Area 51," Chad said. "I'm hoping to have those finished in a couple of days. They were in the best shape. Gabby, you want to wrap up here and then join us?"

"I'll stay with her, just to be on the safe side," Riley said.

"You don't have to do that," I insisted. It was an awfully sweet offer, though.

Riley gave me a "really?" look. He was already getting the shadow of a beard across his cheeks and chin. It was a good look, one that I could live with—as long as it didn't get Nate the Great long.

Nate had ruined me for beards, and I'd never associate them with anything positive ever again.

"After everything that's happened around here lately?" Riley said. "I think I do need to go with you. I'd rather play it safe."

I smiled, happy to have him here. I always felt better when he was close by.

I suppose that Chad wasn't the only one whose thoughts were all over the place. One minute, I was sure I wanted to be with Riley. The next I feared obstacles to our happiness—before those obstacles even materialized.

I sighed. Life could be like a rollercoaster and, at the moment, I really preferred a quiet train ride through the countryside. I longed for it. I was fighting desperately to turn my thoughts around, but it was so difficult sometimes. If I could just play it safe—and not take any chances—for a little while, then maybe my heart could recover, and my actions could match.

Dear Lord, I'm a royal mess. Satan has come in to remind me of every disappointment. He's rubbing them in my face. Flaunting them. And, as a result, my faith is taking a beating. With Your help, I'm going to do better. I am.

"By the way, could you forward me copies of those photos? I'd like to document this, as well," Nate said.

I shrugged, thinking it was weird. But Nate was kind of weird, so whatever. "Sure thing."

As the rest of the gang scampered away, I pulled out some of my supplies from my car. Riley took them from me and carried them back to the spot of the footprint.

"Just put them there for a moment," I told him. "I want to check out something else first."

"What are you thinking?"

"I want to see if I can find any more footprints. I'm also curious about this stream. I seriously think that whatever we saw last night stepped over it in only three paces. Is it possible for a human to do that?"

Riley shrugged. "There's only one way to find out."

We followed a path toward the stream. There were a few other partial footprints there, but the best two were by the cabin, for sure.

When we reached the stream, we both stopped and stared at it for a moment. The water was beautiful as it tripped and fell, as it scampered and scurried. Smooth river rocks playfully blocked the water's path, but the stream didn't seem to mind and it easily played along.

"Shall I?" Riley said. "Since my legs are longer? You said three steps, right?"

I nodded.

"Let's see if we can do this then."

Riley took his longest step and landed entirely short of being midstream. He took another step, and then another and another. He was six foot three, and he hadn't been able to make it.

My heart raced. What if I really had seen Bigfoot? No. Now I was thinking crazy.

Riley bounded back over to me. The bottoms of his jeans were wet, as were his boots. But he didn't seem to mind. He simply shook his legs to get any excess water off and turned to face me, his breath coming out in a frosty steam. "I have to admit, I have trouble imagining someone making it in three steps."

I frowned. "Me too. My best bet for getting some real answers is that footprint, I guess."

As we started back through the thin patch of woods, I paused by a low-lying pine tree. Something snagged on one of the limbs had caught my eye.

"What is it?" Riley peered closer.

"I can't be sure, but I think this is some fur from our late-night visitor. It's too high to have come from a deer. I suppose it could be a bear, but I'd like to know something definitive."

Riley leaned closer to examine it. "The evidence does keep mounting, doesn't it?"

"Absolutely." I pulled out my phone and took more pictures. "Let me document the scene first. Then I'm going to take a sample. We'll find out exactly what was out here last night. The evidence doesn't lie, right?"

"You sound so charming when you talk like that, you know."

"Oh yeah?" I grinned and winked at him. "I'm just getting started."

CHAPTER
SEVENTEEN

MY ASSIGNMENT for the day was to work on the floors in Area 51. Chad apparently thought floors were my specialty, and I didn't bother to mention to him that getting blood out of carpet was more my area of expertise. Either way, I had a job to do.

Chad had driven all the equipment up to those cabins. I thought about driving also, but Riley and I decided to walk instead. Maybe that was a stupid choice, but it was daylight outside. The fresh air and exercise sounded good.

When we reached the Bermuda Triangle, I spotted a familiar face ahead.

Just the person I hoped I would run into again. Bill Brunke. He seemed to be in the know and more than willing to talk. Plus, he and his brothers made me smile, adding some humor to an otherwise frightening trip.

I waved hello and introduced Riley to the Brilliant Brunke Brothers. They were all working hard to freshen up the flowerbeds in the area. All of the garbage had been hauled away, new cement had been poured, and the paths had been edged.

Bill stopped spreading mulch in the flowerbeds long enough to nod. "Gabby."

I stared at the grounds around the Triangle. They'd been

working hard to clear everything. "This looks a million times better than it did just a couple of days ago."

"Thanks. Not to toot my own horn, but my brothers and I are the best in the area." He shifted, leaning on his garden rake. "I heard you had some excitement around here last night."

I shifted to get the sun out of my eyes and get a better read on the man. "You heard? Already?"

He nodded. "Nate stopped and showed us the pictures of Bigfoot's footprint."

Wasn't that interesting? Why would Nate do that exactly? I would think he'd want to stay quiet about it, rather than risk bad publicity.

"We're trying to get to the bottom of it," I finally said. As soon as I had the chance to slip away today, I was going to deliver my evidence to a crime lab guy I knew out in Blacksburg, Virginia. I'd met him through my work at Grayson Tech, and I felt sure he would help me. I didn't trust sticking anything in the mail.

"I can't wait to hear what you find out. Maybe you could clear up some of our local mysteries that folks have talked about for years around here. That might make you a local celebrity of sorts."

"I'm not too concerned with being a celebrity, but I'll see what I can do." I turned again, the sun right behind Bill's head. Looking at him was giving me a headache. "Listen, you were telling me the other day about the money that mysteriously appeared in Henry's account. Do you know if the police ever found any evidence as to where it came from?"

He shrugged. "Apparently it was a cash deposit. That's what I heard, at least. No one knows who gave him the money. Not Henry's parents. Not even his girlfriend."

My internal radar went up. This was the first I'd heard about a girlfriend. "Is this girlfriend still alive? In this area?"

Bill nodded, pulling a handkerchief from his pocket and

wiping a line of sweat from his forehead. "Debby? Yeah, she'll never leave. She loves it here. She's up in Whitehurst still."

Debby. I stored her name away in the back of my mind. It could be handy to talk to her sometime. "What's Debby's last name?"

"Stephens."

"Debby Stephens?" I questioned, surprise rushing through me. "Is she related to Scotty?"

Bill smiled, displaying his bright white dentures—a quality he shared with the rest of his brothers. "As a matter of fact, she is. She married his son, Junior."

"Hey, Gabby!" Chad called as I crested the hill with Riley a few minutes later. "I have a new job for you, if you're up for the task."

"I'm up for anything." Saying that was my first mistake. "But I thought I was your floor girl."

"Huh?"

I shook my head. "What about the cabins?"

"Nate wants us to clean up the funhouse. He thinks it's safe enough and that people will get a kick out of seeing the inside. You want to do an evaluation and let me know what's needed? I'm pretty sure all of this was Clarice's idea—he thinks she walks on water. So does she. Anyway, I'm not the one calling the shots."

Clowns. There had been clowns near the funhouse. Were there clowns inside also? I didn't want to appear to be a wimp, but I was edging closer and closer to that distinction. There was just something about this place . . .

"I'd be happy to do an evaluation," I finally said.

"Great. Riley, why don't you help? You know where it is, right? The Bermuda Triangle."

"What am I looking for exactly?"

"How stable it is. If there are any safety hazards. General improvements we can make while still keeping the rustic, vintage funhouse feel. You know the drill."

At the word "drill," I immediately thought about a clown. With a drill. Chasing me.

I had to get a grip here.

"Oh, and Braxton is still working on the electricity. I'm not sure if it's working there or not," Chad added.

"Even better." With my luck, a mysterious TV would pop on again.

Riley gripped my hand as we walked the rest of the way up the hill. We reached the Bermuda Triangle, and I paused a moment to stare at the lopsided building in front of me. Deceptively cheerful signs hung outside the door, all painted with letters that had once been colorful and inviting. A warning on the front door said "Point of No Return." That didn't make me feel any better.

"Here we are," I muttered, my feet remaining planted.

I really wanted to continue thinking about the fact that Henry's ex-girlfriend had eventually married Scotty Stephens Jr., but I wouldn't have time for that at the moment. Right now, I had to conquer a fear. A clown fear.

"You sure you're up for this?" Riley looked down at me with those warm, blue eyes that I loved so much.

"It's an old funhouse. What could go wrong?" I gulped as the words left my mouth. *So much could go wrong!*

He stared at me another moment before eventually nodding. "Okay. Good for you. I thought you'd be more freaked, especially given your earlier reaction to clowns."

"I was just taken off guard before. You know how that goes sometimes. Clowns . . . coming out of nowhere . . . staring at you like maniacal killers."

"You're kind of cute when you're freaked out." He chuckled and squeezed my shoulder. "I'm glad you're so tough."

If only. I pulled out the clipboard Chad had handed me.

"Let's go see what's inside and take some notes. It's just another day at Mythical Falls, right?"

"Just another day."

I sang a few lines from "Nightmare on My Street." Some of the songs I used to listen to were flashbacks to my childhood, and that song was no different.

Riley laughed. "It's not often I hear you rap."

"Be thankful. Be very thankful."

I pushed open a decrepit-looking door at the entryway. The first thing I reached for once I was inside was the light switch. Unfortunately, the electricity hadn't been turned on in this building yet. Awesome. I guessed that meant we'd be exploring it in the dark.

I pulled a flashlight out of my bag instead. As my beam hit something in the distance, a small gasp escaped from my lips. I backed up, right into Riley.

"It's just a dummy," Riley whispered, appearing at my side.

He followed my gaze to the clown in front of me. One of the figure's eyes had popped out—but not completely. Instead, it rested on his cheek. The red paint around his mouth was smeared. His shirt was torn open, like someone had tried to wrestle with him.

This was the stuff of nightmares.

My mental soundtrack continued to play "Nightmare on my Street."

I shrugged it off and took another step toward the entrance, gripping my clipboard like it was a shield. "Here goes nothing."

I walked toward a maze of mirrors in front of me. As soon as I passed the first one, a terrible sound thundered above me. My skin crawled at the cackling, mocking laugh.

"It's just a soundtrack," Riley said.

"How is it possible that the lights don't work but some soundtrack from twenty years ago does?" I muttered.

"This place definitely has the creep factor going on." Riley craned his neck to look around.

"Yeah, it's real . . . fun." Why would anyone come to this place for pure enjoyment? I had no idea.

Riley squeezed my hand. "We've got this."

"Promise me you'll stay close by."

"I won't leave your side."

His words made my cheeks flush. He meant it, didn't he? Not just at this moment but forever. Or was I hoping for too much?

With that assurance, I took another step. How was it that crime scenes didn't affect me that much anymore, but put me in an old funhouse surrounded by clowns and I fell apart? I was sure there was a great psychological analysis in there somewhere. I didn't have time to dive in now, though.

"We're going to need to replace three of these mirrors." I shone my flashlight on them. The reflective surfaces covered every available wall within eyesight. "They're broken. Definitely a safety hazard."

"My advice to Nate: Burn this building down. The whole thing is one big safety hazard." Riley shook his head. "I'm not sure Clarice's advice is the best—not that she doesn't have some great ideas."

"Tell me about it." I took another step and banged my head on a mirror. I groaned and rubbed the sore spot on my forehead. "These mirror mind tricks really work."

Riley grinned. "They sure do. You want me to lead?"

Honestly, I did want him to lead. But I wouldn't allow myself to say yes. How many times did I have to remind myself that I was a professional? CSIs didn't get scared . . . right?

"I'm all good. Let's keep moving." I shined my light on the floor. It was carpeted at one time, but now dust, litter, and feces covered it. "There's also a spot right here that feels soft. We should replace that as well. It's even starting to buckle some."

"Noted."

I reached a hand out in front of me, determined not to embarrass myself again by walking into another mirror. But, I was disoriented now after looking at the floor. Whatever direction I turned looked the same.

Riley squeezed my shoulder again. "I've never seen you like this before, Gabby."

"This is really messing with my mind." Just as life had messed with my perception of the future. Wasn't it just peachy that this was the time I'd chosen to get deeply analytical about my fears and failures?

"This is a different side of you."

"A weak side," I muttered. I always tried to hide these parts of me, even from the people who knew me best. Strength was admired, as was courage in adversity and wisdom in difficult times. You know what wasn't admired? Succumbing to fears.

"It makes you seem more human."

"Need I remind you of all the other times I've seemed human? I have a whole list of mistakes I've made that will show anyone and everyone just how fallible I am."

He kissed the back of my head. "We've all got those, Gabby. You know mine all too well."

At least he had a good excuse for his—most had occurred while he was in physical rehab after being shot in the head. Mine were just second nature to me.

I came to a stop as the mirror maze ended. My heart slowed for a moment. Whew. We'd made it through the first obstacle.

The cackling clown laughter in the overhead hadn't helped my nerves, but I supposed for most people that was part of the fun. Scares within a controlled environment, similar to scary movies. Only, at the moment, nothing about this seemed controlled.

I shone my light around the walls, trying to figure out where to go next. "Stairs? We have to go upstairs?"

"Apparently."

"Awesome sauce." I gripped the flashlight, searching the steps for any signs of danger. The wide, twisting staircase seemed sturdy enough, other than the cobwebs that were strung across the majority of it.

At the top of the staircase was a cylindrical tunnel. At one time it had probably spun. Right now it just appeared to be a dark abyss that I had to walk through.

A breeze swept across us as we ventured through the tunnel, and I shivered.

"The building is just drafty," Riley whispered in my ear.

"Of course." My throat felt tight as I said the words.

I forced myself to move forward. The clown laughter above us must have been triggered by some kind of motion sensor because, wherever we were, the sound billowed around us.

I stepped into the next room. This one had tiles dangling from the ceiling that I had to skirt around in order to get through. My back tensed at the thought of what might be hiding behind one of those tiles.

At least the floor felt relatively solid in this area. We'd have to check where each of the tiles connected with the ceiling. Certainly some of them would have to be replaced.

I had to agree with Riley, though: opening this building up to the public seemed like just one more on an already long list of bad ideas.

Just then, I heard Riley gasp behind me. I twirled around to make sure he was okay.

He was gone.

"Riley?" I called.

I darted my flashlight around the room. He was nowhere to be seen.

At the moment, the floor creaked only feet away from me. I pointed my flashlight toward the sound, just in time to see a shadow disappear in the corner.

What was going on? I had no idea.

I only knew that Riley was gone. And someone else was in this building.

CHAPTER
EIGHTEEN

I'D STEPPED into an episode of Scooby-Doo. That was all there was to it. Things like this didn't happen in real life. An abandoned funhouse with no lights, spine-chilling soundtracks, and hidden intruders.

Who else was in here? Bigfoot?

My heart shuddered at the thought. No, he wasn't real. But, then, who?

Maybe a real-life killer, a person who'd remained faceless up until this point? The person who'd killed Caleb Kidwell? A hit man hired by Scotty Stephens? Or could a desperate Nate, who had a dark, evil side to his plan that he hadn't let on to, be behind this?

Could it even be someone who had no real connection, but who was simply just fascinated with this place? With murder?

I gripped my flashlight again, feeling like it was my only life-line, at the moment. Other than God, of course.

Please, Lord, be with us now. Keep us safe.

"Riley?" I called again.

There was no answer. Where could he have gone? Maybe this place had one of those trapdoors, and he'd fallen through? That really didn't make me feel better.

I needed to know he was safe. I desperately wanted to be safe. And outta here. Now.

But no man left behind seemed only appropriate at the moment. I couldn't leave Riley.

Another one of the dangling ceiling tiles moved. My flashlight shot in that direction just in time to see a shadow disappear across the room.

My throat clenched and I rubbed it, imagining how it would feel to die by strangulation. Not good. Not good at all.

At that moment, something cackled at my belt. My radio! That was right. How could I have forgotten about that?

"Gabby, how's it going in there?" Chad's voice sounded over the line.

"Chad, I need you in here. Now." My voice cracked with each word.

"Is something wrong?"

My gaze scanned the room for any more sign of trouble or danger. "That's what I'm trying to figure out. I've got a bad feeling. Please. Come fast."

"I'm on it," Chad said.

I had to see if I could get out of here. That meant confronting the unknown and possibly running into a stuffed clown and facing moving shadows.

All of my muscles trembled as I moved forward, one hand outstretched and the other shining a light on my path. I held my breath as I passed each tile. No one jumped out, although my body felt tight in preparation.

That laughter kept winding my nerves tighter and tighter.

Finally, I reached the last ceiling tile.

I stepped out of that room and into another. As soon as I entered it, my head seemed to wobble and the space around me shifted. What was going on?

That's when I realized that the whole room was slanted. But the walls were designed to contrast the tilt of the floor, making the entire space a giant optical illusion.

Brilliant. But not at the moment.

I heard another creak behind me and decided to pick up my pace. I ran across the floor, my head spinning with each step. At the end of the room was another tunnel. I started through it, only to realize it wasn't a tunnel but a swirly slide.

I prayed that there were no parts missing, because if there were, I was a goner.

I froze as I reached the bottom, mentally evaluating myself for any injuries. I was fairly certain I was okay.

I'd made it down in one piece. But where was I now? Certainly I was at the end of this horrific place. Surely the exit was close.

A door opened in front of me. I squinted, the daylight blinding after being in darkness for so long.

"Gabby?"

I recognized that voice. "Chad?"

He stepped inside, blocking the glaring sun. "What's going on?"

I grabbed his arm, the urgency of the situation pressing on me. "I lost Riley."

He squinted. "What do you mean?"

"He was behind me one moment. The next moment he was gone. And someone else was in there with us. Someone who could have done something to Riley."

"I'll check it out. Why don't you wait outside? You look shaken."

The offer was tempting. But I couldn't do that. No way. "I'm going with you. I have to find Riley."

I followed Chad into the entryway of the building. As I did a familiar figure emerged from the mirror maze. Riley!

He rubbed his head and looked slightly disheveled as he blinked. But he was okay! Thank goodness, he was okay.

I rushed toward him and threw my arms around his neck. "Riley! Are you okay? What happened?"

"I'm not sure. One minute I was with you, and the next

minute I was in a ball pit—a nasty, rat infested ball pit. I think I hit my head on the way down."

"A ball pit?"

"The floor must have collapsed. Thankfully I was standing over the area where the ball pit was."

Chad rubbed his chin, looking deep in thought. "There are different paths you can take inside this place. You must have veered off."

"Are there trapdoors?" I asked.

"No, but I think there's another slide that leads to that ball pit."

"That would make sense. I could hardly see my hand in front of my face." Riley looked at me. "I tried to call for you, but you probably couldn't hear me over the soundtrack."

"What's up with that?" Chad stared at the ceiling. "It's unsettling."

Just then, another squeak sounded above us. All three of us looked at each other. Someone else was in here still!

"We should go check this out. End it once and for all," Chad said.

Chad led the way, and Riley held my hand. I had no idea what had happened to my clipboard, but now wasn't the time to figure it out. Now was the time to find some answers.

Chad seemed to instinctively know how to get through the mirror maze. He led us up the steps again, but instead of going into the roomful of swinging ceiling tiles, we ended up in a room full of . . . what else? Clowns.

I froze as I glanced at each of them. Most of the mannequins were in decent condition, all things considered. They stood around the edge of the room, each frozen in a different position. One slapped his knee and laughed. Another pointed toward the ceiling, a gleeful smile across his face. Two others climbed on each other's shoulders to reach a light bulb. Still another attempted to juggle.

The happy scenes clashed with my not so happy thoughts about clowns.

"There's no one in here," I squeezed Riley's hand tighter. "Do you think that sound came from the room with the hanging tiles?"

"It came from directly above us." Chad pressed his lips together in thought. "This room was directly above us."

"Whoever it was must have gotten away," Riley said. "It's empty now."

"Wait one minute." I shined my light on each of the clowns.

Just then, one of them blinked.

I screamed.

THE CLOWN SPRANG to life and took off toward the door across the room. Riley darted after him. As the clown leapt over a metal railing, Riley was right behind him, moving with amazing strength and agility. Chad and I were right on his heels.

That clown couldn't get away.

As we reached the other side of a silly mirror room, the door slammed shut. Something slid across the floor on the other side. Riley rammed his shoulder into the wood, but the door didn't budge.

"He blocked the door," Riley muttered, staring at the exit in contempt.

"We've got to go back the way we came," Chad said. "Follow me."

We all took off toward the spiral staircase leading to the mirror maze. We had to reach the man who'd been hiding in here before he got away.

We darted down the steps, through the lobby, and out the front door. By the time we stepped outside, the man disappeared into the woods.

I slowed to a stop. There was no way we'd catch him now. He had too much of a head start.

To my surprise, Riley continued after him. Instead of skirting around the line corral leading to the bumper-car area, he leapt over the railing there, two or three bars at a time before vaulting over a halfwall into the pavilion. He moved surprisingly fast across the floor.

"That was pretty sweet." Chad stared in the direction Riley had raced, momentarily distracted from our clown problems.

"I concur." I only hoped he was okay. What if Riley came face-to-face with that clown? What if that clown had a gun? This was all just too weird and creepy.

I shivered again as I remembered seeing the person blink while wearing that clown costume. There was creepy, and then there was creepy. That was the creepiest, by far. It would go down in my "Hair-Raising Hall of Fame," All Stars Edition. And I had some spine-chilling experiences up there.

Just then, Riley emerged from the woods. He shook his head and held something red in his hands.

A wig, I realized. He'd managed to get the clown's wig.

I rushed toward him and placed a hand on his chest. "Are you okay?"

He nodded, a rather somber look about him. "I'll be fine. The clown got away—but just barely. He had some kind of ATV waiting out in the woods. Once he got on that, I knew there was no way I'd catch him. At least I got this." He held up the wig. "It must have flown off when he ran away."

I took the hairpiece from him and observed it. Each of the stiff fibers looked old and moldy. Disgusting really. I couldn't imagine anyone wanting to put that on his head.

"Why would someone be hiding up there?" Chad began to pace on the walkway near the carousel of mythical creatures— mostly unicorns.

"I'm guessing here, but what if someone heard us coming and darted into the funhouse to hide," I mused. "When we got closer, he could have grabbed the clothes from one of the clowns and put it on to disguise himself."

"Interesting theory," Chad said.

"But it's also interesting because the clown was slight," I mused aloud.

"What are you getting at?" Riley said.

"If someone is dressing up as Bigfoot, they're large. They have to be to fill out the costume. Whoever was dressed as that clown was small."

"So you think two different people are involved?"

I shrugged. "Or there are two separate crimes going on."

"What are the odds?" Chad muttered.

I raised the wig. "I'll check this for hairs or other fibers. You never know."

"Even if your theory is right, why is someone trespassing here, anyway?" Chad continued. "This goes beyond college pranks."

"Maybe someone's determined to scare us off this property," I said. "Whoever it is seems to be doing a good job."

Chad sighed. "I'm counting on this paycheck. Sierra wants to cut back on her work hours. We need to pay off our cars. Plus, eventually, I know she's going to want a house. Who doesn't after they have kids? And then she'll want a nice-sized yard so we can have dogs. Then there's going to be private school—"

I laid my hand on his arm, things suddenly making sense. "Is that what all of this is about? I was wondering why you seemed so focused."

"I'm a family man now. I have two people who are depending on me. I can't just take odd jobs whenever they come. I need to be out there looking for good leads. Not letting opportunities like this pass me by. If we drop out of this, then all that money I'd been counting on . . ." He shook his head.

Riley clamped down on his shoulder. "We're going to get this done, Chad. No clowns or mythical creatures are going to scare us off. Not even rainbow-colored unicorns." Riley gave a pointed look to the carousel creature beside us.

"I think it's admirable that you want to provide for your family," I added. "But, remember, Sierra is her own person. I've never seen her show any interest in having a nice house or driving the nicest cars or even having her kids attend the nicest school."

"Have you ever been to her parents' place?"

I shook my head. "Nope."

"It's nice. I'm afraid she's going to morph into her mom."

I supposed everyone had fears, even Chad. It wasn't so much having fear, as it was what you did with it. "Like I said, Sierra is her own person. I know her hormones have been a little crazy lately, but you should give her more credit."

Chad paused and shook his head. "You know what? You're right. My mind is just working overtime. I don't want to be a disappointment, you know?"

I knew what he meant all too well. We were having our own little Dr. Phil moment out here in the Bermuda Triangle. "You won't be, Chad."

"Thanks for the pep talk." He straightened, signaling a shift in our conversation. "Listen, be careful out there. I don't know what's going on. You came here to help me fix this place up. But Nate mentioned something about having you investigate Caleb's murder. At first, I discouraged him, but now I'm seeing how it could be a good idea."

"I'm beginning to think that should be more of a priority also. But I think I can squeeze in both investigating and helping you."

"You're the best. You want to go supervise the cabins in Area 51?" Chad asked.

"If it's okay, I'm going to run some samples to a friend of mine who works at a lab a few hours from here. It will take the rest of the day."

He shrugged like it was no big deal. "Sure thing. Let me know when you're back."

As Chad walked away, I turned to Riley. "Those were some fancy moves you did back there."

"I'd told you I'd been training."

"In martial arts," I reminded him.

He teetered his shoulders back and forth. "There's some parkour in that. American Ninja Warrior type of stuff. It's been fun and a great workout."

"I want to see some of those moves sometime." I shifted. "Why haven't you mentioned this more? I mean, I know you go to lessons a couple of times a week and sometimes on your lunch break. But it seems like I would have known about this before now."

He shrugged. "The time never seemed right to bring it up. Plus, apartments and restaurants never seem ideal for these things."

"Well, show me something now then."

He raised his eyebrows. "For real?"

I nodded. "For real."

He shrugged. "Okay then."

He glanced around before seeming to settle on something. With a start, he ran across the pavement toward the funhouse. As gracefully as a cat, he ran up the wall, grabbed the roof, and pulled himself on top. Once up there, he gave a curtsy.

I clapped my hands. "Impressive."

He hopped down and stood in front of me, grinning mischievously. "Is that all I would have had to do this whole time to impress you?"

I grinned, liking that he was standing so close. Close enough to kiss. To forget my fears for a moment. "I've always been impressed by you, Riley Thomas. I think you know that by now."

"Sometimes, I wonder." His voice got the wistful sound again as he turned his full attention on me. "I'm afraid I hurt you too badly for you to fully forgive me, Gabby. That's the honest truth of the matter."

I opened my mouth, not sure what to say or how much to

confess to. But before anything could come out, a horn honked in the distance.

Riley and I glanced at each other before hurrying down the trail toward the entry gate. There, on the other side of the fence, was a news van. Two news vans, for that matter. And someone already had a camera rolling despite the barrier between us.

"Is it true that you spotted Bigfoot?" a reporter yelled. "And that you have proof?"

Riley and I looked at each other. The day kept on getting more and more interesting.

And that wasn't necessarily a good thing.

BEFORE TALKING TO ANYONE, I radioed Nate, who met us at the gate. His eyes lit with interest when he saw the news crews.

"This is most excellent," he muttered.

It wasn't the reaction I'd expected. "What do you want us to do?"

"Talk to them. Just be honest."

"Honest?" I repeated. Perhaps he'd forgotten about everything that had happened. I could simply not answer their questions. "About everything?"

"Of course. Transparency. That's what I want."

"If you're sure." Transparency was great in relationships, but not always in business.

He nodded. "This will be great publicity for the place. We need all the help we can get. Especially once word gets out about what happened here earlier."

Hesitantly, I stepped back. "It's your call, not mine."

"Perfect. I appreciate you doing this. I owe you all big time."

Nate opened the gate, and the news crew flooded inside. Before I could even say anything, a curly haired reporter shoved a microphone in my face.

"Are you Gabby St. Claire? *The* Gabby St. Claire."

I blinked, taken back by her focus on me. "That's correct."

"Is it true you're like a modern-day Sherlock Holmes?"

I nearly snorted. "Modern-day Sherlock Holmes? Who in the world said that?"

"We heard that's the rumor."

"I'm the only one who thinks that. Sherlock was a master. I mean, a fictional master, but still." I shook my head, praying she wasn't catching all of this on camera.

"Is it true that you're a real-life forensic investigator who's looking into Bigfoot?" the other reporter, a woman in her forties, asked.

"What? Who told you that?" Where had these people gotten their information? It had to be from someone here on the property. I had one guess as to whom that might be.

Nate.

I gave him a dirty look, but he shrugged.

"Is it true?" the brunette continued.

I threw Nate another dirty look, wondering exactly what they'd been told. "I'm not here specifically to research Bigfoot."

"But you are researching him? In fact, you saw him here on this property?"

I shook my head. "I saw something that appeared to be a hairy bi-ped. It's unconfirmed what exactly he was. Scientists must be opened-minded." Except when it came to God. Then most scientists rejected the idea in favor of the rational and provable.

At one time, that had been me. Now, I didn't know what I would do without God in my life. My faith had sustained me through some tough times. I didn't suppose the reporter wanted to talk about that, though.

"So you're open to that idea?" the curly haired reporter continued.

I wanted to say, "Not really." But I decided to say something more reasonable instead. "I'm looking at all of the evidence."

"You have evidence?"

I cringed, wishing I hadn't let that slip. "I have a cast of the footprint."

"And?"

I cringed again. "And I'm looking into it."

Wait—had I just admitted that I was looking into Bigfoot? How had that happened?

"What are your initial thoughts? Folks here at WTRO want to hear it first."

I shifted, deciding to just embrace this moment instead of fighting it. "My initial thoughts are that the footprints weren't deep enough to be caused by a Bigfoot. Though the prints were large, the depth wasn't what I would expect from a mammal of Bigfoot's size and weight."

"Couldn't that be explained by the dry weather we've had here lately?"

"Normally, I'd say yes. But I was by a stream where the ground was moister than in other places. These are all things that are taken into consideration when doing forensics."

The brunette thrust her microphone toward me, obviously not wanting to be outdone by her competition. "Is it true that you solved the Mercer family murder up near Cincinnati?"

I almost asked how she knew about that, but I knew it was of no use. She hadn't answered me yet, and I asked twice. Chad must have told Nate, who'd sent out a press release. Or had this been Clarice's idea? "Yes, that's true."

"And you also solved the murder of the senator's wife a few years back?"

"Gloria Cunningham? She was actually the daughter of a senator, and her husband was running for office." Hers had been one of my first cases. Just the mention of her name brought back so many memories. I'd met Riley then also. I'd had ashes on my face, smoke saturated my hair, and crime-scene goo had stained my clothing. It wasn't my best moment.

I'd had many more moments like that since we'd met.

"So, yes?" Ms. Curly Locks waited expectantly.

I cringed. "Yes, that's also true."

The brunette shoved herself in front of Curls. "So you are like Sherlock Holmes."

"I think this interview is over." As I took a step away, she turned her attention on Nate.

I shot Nate and Chad one more dirty look before hurrying toward my car. I needed to get out of here.

"I'm going with you," Riley added, catching up with me.

"You don't have to do that."

"You keep saying that, but the truth is, I kind of do. Everyone needs someone to watch out for them, Gabby."

My cheeks warmed. "Then I choose you."

He feathered a kiss across my lips. "No words could make me happier . . . Sherlock."

It took three hours to get to Blacksburg, but my friend Augustine at The Lab had assured me when I called him earlier that he would be waiting. The Lab was a privately owned forensic lab facility. Sometimes police stations used their services when the state crime lab was too backed up. Evidence could be double-checked independently there for court cases, as well.

I'd met Augustine through my job with Grayson Technologies. The Lab utilized our products, and I had paid a visit to them several times in the past. Augustine had been one of my points of contact. We'd hit it off in a nerdy, "I love microscopes" kind of way.

It felt so good to get away from Mythical Falls. Every time I closed my eyes I saw Caleb's dead body, Bigfoot, or that clown coming to life.

I was going to need therapy after this.

"What's your next step?" Riley asked after we left.

I let him drive my car. I loved my new vehicle. It was neat

and clean. I'd been driving around in an old van filled with hazardous materials for so long that even this basic sedan without any upgrades seemed luxurious. Plus, it felt good to have Riley beside me, like we were really grownups.

I shrugged. "I guess to work on the cabins in Area 51."

"No, I mean in this investigation. Where do you go from here?"

I nodded slowly. "Oh, that. Well, Augustine said he could probably have the results back to me tomorrow—if I'm able to receive his phone call, of course. Tomorrow evening I'm supposed to meet with Marion, and I'm hoping to pick her brain as well. There's one more person I'd like to talk with."

"Who's that?"

"Henry—the man who died twenty years ago—had a girl-friend. That girlfriend is now married to Junior—Scotty Stephens' son. I want to talk to her and hear her perspective on all of this."

"You think she'll talk."

"I have no idea." I cast a glance his way, noting how the moonlight hit his face in swatches between trees as we traveled down the dark mountain road. The area was practically deserted —there was only one car behind us, and we hadn't passed anyone in at least ten minutes.

"What if she's guilty?"

"I have no reason to think she is. Should I?"

He shrugged. "I don't know. The question would be: did she have any connection with Caleb Kidwell? Once we find a connection between those two people, we'll have a lead."

"You said 'we'll.'"

He flashed a smile. "We are a team, aren't we?"

I nodded slowly. "Yeah. We are. I'm really glad you came, Riley."

And I was. Despite all of my irrational fears, I still knew that I loved Riley. I was just so entirely afraid of ruining things.

"Anything to spend more time with you."

Guilt flashed through me again. When would I get real with him? When would I feel like I could speak my deepest fears? I wasn't sure still, but I didn't like not knowing. If I kept my fears secret, maybe they'd never come into the light—maybe they'd never become reality.

"Last year at this time, I saw no hope on the horizon," Riley started.

"You were in rehab. You really had to simply focus on getting better."

"I know. But I was probably depressed, truth be told. And that's not unusual in situations like mine. But I didn't think you would ever love me again. I thought I would be a burden to you. As a result, I almost ruined things for good."

I squeezed his hand. It felt strong in mine, like it belonged there. "But look at us now. Back together and stronger than ever."

He stole a glance at me. "But are we? I keep feeling like you're holding back."

"I've had a lot on my mind. I'm sorry."

"Did I do something?" His voice sounded quiet, tinged with hurt.

I quickly shook my head. The last thing I wanted was for him to feel hurt. He meant too much to me. "No, you didn't. I'm working through issues."

"I want us to be able to work through things together."

"I know. And I appreciate that. Deeply appreciate that. But—"

Before I could answer, something rammed into the back of my car. Our vehicle went careening off the side of the road—and right toward the side of a mountain.

CHAPTER
TWENTY-ONE

I REACHED for the dashboard as the car shifted and tilted and jerked. We slid close to the guardrail. On the other side of the wooden barrier was a cliff that cascaded down to a rushing river a good 30 feet below.

The car behind us zoomed past. I only got a glimpse of black before riveting my gaze back on the cliff in front of us.

Riley jerked the wheel, but it was too late. We were already out of control.

The car began to fishtail.

My life flashed in front of my eyes. The good, the bad, and the ugly times.

I wasn't ready for it to end yet.

I held my breath as we finally came to a stop. The front of my car dangled over the edge of the cliff. But we'd stopped. We hadn't gone over.

My heart pounded in my ears as I realized just how close we'd come.

I glanced at Riley. "Are you okay?"

He touched his forehead. A slight trickle of blood had started there, but he otherwise appeared fine. "Yes, I'm okay. That was unexpected."

"Someone was trying to kill us," I whispered as reality set in.

Riley stared straight ahead, his breathing still labored. "They almost succeeded."

As he said the words, our car teetered like a seesaw on the playground in elementary school.

I froze. "We're not safe yet."

"We need to get out of this car. Carefully."

I started to nod but then thought twice of it. No movement other than what was absolutely necessary, I told myself. Absolutely necessary.

"I'm going to open my door and slide out," Riley said. "You're going to hold my hand the whole time."

I knew what he was getting at. He didn't want to shift the car's weight when he got out and leave me inside to topple to my death. "Got it."

"Come closer to me. Slowly."

The car rocked again, and I held my breath.

This wasn't good. It wasn't good at all. Of all the ways I'd envisioned dying, this wasn't one of them. And I'd envisioned death a lot of ways. Way more than the average person.

As Riley stood, the car wobbled again.

I froze, only moving my eyes as I glanced up at Riley.

"It's going to be okay," he murmured.

He still gripped my hand, and that was my only comfort at the moment.

"We don't have time to waste here, Gabby," Riley urged. As he spoke, the car rocked again.

I gasped as the jostle strengthened.

"Now!" Riley shouted.

As he said the words, he jerked my arm. I darted out of the car, diving onto the rocky ground on the other side.

Just as stones and pebbles dug into my flesh, I heard a groan. I turned around in time to see my car fall to the cliff below. A horrific crash sounded. My precious car that I saved so long and hard to buy was gone. Thank goodness, we weren't inside.

I sucked in a long breath.

That had been close. Too close.

My head fell to the side, and I spotted Riley lying beside me. He was okay also. Thank goodness.

I threw my arms around him, so grateful that we were both safe. That was the important thing.

Riley pulled me close, and I could feel his heart pounding against my ear. "That could have been catastrophic."

"Why is someone trying to run us off?" I asked.

"Usually it's because you're getting closer to answers."

"That's true. But I really don't feel like I'm getting close to anything. I only have theories."

"Someone else begs to differ."

Whom had I encountered who might be feeling threatened? Junior? Nate? I had no idea.

"You know the only thing that could make this worse?" I asked.

"What's that?"

"No cell phone service."

Riley and I had to walk a half a mile down the road before either of our phones picked up one bar. We managed to call the state police and they promised to send someone out. Then we hiked the half-mile back to where my car had gone over the edge.

We hadn't passed a single soul since all this had happened. This was why I could never live in the middle of nowhere. My imagination was too big.

Holding Riley's hand, I peered over the broken guardrail.

It was so dark that it was hard to see. But, there, at the bottom of the ravine, I could barely make out the car that I'd worked so hard to buy.

"I'm sorry, Gabby." Riley squeezed my hand.

"It's like you said. This could have been much worse."

"I know how proud you were of that car."

"The Bible says to store up treasures in heaven, not on this earth, right? As long as everyone I love is okay, then so am I."

He turned toward me, the full moon hitting his face as he brushed my hair away. "Who would have thought three years ago that we'd end up here?"

I settled in his arms, feeling safer there than on the desolate roadside. "I was just thinking about that earlier."

He smiled softly. "I thought you were so beautiful when I saw you in the parking lot that first day."

The memories hit me at full force. The arson. My disheveled state. My curiosity about my new neighbor. "I looked awful."

"I didn't think so."

My heart fluttered. "You're incredibly sweet."

He kissed my forehead and pulled me into a gentle, sweet hug. Nature sang its song around us, the darkness enveloped us, and solitude, for a moment, felt like a friend.

Riley pulled back and studied me a moment. "Do you like rollercoasters?"

I blinked in surprise at his question. I hadn't been expecting him to say that. "Yeah, I guess I do. Why?"

"We've talked about a lot of things, but we've never talked about that. We've never even been to an amusement park together." He rubbed his lips together a moment. "Do you remember the first time you ever rode a rollercoaster?"

I nodded. I remembered it clearly. My parents had taken me to King's Dominion, an amusement park near Richmond. My brother had only been four or five at the time. It had been back before my family fell apart. Before my brother had been kidnapped. Before life felt like a burden.

"It was the Rebel Yell. Did you ever ride it?"

"You better believe it."

I smiled, as I remembered my dad talking me into going on it while my mom stayed with my brother. "I was terrified. I remember going up the first hill for the first time. I was literally beside myself. I couldn't even talk I was so scared."

"And then . . . ?"

"Then we went down the first hill. I thought I was going to die. I vowed to never speak to my dad again or to believe a word he told me. I literally felt paralyzed. Then we got to the next hill and the next. By the end of it, I loved it. I wanted to do it again. Why do you ask?"

Riley's smile widened. "I was looking at the Vomit Comet, as Chad called it. My first experience was similar to yours. I was terrified, excited, all of those things. I started thinking this week about how life is like that sometimes. It's a bit of a rollercoaster ride. You have ups and downs. Times on the mountaintop and times in the valley. You never really know what's around the bend. You just have to be ready to roll with it. Our only assurance is that God will be there with us to face whatever we have to face."

"Wise words, counselor." I swallowed hard, wondering exactly what he was getting at.

"I know that life has been difficult over the last year, Gabby," he lowered his voice. "I wish I could promise you a future that was full of certainty. Then I realized that I could. I can give you the certainty that I will always love you."

His words seemed to melt my heart. "Riley, there's been something I've wanted to tell you—"

Before the words could leave my lips, a police cruiser pulled up.

It looked like we'd have to save this conversation for later.

Which was good, because then it would give me time to think about his words. Because, when it came to the rest of my life, I didn't want to live in fear or make promises I couldn't keep.

"What do you mean someone rammed into you?" Chad repeated after we'd returned to Mythical Falls. The gang was all gathered in the guys' cabin playing cards and eating popcorn when we arrived.

Well, not everyone. Not Nate.

"Someone tried to run us off of the road," I repeated. "He or she almost succeeded."

"How'd you get back here?" Clarice asked, pausing for a moment from painting her nails.

"The state police showed up," I told them, recalling the long, chilly wait. "We were informed that it would take special equipment to get my car out of the river it fell into."

"I can't believe it," Chad said. "You worked so hard to buy that car."

"Tell me about it," I muttered, remembering all the extra jobs I'd taken. At least insurance should pay for this—eventually. I wasn't sure what I'd do in the meantime.

"I'm glad you're both okay, though," Chad said. "It could have turned out much worse. I just don't get it, though. Why would someone do this?"

I glanced at Riley. "It's like Riley said: we must be getting too close to the answers. Since the scare in the funhouse didn't deter me, someone decided to get more aggressive."

"But who would that be?"

"That's the question of the hour." I sighed before drawing in a deep breath. "What did you guys do while we were gone? Did you make a lot of progress?"

"Braxton finished rewiring three cabins. Clarice scrubbed them down. I finished putting up some drywall. By the way, I talked to your father. He might come this weekend and help us paint."

There was a time when I would have rebelled against that idea. But my dad and I had come a long way, in part thanks to his fiancée, Teddi. I'd learned to forgive and put the bad memories from a childhood growing up with an alcoholic father behind me.

"I'm sure he'd appreciate the work." I glanced around the exhausted looking group one more time and noticed someone was missing. "Speaking of which . . . where's Nate?"

Chad nodded. "He was here, but then he had to go into town again to meet with a client."

Something about his words caught my interest. "When was that?"

Chad shifted, narrowing his eyes. "I don't know. Around seven. Why?"

Around seven? We'd been run off the road around eight thirty. The area where we'd been traveling was about an hour and a half from here. Was that a coincidence? "I was just wondering."

"I know you better than that. You're still wondering if Nate is guilty."

I shrugged. "He may be the only one who knows exactly what's been going on around here. He knew we left. He knew what we were doing when we left. He even knew we were in that clown house." I straightened. "Speaking of which: Where was he when that psychotic clown started chasing us?"

"He was with Clarice," Chad said.

I looked at Clarice. She shook her head. "No, he wasn't. I was scrubbing baseboards while Braxton worked on wiring the cabins in Area 51. I don't know where Nate went."

Wasn't that interesting?

No alibi. No alibi. You ain't got no alibi.

I did a mental cheer in my head, complete with pompoms and a cupie.

"He wouldn't do something like this," Chad said.

"You have to admit that Nate makes the most sense," I said. "If I looked hard enough, I could find motive. Maybe he wants to bring attention to Mythical Falls. Maybe he's hoping for an insurance payout. Who knows? But he was around here twenty years ago."

"He was only ten years old." Chad crossed his arms.

"Maybe it's been passed down generationally, and his father started all this."

"Killing two people wouldn't up the tourism antennae for the park," Chad said. "Listen, Gabby. I really need you to lay off Nate. I know him. He'd never do something like this. If you keep pushing, I'm afraid I'm going to be the biggest loser here."

"What do you mean?"

"Nate could find plenty of other people to do this work. He could probably hire them for cheaper. I can't afford to lose this job. So do me a favor and back off. Okay?"

I stared at Chad a moment, desperately wanting to argue. But I didn't. I had to respect his wishes here.

Finally, I nodded. "Fine. I'll lay off."

Until the evidence demanded I raise a ruckus.

CHAPTER
TWENTY-TWO

THE NEXT MORNING, after everyone else got busy with their jobs, I sneaked away for a moment to check my phone. I decided to be the smart girl, and I brought Riley with me. As I reached the magic spot of cell reception—which really should be labeled as one of the park's attractions—I had my *bingo!* moment.

I found my cell signal, and I had a voicemail from Augustine asking me to call him back. Oh, boy, would I. I couldn't wait to hear what he'd learned. Maybe I'd finally have a decent lead.

"Here goes nothing," I told Riley. I dialed Augustine's number, and he answered on the first ring.

"Just the person I was hoping to speak with," he said.

"You've got me curious. What did you find out?"

"First, let me say that I agree with your initial assessment about the footprint. It's not deep enough to support the weight that a supposed Sasquatch would carry. Plus, the impressions toward the center of the foot were deeper, which leads me to believe that the weight wasn't evenly distributed."

A theory was already forming in my head, but I wanted to hear what else he had to say first. "Good to know."

"But, of course, there's more. I tested the hair you collected. It's synthetic."

I nodded, giving one of the Bigfoot figures in the distance a "take that!" look. He stared back with one eye and a grimace on his face.

"I thought it might be," I said.

"I can test it further and try to match it to the exact brand, but it's definitely a costume."

"You don't have to do that. I suspected that someone was simply trying to scare us away this whole time—or to drum up publicity. This only confirms it. Thank you, Augustine."

"No problem. Let me know how everything goes. I saw a little news clip about what was going on. I'd like to say you looked good on camera, but . . . "

I narrowed my eyes, but I knew he spoke the truth. "I know. I was caught off guard. After being trapped by psychotic clowns, what do you expect? It's a long story."

He chuckled. "I look forward to hearing it one day. It seems like your life is full of adventures. You always have interesting stories, way more interesting ones than I have being in the lab all day."

"Full of adventure is one way to put it." But he was right. I'd always thought I wanted to work in the lab, but I was so much happier out in the field.

I hung up and relayed the conversation to Riley.

He put on his thinking face—his contemplative "I like to give wise legal counsel" look. "So someone planned all of this. Maybe Caleb wandered into the middle of something—something illegal perhaps?—and someone killed him to keep him quiet."

"But then what about the money?"

He slowly shook his head. "I haven't figured that one out yet."

I frowned as my thoughts churned inside. Henry and Caleb both paid off with the same sum of money. Probably untraceable, if I had to guess. Whoever was behind this was too smart to cut a check.

Riley and I had to be getting closer to the answers, though. Otherwise, why would someone be desperate to keep Riley and me silent? Would we be the next victims of this Bigfoot Strangler?

The even bigger question I had to ask myself was: Who had the most at stake here?

The answer seemed clear.

"I wonder where Nate's car is . . ." I muttered.

Riley raised his eyebrows. "You think he tried to run us off the road last night?"

"The likelihood is that the person who's behind Bigfoot is also behind the other crimes that have been occurring around here. It's worth looking into."

"I know he has more than one car. He's mentioned them to me during his long, bragging homilies. I've only seen him driving his truck. Either way, he left early this morning." He readjusted his legs, that lawyer look still present. "We're going to dinner tonight with your friend, right?"

I nodded, wondering where he was going with this.

His eyes sparkled. "Then finding out exactly what kind of cars Nate has might be something to look into."

While pest-control people sprayed all of the cabins, the Squeaky Clean gang had moved down to the Loch Ness area to work on it. Thankfully, the day had turned out to be nice. The sun was out; the sky was blue; and the air felt warm. I'd even stripped off the flannel shirt I'd worn and tied it around my waist. The black T-shirt underneath was perfect.

There were no cabins in this area—only two small bathrooms that were more like outhouses. Chad and Braxton were conquering them.

Riley had been put to work fixing the railing that overlooked the waterfall while Clarice and I picked up trash from looters.

Nate, of course, wasn't back yet, so I hadn't been able to talk to him. Before I shared my suspicions with Chad, I wanted to speak with Nate and give him a chance to explain himself.

Clarice paused and stretched her back. She was always the pretty girl, even when cleaning up trash. Her hair was in a neat, perky ponytail. She wore her oldest designer jeans, a scoop-neck T-shirt that probably cost more than my leather coat, and loafers. "This is really beautiful, isn't it?"

I stared out at the waterfall. Mist rose up around it. The changing leaves, rich in orange, red, and yellow, made a beautiful backdrop, and the water almost had a greenish tint. The scientific side of me realized that the green probably came from algae, but, still, the effect was beautiful.

"I agree. I'm glad this area will get some use again. It shouldn't be hidden away."

Clarice snapped her neatly trimmed, pink-tipped fingers. "You know what Nate should do?"

I shook my head, having no idea where she was going with this. I could think of a lot of things, none of which applied to her train of thought right now. Things like . . . Nate should abandon this whole idea. Nate should possibly go to jail. Nate should take classes on how to talk to women.

Instead, I said, "No idea."

She spread her arms out wide, as if painting a picture. "He should advertise this place as a destination wedding area. People love stuff like that, and this would be the perfect location."

I thought about her idea for a moment and then nodded. "You know, that's not a bad idea."

She spread her hand across the overlook again. "I can see it now. The bride and groom can stand there. The seats can be set up behind them, facing the waterfall. The reception could be right over here. People could string up some lights through the trees. Have a band over there on the patio."

I nodded again. She really might be onto something. "Getting people down here could be a challenge. The hill is kind of steep."

"You could provide transportation. That's what Nate is thinking about doing. He's going to widen that path and flatten it out some. He should be able to get a Jeep down the path with no problem. It would be the perfect solution."

Clarice and Nate had really talked this through, hadn't they? Maybe there was more to their attraction than I'd given them credit for. "You should share your idea with him. I think he'll like that. I think a lot of people would."

Not to mention the fact that she obviously had his ear.

She beamed. She did that whenever someone complimented her. For years, she'd been known as the pretty airhead. It was good to see her coming into her own and feeling good about herself.

"Nate's really great, isn't he?" She swooped down to pick up another abandoned can of soda and shoved it into a bag.

"He . . . is. You two have seemed close lately."

"It's been a lot of fun getting to know him. He's got so much life inside him. So many ideas and plans. It's invigorating to be around him."

I paused, an old fast-food cup in hand. When I saw all the ants inside it, I quickly tossed it into the trash bag. Ew. "You really like him, don't you?"

She shrugged and giggled. "Maybe a little."

"I thought you were dating someone else."

"You mean Steve? No, we just went out a few times. He may have been handsome, but he had terrible breath."

Clarice had a tendency to go out with a lot of guys "just a few times." But at least she was being picky. That beat just committing to anyone who showed interest in her.

"I see. I hope things work out." I changed gears as I pulled an old shirt out of the underbrush. "By the way, you know that whole funhouse incident? Where was Nate when that happened? I figured he'd come when he heard over the radio what was going on."

She shrugged. "I dunno. Why?"

I didn't say anything, I just continued with trash pick up.

She froze and her mouth dropped open. "You think he's behind the whole clown incident, don't you?" Outrage filled her tone.

I shrugged, hoping she wouldn't get too worked up over this. "I didn't say that. I mean, why would he be guilty? For that matter, why would anyone do something like that?"

Clarice shook her head. "Because they're crazy."

I nodded. "Was he the one who called the news?"

"No," she said quickly.

I slowed my movements. "Why are you so certain?"

She shoved her tiny little chin into the air. "Because I did it."

"Why would you do that?" Outrage filled my voice this time.

She busied herself with work and didn't make eye contact with me. "We were talking, and I was telling him about you. I had one of those "ah ha" moments where I realized it was an opportunity for publicity. I'm not going to lie—it was a good chance to make myself look respectable. Nate was all on board. I almost didn't do it, but then I realized it was great publicity for you too. Those reporters called you Sherlock."

I let out a long sigh. "I'm not Sherlock. And now I'm a target."

"Why would you be a target?"

"Because someone thinks I'm going to discover them! It was right after that I nearly careened to my death off the mountain."

Her expression fell. "Oh."

I glanced at my watch. It was time for me to wrap up for the evening and get ready for dinner with Marion. Plus, it was a good excuse to finish this conversation before I said something I regretted.

Besides, I couldn't wait to hear Marion's insight on everything.

TWENTY-THREE

"TURN HERE," I told Riley, glancing at my GPS. We'd taken his car. Of course. All of that saving and working so I could buy my own vehicle, and now it was gone.

The one thing I loved about Riley's car, though, was the well-used Bible he kept between the seats. He had another one he took with him. But he always kept the brown leather one here, and in its pages were notes he'd written and insights he'd gathered. It was a great testimony of his spiritual life.

"As you wish," he murmured. "Are you going to confront Nate if he's there?"

I thought about his question for a moment. "Confront is a strong word. I really just want to talk with him. But first I want to see if there are any cars in his driveway. I need to know if he's the one who tried to run us off the road last night."

And if I saw a clown costume in his backseat, I might pass out right then and there.

A few turns later, we pulled to a stop in front of a red brick house sporting two columns that ran up both levels to the roof. A large porch, simple but neat flowerbeds, and a cheerful-looking American flag completed the scene.

This was a pretty nice home for Nate. Of course, he had a

nice job, and money must not be a problem for him since he was investing hundreds of thousands into Mythical Falls. Maybe he came from a wealthy family.

"What now?" Riley stopped and put his car into park at the curb.

I craned my neck for a better look. "I don't see Nate's usual truck here. I'm going to assume he's not home. But I'd like to search the perimeter of the property."

"I'll go too."

We climbed out and walked toward Nate's. Rule number one for being nosy: Look like you know what you're doing. For that reason, I kept my chin up and my hands tucked snuggly into the pockets of my black parka.

We followed the driveway toward a detached garage at the back of the property. There were no cars back here or anything else that seemed out of the ordinary.

"I want to check out the garage," I whispered, stepping into the shadows.

"Let's go." He put his hand at my waist as we hurried through the darkness. Dogs barked from a distant yard. Cars drove past. Someone rattled a trashcan.

Even after knowing Riley for nearly three years, he still managed to send tingles up my spine. But that was something to think about later.

Cautiously, I twisted the door handle. To my surprise, it opened.

I pushed it just enough that Riley and I could step inside the space. I knew turning on the overhead light was a bad idea, so I pulled up my flashlight app on my phone.

As a beam of light filled the room, my eyes focused on what was in front of me. Sure enough, two cars were in the garage. One was a classic Corvette that I could tell, even in the darkness, was well taken care of. There was something about the shiny coat and the spotless trim that made it clear this was a prized possession.

"Nice," Riley muttered.

"Apparently Nate has a lot of expensive hobbies. Cars. Big-game hunting. Restoring ramshackle amusement parks." Those were just a few of the things he'd mentioned since I'd met him.

"Must be nice to have money to burn. If I had that much money, I'd do the same thing."

I moved beyond the red Corvette to see the vehicle on the other side. It was an old black Buick. My blood spiked . . . *Could this be it?* I skirted around the back, squeezing by a lawn mower and other equipment. Finally, I reached the front.

My eyes widened. Sure enough, there was a dent in the front bumper. I leaned closer. Flecks of white marred the chrome.

"Nate hit us last night," I whispered.

Riley shook his head. "I have to admit—I don't know what to say. I didn't think he could do something like this."

I took a few pictures and then we slipped outside. We needed to get out of here before Nate returned home. Otherwise, he just might finish the job he failed to complete last night. The big jerk. And that was putting it lightly.

"Let's go," I said.

Riley took my hand and pulled me toward his car. Just as we cleared Nate's yard and set foot on the sidewalk, a voice sounded from the neighbor's yard.

"Nate's friends?" An older woman peered at us over the top of her bifocals. She had a watering can in her hands, even though it seemed awfully dark to be tending flowers. But to each her own, I supposed. I'd seen stranger things.

"Yes, we are," I said. "We were looking for him, but it doesn't appear he's home yet."

"He hasn't been home much lately. He's working at Mythical Falls. Then, again, you probably know that already, don't you? Since you're friends and all."

I nodded, unsure if she was trying to call my bluff or what. I decided to roll with it. "That's right. Hopefully it will open before Halloween."

"Are you two connected with the college also?" she asked.

I tilted my head, still unsure of where she was going with this. I really wanted to find out. "You mean Whitehurst College?"

She studied us a moment. "I'm guessing you're too old to be students, but maybe professors?"

I was halfway insulted because in my head I was still twenty-one years old. But I forced a smile. A professor wasn't that bad. At least she hadn't suggested we were the parents of college students. "No, but we are from out of town."

"I see. Nate's had several people from the college over lately. I just assumed he was doing another class there or something."

"Another class?" Riley asked. "He's never told us he taught there. He's so modest like that."

"You know, Nate. He's always up for new adventures. But about a year ago, he taught a financial class. I heard he was quite popular on campus."

"I can imagine. He has a magnanimous personality." I mentally rolled my eyes as I said the words.

"Yes, he does."

I shifted. "Did some of his friends who came here happen to be big guys? One a blond and the other have dark hair?"

She nodded. "As a matter of fact, yes. I just saw them here a few days ago. I guess you know them."

Satisfaction burst inside me. I finally had a connection. "Yes, I do. I was hoping I might run into them again also. Maybe I'll have better luck next time."

"Gabby! It's so good to see you!" Marion pulled me into a hug. "And who is this with you?"

"This is Riley. He's my . . ." Husband? Boyfriend? Fiancé? It was all so confusing.

"I'm the man she's going to marry," Riley said, giving me a wink.

Well, that was one way to say it.

"You're one lucky man," Marion said. "Gabby's a special, special girl."

"Believe me—I know it." Riley gave me a little squeeze.

"Come in, come in. I'm so happy you could make it. Did I hear that Caleb's parents called you?" She ushered us inside, took our coats, and led us into the living room.

I nodded, lacing my hands together in front of me and standing on a well-worn oriental rug. "They did. I told them I would work on the case in my spare time. I'd love to find answers for them before I go back to Virginia."

She offered a grateful smile. "Wonderful news. I was hoping all of that would work out. It means so much to them."

"Do you know them?" I asked, ignoring the tantalizing smell that curled around me. Pasta? Freshly baked bread? Those were my guesses, and I hoped they were right.

"No, but I talked to them for quite a while when they came into the office. They seemed like such a nice couple." She paused from filling some goblets with ice. "Now when do you go back to Virginia?"

"I originally was heading back on Saturday or Sunday, but I have a feeling I'll end up staying longer. My next job back in Virginia isn't until Wednesday, so I do have some time."

I hadn't told Chad that yet, but I figured he'd need the help. However, I would be at the mercy of whoever could give me a ride back.

"I hate to see you doing construction when you could be using that wonderful brain of yours for other pursuits."

I shrugged. "It's like I said: I do this and that. Between Grayson Tech and all of the side jobs I've gotten doing P.I. work, I've stayed busy. I can't complain."

"Well, I'll put in another good word for you with the Virginia

Medical Examiner's Office, if you'd like. You never know when things will turn around."

"I'm never opposed to having good words put in."

"This is my husband, Duke," Marion continued. A large, tall man with the most massive hands I'd ever seen stepped in from outside. I swallowed hard when I spotted him.

No, there was absolutely no connection between this man and the Bigfoot Strangler. Why would there be? But I'd never seen hands that large. Never.

"Nice to meet you both," Duke said. He had a low, gravelly voice. His hair, which was peppered with gray, was curly and too long. Thick hair also extended out of his collar and on top of his hands.

This man appeared to be the human form of Bigfoot. I had no doubt about that. He even seemed quiet and brooding.

But Nate was the one behind those Bigfoot sightings at Mythical Falls, and he was the one who'd tried to run us off the road. He'd somehow connected with Franz and Tobs to do this. I couldn't forget that. I knew exactly how to get the evidence I needed to prove he was guilty. I just needed a little more time.

"We're having something easy—baked spaghetti. It's already on the table, along with salad and some garlic bread. I didn't want anything fancy—just a simple dinner with time to catch up," Marion said. "So why don't we all go sit down?"

We did just that. The first hour, we chitchatted in general about life and let yummy pasta fill our tummies. But, just as I'd hoped, while having dessert the conversation finally took a turn toward the mystery at Mythical Falls.

"What do you think is happening at Mythical Falls?" Marion gingerly cut a piece of cheesecake and raised it on her fork. "Do you believe in Bigfoot? I saw you on the news, by the way. Very nice."

I offered a half-hearted smile and pushed a hair behind my ear. "I was ambushed. But thank you for being kind. No, I don't believe in Bigfoot. I do believe that someone dressed as Bigfoot in an attempt to scare us away."

But why would Nate want to scare us away? Why bring us here only to frighten us? And was he also guilty of—

"Do you think this same person is responsible for the murder of Caleb? And for the murder of Henry before him?" Duke asked, almost as if he'd read my mind.

"That is something I don't know. Unless Henry or Caleb discovered something they shouldn't, and this person decided to silence them once and for all."

"But death by strangulation?" Marion frowned. "You know what they say about that. In cases of strangulation, it's usually someone the victim knows."

"I thought about that, but both Henry and Caleb were strangled from behind. I think that could be telling. Sure, the murderer didn't want to look his victims in the eyes. Maybe he even ambushed them. But I'm not convinced he knew the victims."

"Why not use a knife or a gun? That's what most killers do."

I rubbed the white ceramic of my coffee mug, deep in thought. "Maybe he wanted to give the appearance that Bigfoot had done it," I said. "And, if that was the case, it worked. For years, people have believed that Bigfoot was roaming the woods, looking for more victims. Maybe someone knew that and wanted to exploit it."

Marion shifted before nodding thoughtfully. "That's a very interesting theory. I certainly wouldn't want to encounter this person in the dark, though. I can only imagine what goes on in their heads."

I wiggled in my seat a moment, getting out my nervousness before asking my next nosy question. "I know I'm not supposed to ask this, but how is the investigation coming? Are the police tracking down any promising leads?"

Marion ate her last bite of cheesecake and shook her head. "Not to my knowledge. They were unable to obtain any fingerprints from the gloves or gasoline cans. You know how difficult it can be to draw prints from leather."

I straightened at her statement. "I bet I could."

She twisted her neck in curiosity. "What do you mean?"

My mind raced with possibilities. "There's a new product called Polyvinylsiloxane. It's amazing at getting latent prints from difficult surfaces."

She twisted her head as she considered my words. "I wonder if the department knows about it."

I shrugged. "It's a relatively new product. It's one of the presentations I do for Grayson Tech."

She leaned closer. "Gabby, would you mind if I told some of the guys at the station about this Poly—?"

"Polyvinylsiloxane," I finished. "No, feel free. I try to spread the word about it. Whatever I can do to help."

She leaned back and smiled. "Great. I have a feeling it's no coincidence you're here now. No coincidence at all."

"We've got to go talk to the Tobs and the Franz," I told Riley after we left Marion's.

"The Tobs and the Franz?"

"Frat boy nicknames. They're the friends of Caleb's. I spoke with them a couple of days ago, and they match the description that Nate's neighbor gave us. I want answers from them before I confront Nate."

"How about we just call the police?"

I shook my head. "If my accusations are wrong—and I'm confident they won't be, especially after seeing Nate's car—but just in case, I need to know for sure. This could ruin my friendship with Chad, otherwise."

"Let's go then."

Thankfully, the college wasn't far away. As we cruised down the road, Riley said, "They seem like a really solid couple."

I nodded. "They do, don't they? And to think they met on an online dating site."

"It's not how you meet. It's about who you are and who your partner is, right?"

I nodded. "That's what I've always thought. But, then, I look at Stephen and Patti at church. If they can't make it, is there any hope for the rest of us?"

I hadn't intended on bringing them up, but they'd been on my mind a lot lately.

Riley grimaced. "I know. I hate to see their marriage fall apart. I keep praying that things will turn around for them."

"How does that happen, Riley? How does a couple go from being the leaders of our Bible study, model parents, and whispering the sweetest, most sincere sounding prayers ever to getting divorced?"

"It's enough to shake anybody up. I get it. All I know is that your foundation in Christ has to be solid. Divorce and giving up can't be an option. It can't even be on the table."

His words remained on my mind as we pulled into campus. We found parking, hiked across the campus, and were able to slip inside the dorm when someone else emerged. I walked up the stairs, acting like I knew what I was doing. A few minutes later, I was knocking on Tobs' and Franz's door.

Tobs answered a moment later. His eyes widened when he saw me.

"We're not supposed to have visitors here, you know," he said. "It's past hours."

"Thankfully one of your fellow students let me in," I responded. "We need to talk."

His gaze flickered back to Riley, and finally he nodded hesitantly. "About what?"

"About how Nate hired you to go to Mythical Falls disguised as Bigfoot," I stated.

He stared at me a moment before laughing. "That's ridiculous. Why would he do that?"

"He hired Caleb first, but something went terribly wrong. Were you there when it happened?"

"I don't know what you're talking about."

"I'm guessing he paid you ten thousand dollars because he knew Henry had been paid that amount. It would stir up more interest in the place if current events matched past ones."

Something flickered in his gaze. "First I've heard of it."

"For that matter, maybe you were the one who killed Caleb. Did he threaten to spill the beans on the whole mission? Maybe you needed the money—so badly that you'd kill to keep him quiet."

His eyes widened again, this time with a tinge of panic. "That's crazy. I would have never killed Caleb. He was my bro." He hit his hand on his chest in some kind of bro loyalty ritual.

"Then what happened? Because when I leave here, I'm going to the police with my theories. This is your one chance to explain yourself. You have to the count of ten or I'm leaving." I had to talk tough to get through to him. Tobs wasn't the type who'd easily confess. Most people weren't.

"Whoa, whoa, whoa. Slow down, Missy."

I cocked my hand on my hip. "Missy?"

He nodded, all ghetto-like. "I know who you are. I saw you on the news. You're like the female Sherlock Holmes. And you're trying to mess with my mind."

I almost rolled my eyes, but, then again, maybe I should be flattered by the title, even if someone who'd wanted to draw publicity to an aging theme park had fabricated it.

"Your time is ticking away," I told him. I glanced at my watch just for dramatic effect.

He raised his hands. "Okay, okay. I didn't kill Caleb. That's the truth. I would never hurt someone. Especially not Caleb."

"So what really happened?"

He looked down the hallway and then motioned for Riley and me to come inside. I would have said no, except that Riley was with me. But I made sure to keep the door open this time.

People, when threatened, could react horribly, and I didn't want to put myself in that position.

"So?" I crossed my arms, knowing I couldn't back down and that compassion would only be seen as weakness.

"We were hired to wear a Bigfoot costume. We were supposed to leave some footprints, do some wood knocking, maybe scare a few people. That was it."

"Were you the one peering in my window?"

He frowned, his shoulders slumping. "I was."

"How did you make such a quick getaway?"

"We rehearsed how to walk like Bigfoot. I had to take leaps to get across that stream like I did. After that, I said, 'No more.' There are too many creepy things going on. I finished my contract, and that was it."

"Contract?"

He nodded. "That's right. I had to sign a contract. If I didn't fulfill my portion of it, I would have to pay back the money. I can't do that. I used it to sponsor a party in my room last week-before Caleb died."

"So Caleb was originally hired to do this?"

He nodded again. "That's right. It was Caleb, me, and Franz. All three of us. Caleb went out to take his turn. But he never came back." His voice caught.

"Why didn't you tell the police any of this?"

His eyes sparked to life. "Because I know how it looks! It looks like we're guilty. I can't afford for people to look at me as if I'm one of the bad guys. I was just in the wrong place at the wrong time."

"So no one was there with Caleb that day?" Riley asked.

He shook his head. "No one. He wanted to go by himself to check out the property. We weren't supposed to start until the next day."

The day the work crew arrived. What perfect timing.

"Who hired you?" I already knew the answer.

"Nate. He said he wanted to drum up publicity."

Nate was way sneakier than I'd given him credit for. But was he sneaky enough to murder someone? "Did Nate kill Caleb?"

"Why would he? I don't know. I don't know anything about him. We met him at a workshop. We knew he owned Mythical Falls so we asked him some questions. He took us out there to see the property. That's when he mentioned a prank he wanted to play. He said it would be like one of those reality shows. We didn't think anything of it."

"Is there anything else you're not telling me?"

He shook his head. "No. Nothing. What are you going to do now?"

"I will have to share this with the local police, but I don't think you'll have any repercussions—not if you continue to tell the truth."

He nodded. "Of course. I want to make things right."

"What about your friend, Franz?"

He shrugged. "I don't know. I thought he'd be back by now."

"Where did he go?"

"To Mythical Falls. He was going to tell Nate he was done. No more. But he's not answering his phone."

"WE'VE GOT to get back to Mythical Falls and find Nate. Right now."

"Should we call the police?" Riley asked as we sped down the road. We were still at least thirty minutes away from the old theme park. I really hoped that Nate was there—or, if not, that someone knew where he was. I was beyond the point of being polite—Nate had betrayed all of us.

"We have nothing but theories now," I finally said. "I promise —I'll call them. I don't want to deal with this on my own. But I'm not sure how seriously they're going to take us at this point."

"Do you really think Nate murdered Caleb?"

I nibbled on my bottom lip for a moment. "I see very few other possibilities here. If Nate's not guilty, he's put himself in an awful position."

"What about this Franz guy? Are you worried?"

My stomach tightened at the thought. "I hope Franz is okay. But everyone has secrets, Riley. Everyone."

He opened his mouth then shut it again. Had he been about to ask if I had secrets from him but then stopped? Maybe he didn't want to know the answer. Maybe he didn't want to know how much I feared that all the good things in my life would slip away. That I was destined to mess things up. That I didn't know if I deserved to ever be truly happy.

Finally, we pulled into Mythical Falls. As soon as Riley parked, I hopped out and burst into the cabin.

My eyes immediately fell on Nate. He sat on the couch, his arm stretched behind it. Clarice giggled beside him, and Nate looked totally relaxed, like he didn't have a care in the world.

"Guess what, Gabs?" Nate rushed before any accusations could leave my lips. "We're now booked through the end of January. Can you believe it? The publicity has been amazing. *Amazing.*"

I ignored him and got right to the point. "Did you kill Caleb?"

The room went silent. Braxton paused from whittling at the kitchen table. Chad froze from stoking the fire.

"Gabby!" Chad finally said, reprimand in his voice.

I didn't care about this job right now. There were bigger issues at hand. My gaze remained locked with Nate's. "Did you?"

His entire body tensed, and the smile disappeared from his face. "That's crazy. Why would I do that?"

"To keep the rumor mill alive. To keep people's interest in this place and its morbid past."

He swallowed hard, his Adam's apple bobbing up and down. "I would never do that."

I stepped closer, anger flashing through me. "You hired Caleb to pretend to be Bigfoot."

Painful silence followed. I could feel everyone's gaze volleying from me to Nate like we were part of a bad soap opera.

Finally, Chad stepped toward me. "You're out of line, Gabby."

"She's telling the truth," Riley said. "Caleb's friends admitted to everything. The Tobs told us what happened."

"The Tobs?" Chad repeated.

I shook my head. "A college kid Nate got to know through a

class he taught at Whitehurst. He was friends with Caleb Kidwell."

Nate stood, his hands raised as if to ward off an attacker. "It's not what you think, Gabby."

I raised my chin, letting him know I had no intention of backing down nor would he be able to pull the wool over my eyes again. "You have no idea everything I'm thinking right now, Nate."

I remembered the gun in my purse. I hoped I didn't have to use it. After almost being killed by a serial killer, I got a concealed carry permit. I never wanted to be in that vulnerable position again.

However, I really didn't ever want to use the gun either. My life or the life of the bad guy? The life of a loved one or the life of a killer? When it came down to it, I knew what my decision would be.

"I may have hired three college guys." Nate's shoulders slumped.

"What?" Chad fell back into a chair, looking absolutely stupefied.

"None of this was ever supposed to happen." Nate squeezed the skin between his eyes. "Everything's gotten out of hand. Totally out of hand."

"I'd say that was the understatement of the year," Riley muttered. "You need to start talking, Nate. This is serious. We're talking murder, at most. Harassment, in the least."

I liked it when Riley talked all tough like that. I also liked someone having my back. It felt good.

When Nate looked up, his gaze was haggard. "I hired them to pretend to be Bigfoot. I just wanted to stir up some publicity for the place. It seemed cheaper than taking out magazine or TV ads. It was all just supposed to be for good fun."

Chad's mouth dropped open. "I can't believe this."

I kept going, having a Perry Mason moment where I laid out

all of the evidence before the jury. "You arranged for them to come right when we arrived."

He offered a half shrug. "It's true. I did. I had to have witnesses, and you all made the perfect subjects. Then Chad told me about your kick-butt investigations, Gabby, and I knew that could work to my advantage—if you didn't discover my plan first."

"My guess is that you led Clarice to believe that calling the media was her idea when all along that was your plan. You just had to convince her to do it so you could have plausible deniability." My mind was made up that this was true. I just wanted to hear him confirm it.

His eyes narrowed. "Okay, okay, you're right. I did. I admit it. But again, it was a banging business move. No one was supposed to get hurt. No one."

"What happened to Caleb?" Chad's expression turned from stupefied to horrified. "Did you . . . did you . . . kill him?"

Nate gasped and ran a hand over his face. "No! Of course not. I would never do something like that. *Never*. Who do you think I am?"

A liar. A manipulator. A cheat. I kept those thoughts silent, and instead asked, "Then what happened?"

Every movement Nate made seemed neurotic, like his muscles were all tightly wound and causing him to jerk and talk fast. "I have no idea what happened to Caleb. You've got to believe me. No one was supposed to get hurt—that's the truth. I was just as surprised to find Caleb dead as anyone."

"Why didn't you tell the police this information?" I continued. "Why waste their time? While you do, the real killer could be getting away."

"I didn't want to be a suspect. That's not the kind of publicity I want. I mean, really, Gabby, think about it." He tilted his head and gave me the "duh" expression I was getting to know all too well.

Again, he treated me like I was the one with no brains. I wanted to throttle him with a big, old Bigfoot hand.

"Yet you didn't call off the troops after Caleb died. You still made Tobs and Franz honor your contract and act like Bigfoot." I wasn't letting him off the hook this easily.

His shoulders slumped even more as his dirty look deepened. "What happened to Caleb was terrible. But I've staked everything on this place. If it fails, then I lose everything. *Everything*. I desperately want to give up that awful job in finance. I abhor it. *Abhor* it."

"Then why haven't you changed careers?" I asked. Hadn't he ever heard about how the average person had three different careers in their lives?

"My dad passed on his bore-of-my-life business to me and expected me to take over. I have to admit that the job pays good money—hot-diggity-dog good money, for that matter. But it's not worth doing for the rest of my life. This project has to work. It *has* to."

My initial impression that he wasn't a desk job guy was correct. He wanted to take risks. To experience adventure. To live free.

He might have a viable explanation for that, but I wasn't done yet. "What about last night? Why'd you try to run Riley and me off the road?"

"What are you talking about?" He looked earnestly confused with his wrinkled forehead and narrowed eyes. His hand went to his hips and he stared at me.

I leaned closer. "I saw your car in your garage. The dented front bumper. The flecks of white paint from my car. You weren't here during the accident. Maybe that's because you followed Riley and me and tried to silence us for good."

Clarice stood and looped her arm though his. "Nate would never do the things you mentioned."

He'd just admitted to half of them! Clarice was going to have to figure her love life out on her own, though. I had bigger issues at hand.

He shook his head quickly—too quickly. "No way. I would never do that. You're off your rocker."

"Then explain your car," Riley said.

"I haven't driven it in months. It's stayed parked in my garage. Wait—which car? My Corvette?" He shook his head, as if hoping his thoughts might fall into place.

"The Buick," I said.

"The Buick?" He pulled his lips back in revulsion. "I hate that car. It was my granddad's though. That's why I've kept it."

"Where were you last night?" Riley asked. "Around eight thirty."

"I . . ." He hesitated and stole a glance at Clarice before his chest deflated even more. "I was on a date."

Clarice gasped. "What? What about all of those talks we had about the future?"

"Babe, you've got to believe me. I meant all of those things—"

"You're a liar!" Clarice let out a sob before running to the bathroom.

Nate scowled at everyone who'd witnessed his humiliation. "It wasn't like that. I scheduled this before I met Clarice," he said. "This woman's father owns a travel magazine. I almost canceled, but it was such a good opportunity."

"You'll do anything for publicity . . ." I let the implications of my statement rush over him.

"But not murder!" he quickly added. "Never. No way."

"I thought more of you, man." Chad's face was all tight lines, and a cloud of disappointment hung around him.

"We'll have time to talk more about all of this later—I have more questions. I want to verify that alibi. Right now, Franz is missing. Have you seen him?" I asked.

"Franz? No way, man. I haven't seen him. Why would I?"

Tension crackled in the room, right along with the wood being eaten away by the blazing flames in the fireplace.

"He was backing out of your contract."

"That would have been fine. I already got the attention I needed."

"Maybe you had to kill him off so he'd stay quiet." Riley's words sounded grim, serious.

"You're talking crazy." Emotion grew in Nate's voice. If it got any bigger, the man might explode.

"I'm talking crazy? I think there's a better case in your favor." Riley's lawyerish tone emerged and sent tingles up my spine.

"I haven't seen him. But I know where he parks when he comes here," Nate said. "Let's go check it out before more accusations come flying my way."

I only hoped we weren't walking into the woods with a killer, I mused when we all departed a few minutes later. But I figured there were enough of us to take Nate if he turned crazy. Plus, I'd stuffed my gun into the waistband of my jeans, just in case we ran into trouble.

Nate and Clarice spoke in low tones up ahead. Clarice's arms were crossed, and it was obvious she wasn't happy. She hadn't wanted to come, but we couldn't leave her in the cabin alone.

I imagined that Nate was trying to explain things to her. He was a charmer and Clarice loved attention, so the two could very well be back together by the end of the night. Chad and Braxton walked in the middle, and Riley and I trailed at the end. I was glad to be at the end—it gave Riley and me a chance to talk.

The dark trail was narrow and underdeveloped, the kind where it would be easy to lose our way, especially at night. The moon and stars were all but blocked by the thick canopy of trees. Driving down this way hadn't been an option, which didn't thrill me.

The blackness around was incredible and intense and unlike the darkness back home in Norfolk. If I'd been able to glance at the stars, I bet they'd be remarkable—unobstructed by the city or streetlights even.

But I wouldn't be enjoying that tonight.

Ten minutes into our walk, I noticed that Clarice had forgiven Nate because she began to chatter about mountain lions, bears, and any other beast she could think of and she felt threatened by. Her babbling was driving me crazy, probably because I was already on edge. "Living on a Prayer" repeated over and over in my head. The words to the Bon Jovi song seemed appropriate for my life.

Chad looked tense in front of me. I wasn't sure if he would ever forgive Nate for his deceit. But, again, we'd have to deal with that later. Right now we could have another potential victim on our hands.

Dear Lord, please let Franz be okay. No more people hurt. I don't know what's going on, but give us wisdom. Lots and lots of wisdom.

Riley grabbed my hand as we wrestled with underbrush and as skeletal branches reached for us in the dark.

"You okay?" he whispered.

"I'm okay. I hope I can say the same for Franz."

"Do you believe Nate?" he whispered, throwing a glance at our "wilderness guide."

I thought about the question. I knew my gut wasn't always right—guts were really just a fancy word for strong emotions, and emotions couldn't be relied on. But I could rely on my powers of observation.

"He truly looked surprised when I'd brought up Franz missing," I whispered back.

"I agree. At least he owned up to being desperate for publicity. However, I don't think he'd go as far as to murder someone."

"I'm inclined to agree, but I'm reserving my judgment. Once someone lies about one thing, I have a hard time trusting that they won't lie about whatever they want."

"Once someone hurts you, you have trouble believing they won't hurt you again," he said softly.

I couldn't argue or deny it. Riley could read me better than I thought. He knew my trust issues went deep—deep enough that he wasn't immune. "I think anyone would say that. Our experiences condition us for our future reactions. I think that's healthy."

"I want to spend the rest of my life proving that hurting you is the last thing I'd ever want to do."

His words sent my heart fluttering. I hadn't told him what was wrong, yet somehow he seemed to sense my issues. That was just one thing I loved about Riley—he had the ability to see through to the real me. There weren't many people I could say that about.

I squeezed his hand. "Thanks, Riley. I think you know how much you mean to me. I hope you do."

Before he could say anything else, Nate stopped ahead of us and rallied the troops. "We're here."

He shone his light on something. I stepped closer to see. I sucked in a deep breath as I realized what it was. An old, gnarled chain-link fence stood in front of us. A hole had been cut, which had obviously allowed people to easily come and go.

Just beyond the fence was a maroon Toyota Camry. In the windshield dangled a parking pass with "Whitehurst College" on it.

This was Franz's car. I didn't have to ask. I just knew.

Nate climbed through the fence and shined his light inside. "He's not here."

At first, I wanted to tell him "duh." Then I felt relief that Franz wasn't dead inside. But where was he?

"We certainly didn't pass him on the trail," Chad mumbled. "Where could he have gone?"

"I have no idea," Nate said. "I hope he's okay."

"Did you ask him to come here and meet you?" I still wasn't

ready to let Nate off the hook. He'd done nothing to indicate he was trustworthy.

"No, I promise. I didn't. I have no idea. No blessed idea."

I examined the fence. "Is this the way he always came here?"

Nate nodded. "I showed him, the Tobs, and Caleb this entrance. There's a little service road they can take off another smaller back road. I plan to eventually widen all of this and use it as a maintenance road for the park, especially for disabled guests."

"Well, if he's not in his car, that most likely means he's on the grounds of Mythical Falls," I mused. "If what Tobs said was right, then he's looking for you."

Before anyone could respond, movement in the distance caught my eye. I shined my light back on the path we'd just come from in time to see a tall, hairy figure step onto the trail.

I was done with this. It was time to get some answers.

Or my name wasn't Sherlock . . . er, Gabby St. Claire.

TWENTY-FIVE

"WHAT ARE YOU DOING, GABBY?" Riley yelled.

"I'm ending this." I darted toward the Bigfoot wannabe. As soon as he saw me coming for him, he took off into the woods, moving faster than I thought he'd be able to.

Gripping my flashlight, I followed him. There was ridiculous, and there was *ridiculous*. This was beyond the reasonable and into the plain crazy. If Bigfoot was real, I was about to find out.

Riley stayed on my heels, and I sensed someone else had come along also. I didn't turn to see whom. I couldn't risk taking my eyes off Biggie, who could easily blend in with the shadows and disappear out there. Wasn't that what people said he'd done for years? He had the uncanny ability to hide, to elude truth seekers, and thus conceal evidence of his existence.

I didn't buy it.

Branches slapped me. Rocks threatened to twist my ankles. The incline made my lungs ache with exertion.

I moved as quickly as I could, but Bigfoot was fast and agile. He seemed to know these woods much better than I did. Typical.

"Ow." I heard someone grunt behind me.

I slowed long enough to glance back. Chad had fallen and

was on the ground, holding his ankle and his face was twisted in agony.

"Are you okay?" I called, my steps faltering.

"I'll be fine. Keep going."

I hesitated, hating to leave him while injured.

"I'll stay with him," Nate said, kneeling beside him.

Finally, I nodded. Riley and I started through the woods again. But just that brief reprieve had disoriented me. I paused a moment, trying to remember which direction Bigfoot had been headed.

"This way." Riley took my elbow and led me in the direction of the stream. A roar sounded in the distance.

I knew what that was.

It was Mythical Falls. The thought unnerved me. We would need to watch our steps. It was so dark out here. If we weren't careful, we could step off a cliff and . . .

The thought made my throat go dry. Why did I always find myself in these situations, even when I tried to do the responsible and safe thing?

Something rustled the underbrush in the distance. Was it our suspect? Or could it be something more along the lines of what Clarice had suggested: a mountain lion or bear?

None of those options seemed comforting.

Riley paused and held me back. He put his finger to his lips.

The darkness provided the perfect cover for someone hiding out and planning a sneak attack. We remained where we were, waiting, anticipating.

The scampering continued. My head jerked from one direction to the next. Where was the sound coming from? Was my mind playing tricks on me? The sounds seemed so rapid, like it came from multiple areas.

It was a whole family of Bigfoots.

I shook my head. Now I was thinking crazy.

But I didn't have any idea which way to run, to get away. So I stayed where I was, trying to anticipate what would happen next.

Finally, the noises faded until silence surrounded us.

"I think we lost him, Riley." I frowned.

"That was . . . freaky, for a lack of a better word. Agree?"

"Unfortunately. I'm still not sure what just happened. Was there more than one creature—er, person—out here?"

"Or it was someone who knew these woods so well that could move quickly across this landscape." Riley shook his head again. "We should head back."

I glanced at the darkness around me and shivered again. For a moment, I lost all sense of direction, and I had no idea which end was up or which way we should go. "Provided we can figure out how to get back."

Riley tapped on his watch. "It should be southeast from here. I checked right as we started through the woods."

"You're brilliant. Have I ever told you that?"

"A guy can't hear that enough."

As we walked, I could see a subtle path that we'd left. There were some broken branches. Some footprints.

Including a few of Bigfoot's prints.

I pointed to one with my light. "Look at that. I wish I had a casting kit with me."

Riley squatted closer. "You can, at least, take some pictures."

"Good idea." I used my phone to take a few snapshots. Riley knew me well enough to place a dollar bill beside the print to give perspective to its size.

I shivered as I looked at the print. This case just couldn't get any weirder. It wasn't possible. And that meant a lot coming from someone who'd spent time on a deserted island full of old graves and a creepy lodge.

After I got my photos, we continued to follow the footprints.

Ten minutes into our trek back, I stopped. "This is where we left Chad."

The evidence on the ground told the story. There were signs

of a scuffle. Was that because Chad had fallen and hurt himself here? Or had something else happened after we left?

"Nate probably just helped him back," Riley said.

I nodded, mostly just to acknowledge his words. Because, deep inside, I had to wonder if Nate had done something to my friend. Leaving Chad had been a mistake. I should have stayed with him.

Just then, something cracked behind us. Like a stick breaking under the weight of something large. Something human.

I turned around, ready to pull my gun out if it came down to it.

Instead, I saw Franz buried in the underbrush mere feet away from us.

I RUSHED toward the college boy and knelt beside him. Just as I put my finger to his throat to search for a heartbeat, his eyes fluttered open.

"You're alive," I muttered, relief flushing through me.

He moaned and tried to push himself up. Instead, his hand went to his head and he collapsed to the ground again.

"I'm alive?" he repeated. His eyes were dazed and confused.

I nodded. He was alive. Against all odds. I'd thought for sure his name would be added to the list of Mythical Falls casualties.

"I thought I was going to die." He turned over in the underbrush and moaned.

"What happened?" Riley asked.

"One minute, I was going to confront Nate. I saw that everyone was together in the cabin, so I decided to wander around in the woods for a little while, until I could talk to Nate privately."

"What happened next?" I asked.

"The next minute, someone tried to choke me . . . someone hairy. A noise in the woods stopped him. It sounded like people walking toward us."

The bad guy must have heard us coming. We'd interrupted him before he could strangle the Franz.

"He didn't have time to finish the job. Instead, he knocked me on the head and ran," Franz continued, brushing some twigs from his face.

Our little tromp through the woods may have saved Franz's life.

"We need to get you to safety," I said. "Do you think you can stand?"

He grimaced. "I'll try."

Riley approached Franz from the other side, and together we were able to help him to his feet.

"Can you walk?" Riley asked. "We need to have someone check you out."

"I can try." Franz flinched as he took his first step. He'd be sore, but I thought he would be okay. "It's mostly my throat and head that hurt. I should be fine."

"Did you get a look at your attacker?" I asked, keeping an arm around him. My back ached under his weight. He had to be closer to two hundred fifty pounds of mostly muscle.

"Not really."

"Let me guess: He looked like Bigfoot?" I said.

We moved carefully through the dark woods. Riley held a flashlight to illuminate our path, but every step felt like five minutes had passed.

Franz nodded. "That's right."

"Did he say anything?"

Franz shook his head. "He just grunted."

Grunted? Convenient. "Any idea who might have been in that costume?"

Franz jerked his head toward Riley, his voice tinged with disbelief. "Costume? Who said anything about a costume?"

I let out an inward sigh. "You really think it was Bigfoot?"

I wanted to add, *Really? Really?* But I didn't.

Score one for maturity. At the moment, at least. It was an uncertain battle each time.

"It didn't feel like a costume," Franz said. "I know what a costume feels like."

"Because you're used to wearing one," I quipped.

"Exactly. I was coming here to give it all up. But before I could get to Nate, someone grabbed me."

One thing was for sure: Nate hadn't grabbed him. He'd been with us when all of this had played out. But had he hired someone else to do his dirty work? I couldn't be sure.

Finally, we found the worn path that would lead to the parking lot. I spotted Chad leaning against the car there. His face looked strained, like his ankle was still bothering him. That wasn't good. It was going to be hard for him to work with an injury, and I knew how important this job was to him.

Nate rushed toward us. "Franz? Are you okay? What happened?"

"I'm done with this," Franz said. He pressed down on me with all of his weight until my shoulder and back throbbed. "I will go to the media about what you've done if you don't let me out of my contract."

Nate raised his hands. "You're done. I understand. Just give me some time before you go public. Please. I've staked my whole life on this."

The Franz pressed down on my shoulder again until I thought it might break. "I'll think about it," he grumbled. "I dropped the costume in the woods somewhere, and I have no intentions of searching for it or paying you for it. Sorry—not!"

With that said, the Franz let go of his crutch—that would be me—and stomped toward his car.

"You shouldn't drive," I called. "You should go to the hospital. Then call the police and file a report. Someone attacked you."

"I'll be fine," he muttered. "I don't need to involve the police in this. Then I'll have to explain myself. And I'll be fine without a doctor. Doctors are for wusses."

"But you hit your head," I reminded him. "You could have a concussion."

"I'll be fine."

"You should go back to the cabins and wait this out for a little while." Riley grabbed Franz's arm. "I know you want to get away from us, but you have to be smart here. You don't want to get into an accident on your way home, and these mountain roads are tricky. We don't know the extent of your injuries yet."

Franz paused and seemed to actually consider Riley's words. Finally, he nodded. "My cousin died in a car accident. My family can't go through that again. That's the only reason I'm agreeing."

Riley extended his hand. "I'll drive."

Franz frowned but handed over his keys.

"Chad, Clarice, and Gabby—I think we can all squeeze in. Why don't we all ride around to the gate? Nate and Braxton, I can come back and get you," Riley said.

"I'll walk," Nate said. "I'll be fine."

"I can walk, too," Braxton added. "If my calculations are correct, we'll arrive back at the cabins before you do, and the exercise will only help my heart health."

Unless whoever had attacked Franz attacked him also. I kept the thought silent.

"I'm not sure it's a great idea for you guys to be out there," Riley said. "Whoever did this to Franz is still in the woods."

"I'm telling you—it was Bigfoot." Franz's eyes looked unwavering and determined.

He really believed it was Bigfoot, I realized. He wasn't playing a game or trying to psyche me out. He was a believer.

My heart thumped against my ribcage at the thought. Whatever was going on here most likely ran deeper than Nate trying to drum up publicity. Someone else was involved, whether it was someone paid by Nate or someone acting independently for some reason.

"Let's go, guys," Riley said. "I, for one, am ready to get out of these woods and back to the cabin."

But I knew the truth: I wouldn't even feel safe in the cabin. Not after everything I'd seen and heard.

The next morning, I felt like I hadn't rested at all. I'd tossed and turned all night, both with compelling mental arguments that warred internally and because of fear of whoever was out in those woods.

Riley and Chad had driven Franz back to Whitehurst College last night. Nate had volunteered to go also, but Franz didn't want anything to do with him. Chad's ankle was most likely sprained, but he could still drive.

Clarice and I had been able to talk last night. She'd forgiven Nate, of course, offering excuses about how stressed he was and how he'd said he was sorry and how he was such a great guy. I wanted to tell her she was wrong, that Nate couldn't be trusted and she should run far and fast. However, I decided instead to keep my mouth shut. Advice from me, at this point, would more likely make her run directly into Nate's arms.

Today was my second workday, and I had to travel to a police department about two hours away. However, my training workshop didn't start until the afternoon, so I still had a little time.

When I came from my room, I saw Nate at his computer at the dining room table. He frowned and rubbed his chin as he stared at the screen.

"What's wrong?"

"Well, I had someone come out on Tuesday to begin installing security cameras. It seemed like a logical next step."

"Funny you didn't mention that earlier." There were so many things he failed to mention. Over and over again.

Nate shrugged. Usually, his beard made him look young and hip. Today, as his shoulders hunched, it made him look old. "I was afraid the cameras would pick up on Tobs or Franz doing something. I didn't want to set myself up. But now that everything is out in the open, why keep it a secret?"

Nate had all kinds of tricks up his sleeve, didn't he? It didn't help me build any trust with him.

"Did you see something interesting?" I asked after a moment of hesitation.

"As a matter of fact, yes, I did. I checked the footage from last night." He rewound some images. "This was the first thing I saw."

I leaned in closer and saw a shadow lurking in the woods near the cabins. As the silhouette emerged, someone who clearly looked like Bigfoot stepped out. He walked toward the cabins and peered inside.

Again, a chill frosted my insides. Had we been in the cabin when he came? What was he doing exactly?

"Weird, right?" Nate said. "It gets weirder. Check this out, two hours later."

He fast-forwarded and then stopped. I looked at the time stamp: 11:43. This had happened after we'd gotten back to the cabin after the fiasco with Franz in the woods. A man appeared in the shot. Definitely not Bigfoot or even anyone pretending to be.

No, it was a man wearing camo.

I peered closer and squinted. The man looked vaguely familiar.

I sat back as I realized who it was.

It was Marion's husband, Duke. Could he have been behind this the whole time?

TWENTY-SEVEN

BEFORE I LEFT for the training workshop, Riley and I set out to find the Bigfoot costume that Franz claimed to have left behind. I also wanted to see if any other clues had been left in the woods from our ordeal last night.

I wasn't 100 percent on board with being out in these woods again. In fact, I didn't really care if I ever took a walk through the woods again. But, for the sake of evidence, I would make sacrifices.

"You think we'll find anything?" Riley asked as we hiked along.

"I can only hope so." I hesitated a moment as I considered sharing what I'd seen on the video about Duke. I hadn't mentioned to Nate that I recognized the man, and Nate didn't seem to identify him. Part of me wanted to. The other part wanted to give my friend's husband the benefit of the doubt. I was going to go to Marion first.

At some point this morning, I also needed to go to the police about everything that had happened. It would be an injustice to keep what I learned to myself. Nate might hate me. He might even fire me. But I was going to have to share.

"I think it was around this area where we veered off the

trail." Riley touched a broken live-oak branch. "This seems to be a good indicator. The break looks fresh."

"Let's walk this way then." I'd brought my casting kit, just in case we found the footprints again. However, a soft rain had fallen last night, and I wasn't hopeful. The ground was already damp because of its close proximity to the riverbed.

"Did you hear from the insurance company yet?" Riley asked.

I shook my head as we continued down the path. "If I did, I haven't gotten the message. You know how that is out here in the mountains. I'll call again when I get into town."

"So, if it wasn't Nate who ran us off the road, who could it have been? Who would have had access to Nate's cars?"

"His garage was unlocked. It's probably not unusual around here, right? I mean the crime rate, at least until we came to town, was pretty low."

"Then, who?" Riley repeated.

I thought about his question for a minute. "How about Seamus?"

Riley turned his head sharply toward me. "Seamus? That came out of nowhere."

"He's stayed under the radar, but he knows Nate somehow. Maybe he knows him well enough to know where he keeps a spare key."

"Why would Seamus want to kill us?"

"The bigger question is why would anyone want to kill two people so perfectly lovable like you and me?" I flashed him a smile.

"I can't argue with that. But whoever is behind this does have some kind of connection with Nate. If Nate's not guilty, then someone else wanted desperately to make him look guilty."

"There are a lot of people who might have a reason not to like Nate. There are a lot of people here right now who have reason. Chad, me, and you. Not that any of us are guilty."

"I keep feeling like instead of the net getting smaller, it's getting bigger."

"I have to agree." Riley paused and squatted near the ground. "I think this is where Chad fell. Franz was found not far from here."

"Let me look at that area first." I walked several feet until I found a spot where the underbrush had been trampled. This was definitely the area. In fact, there was even some blood on a rock. Franz had a small scrape on his forehead. Maybe the blood was from that.

I took a photo of it and even considered collecting a sample, but then I'd essentially be compromising a crime scene. I fully intended on sending the police out here as soon as I got cell reception.

"Let's see. Assuming Franz was on the trail when this supposed Bigfoot grabbed him, he somehow ended up a good twenty feet off the path and over here. There's probably a more direct path than the one we took. Let's head back toward the trail, but go this route instead."

"Sounds reasonable to me," Riley said.

We pushed through the underbrush until finally I hit the jackpot: thrown underneath a swath of bushes was the costume we'd been looking for. I leaned down and studied it. It looked like it had been dropped in a scuffle. The arms and legs were strung out with patches of dirt and leaves atop it.

"Sure enough. Here it is, just like Franz said," I mumbled. "I'm not risking losing this evidence. I'm putting it into a bag and taking it back with us."

I picked up the mask, as well as the body of the outfit. As I did, I noticed a Bigfoot shoe, for lack of a better word, remained on the ground, separate from the rest of the costume.

I tilted my head. Interesting.

"Does it belong to the other costume?" Riley asked. "Maybe it got ripped off or something."

With Riley's help, I held up the Bigfoot suit. The deluxe getup was heavy and hard to manipulate. I couldn't even imagine trying to run with this covering my limbs.

Once I reached the bottom of the legs, I paused. Both feet looked intact.

That meant . . . "The person who attacked Franz somehow lost part of the foot of his costume when he struggled with Franz."

I used gloves to pick the gnarled, ape-like foot up, and I placed it in a separate bag. I would be taking all of this to the police.

And after that, I'd pay a visit to Marion.

I leaned back in the chair as I talked to the Whitehurst police chief, Rusty Abel. He'd been a friendly man—probably in his mid-fifties—who was slightly overweight and carried his weight in his belly area. Thick blond hair and red cheeks adorned his square face.

He had a neat, plain office that smelled like cinnamon and afforded a nice view of Main Street. Pictures of him with various town dignitaries graced the walls, along with certificates from his police academy training and a community college degree. All in all, it was pretty typical.

He straightened some folders on his desk. "As soon as I know anything more about the accident, I'll be sure to let you know. I know you're anxious to get everything worked out with your insurance company, and I imagine it's unsettling not knowing who would do this."

I nodded. "To say the least. Whoever did this did it on purpose. He or she wanted Riley and me to go over the edge of the road and crash into the river below."

"Any idea why?"

"The only thing I can figure is that it's because I'm looking into what's happening at Mythical Falls. I've been asking questions, and maybe someone wants me to stop."

"Nate Reynolds' date confirmed that he was with her from seven thirty to ten. They were out by Beckley, so there's no way he's guilty. We're checking his car for fingerprints or other evidence of who may have borrowed it."

"Good to know."

"Marion Edwards told me about you." He leaned back in his chair. "She said you have quite the reputation."

"Did she?"

"She said you were really good."

I shrugged, feeling like I was breaking some kind of rule by not boasting about my talents. "I don't know about that. But I'm determined."

"We were hoping to get some prints from the glove left at Caleb Kidwell's crime scene. Unfortunately, the surface was too difficult, so we're right back to where we started. Not many leads. Not many motives. The kid seemed like he didn't have any enemies in the world."

I nibbled on my bottom lip for a moment. "There's something you should know."

"What's that?"

I poured out the story about Nate hiring Caleb, as well as Franz and Tobs. I even mentioned the attack last night and handed over the Bigfoot "shoe." The chief deserved to know what had happened. I certainly didn't want to withhold evidence.

"Why haven't we heard about this before?" Chief Abel said.

I shook my head. "People keep trying to convince me that it doesn't have anything to do with Caleb's murder. People are afraid they'll look guilty. Other people are afraid Mythical Falls will shut down before it even opens."

"You did the right thing by letting me know. I'll look into it."

I started to stand but stopped. "And about those fingerprints you mentioned . . . "

"Yes?"

"There's this technique I train CSIs on for my job with Grayson Tech. It's a substance almost like caulk, but it can get fingerprints from surfaces that were out of reach only a couple of years ago. It's amazing. You should try it on those gloves."

He raised a thick eyebrow. "I wish we had that in our inventory."

I hesitated, but only slightly. "I actually have some in my car."

Thank goodness, I'd taken my supplies out of my trunk before I left to meet Augustine a couple of days ago. I'd actually taken everything out to carry some supplies from Loch Ness Lake to Area 51, and I'd needed all of my trunk space. If I hadn't done that, I would be in a real bind right now.

"I can't handle the evidence myself, but I could show one of your techs how to use it," I offered.

He sat up and nodded slowly. "You'd do that?"

"Of course. For the sake of justice."

"Let me go talk to my guys then."

"I'll go get my supplies, just in case they're interested." I had packed all of my equipment for Grayson Tech into Riley's car this morning. I let out another breath of thanks that I'd taken it all out before the trip that had ended with my car in the river.

As I stepped out of the office and into the bright sunshine, a familiar figure at the curb caught the corner of my eye. The man stood by a yellow BMW coupe wearing a pressed suit and a frown. He obviously recognized me too because he stormed toward me with a fiery look in his eyes.

"You're not a consultant for Nate Reynolds," Scotty Junior sputtered, raising a finger in the air. "You're helping him."

I cringed. That was the thing about covers: it stunk big time when they were blown. To buy myself some time, I muttered, "Why would you think that?"

"I saw you on the news. They said something about you being like Sherlock. A *detective*!" His nostrils flared. He was obviously taking this very personally. I'd blown his big plan to impress his dad.

"The Sherlock thing was an exaggeration. A deep exaggeration."

"But you're an investigator." His face reddened, looking even more off color because of his thin golden hair that was slicked back from his face.

I wondered for a moment if he wore his hair that way to make himself look older and more respectable. His slight frame and whiny voice didn't exactly lend themselves to being powerful or authoritative.

I remembered his accusation. "I'm only an investigator unofficially."

He looked behind me, as if he wouldn't be outdone by me again. "But you're leaving the police department. Do you think I'm stupid?"

"It's a long story." And by that I meant both my reason for being here at the police department and my opinion of him.

He crossed his arms, revealing an expensive-looking watch and well-manicured fingernails. "I have time."

I didn't have to explain everything to him. Or did I? Did I owe him that much for my deception? It was such a thin line. "I'm just trying to find answers."

His eyes brightened. "Ah ha! You were deceiving me. But why?"

"Can't you see it?"

"See what?"

The conversation seemed to just keep going in circles. "If anyone has motive to shut down Mythical Falls, it's your father."

His eyes widened and he took a step back, shaking his head. "He would never do something like this."

"He might if he wants the land bad enough."

"He doesn't want it enough to do anything illegal."

"That's what everyone says."

"He wouldn't."

"No one buys the idea that he has to have that land to open his retirement community. There are plenty of other parcels he could go after. Why Mythical Falls?"

He shrugged. "I don't know. He says there's something magical about the place."

"Sounds like mumbo jumbo to me."

"Well, it's not mumbo jumbo." He paused, as if he wasn't quite sure of what he'd just said before recovering enough to finish the argument. "My father has always liked that property."

I stepped closer, maintaining eye contact and lowering my voice. "You've never asked yourself why?"

Junior nervously stepped back and shook his head. "Just because he does. It's a beautiful place."

"You married the woman who was engaged to Henry McClain."

His eyes widened again. If they got any wider, they might pop out. "So?"

"Maybe you have something to do with all of this."

"Are you making accusations?"

"I'm just making conversation."

"Debby is a wonderful woman. She mourned for years for what happened to Henry."

"Can I talk to her?"

"Why would you want to do that? So you can find information that makes my dad look guilty?"

No, so I could find information that made *Junior* look guilty. I kept my mouth shut. Of course. "I'm just interested in her perspective on what happened."

"She's always believed it was a random crime."

"There's no reason anyone would have wanted Henry dead?" Like maybe so he could steal his girlfriend?

"No, why would they? Henry was a great guy. He'd just taken a job in Charleston, and he was about to leave this area."

I narrowed my eyes. "You knew him?"

"Of course, I did. He was my best frie—" He stopped

midsentence, as if he knew how it would sound. "I didn't have anything to do with this."

"Are you sure about that, Junior?"

His cheeks reddened. "No one calls me Junior. And no one threatens a Stephens. We run this town."

"I'm sure you think you do."

"No, we do. I have the power to bring you down."

"But I don't live here."

"It doesn't matter. I can make your life miserable."

"Someone who's willing to say something like that might be willing to kill to get what he wants or to impress his father. I'm beginning to think you're the missing link here, Junior."

His face looked like it might explode. He leaned toward me, his finger in my face. "You have no idea what you're saying, lady. You're going to regret it. I'll make sure of it."

CHAPTER
TWENTY-EIGHT

BY THE TIME I got done with Junior and I retrieved the fingerprints for the police, I didn't have enough time to swing by and talk to Marion. I was going to have to save that until after I finished my workshop.

Excitement spiked my blood. As much as I might deny it, I loved being in the middle of a good mystery. At least, I did when things turned out the way I wanted them to.

I still remembered Junior's threats, though. Could he be behind what was going on? He was too slight to fill out that Bigfoot costume, but that didn't mean he wasn't somehow guilty in all of this.

As soon as my workshop was over, I headed to Marion's. It was past five o'clock, so I hoped she would be home. Part of me hoped she wouldn't be, though.

This was the worst part of my job: making accusations against people I actually liked and appreciated. People who'd treated me kindly. That's why I had to be careful not to make it an accusation as much as an inquiry.

I hesitated for a moment as I stopped in front of Marion's house. A shudder of nervousness rippled through me. I just needed to get this over with.

Gathering my courage, I approached the front door and knocked. Marion opened it a few seconds later. Her face lit with a smile when she saw me. "Gabby! I wasn't expecting to see you here. Is everything okay?"

"Hopefully."

She squinted a moment. "Come in then. Would you like to eat some dinner? We're just about to sit down. Roast beef and mashed potatoes."

"That sounds delicious, but I'll pass. Thank you."

Marion rotated her weight from one foot to the next. "Then come into the kitchen while I finish up and tell me what can I do for you. You look like you have something on your mind."

I cringed inwardly. "I was actually wondering if I could talk to Duke."

She blinked in surprise. "Duke?"

I nodded. "It's complicated, but I have a couple of questions for him."

She stared at me a moment before nodding. "Well, of course. Come on in and I'll go get him."

I held my breath, hoping this wasn't some kind of trap. That was the bad part about working on crime scenes so much—everything could seem dangerous and deadly or like a twisted game.

A moment later, Duke appeared, looking just as big as ever. He was definitely large enough to be in that Bigfoot costume and sell the role.

"Gabby." He crossed his thick arms. "What's going on?"

I glanced at Marion and licked my lips. I really wished she wasn't here for this.

Lord, please give me wisdom. Give me the right words.

"I don't know how to say this, so I'm just going to jump in," I started. "We had some security cameras installed at Mythical Falls. As we were reviewing some footage after the incident last night, I saw your picture, Duke."

He blinked with shock or surprise. "My picture?"

Marion gasped. "Gabby! What are you saying?"

"I'm not making any accusations. I just want to find out some answers. That's why I came here instead of going to the police."

Marion looked at her husband. "Well, of course, you weren't there last night. You were playing cards with your friends, just like you do every Wednesday evening."

Duke shifted. Uh oh. That was never a good sign.

"Duke . . ." Marion put a hand over her mouth. "You weren't, were you?"

Duke frowned. "Truth is, I haven't been in months, Marion. The games were getting out of hand with everyone taking their bets too seriously. I had to get out."

She draped a dishtowel over her shoulder. "But . . . where do you go?"

He shuffled his feet. "I've always been fascinated with Bigfoot. I've been going out to Mythical Falls to see if I could spot the old guy."

"Duke . . . are you serious?" Marion leaned against the counter, as if she might collapse.

He nodded. "Unfortunately, I am. I joined this online society, and I haven't been able to get enough since then. Since the mines closed, it's been hard not working. I need something to keep me occupied. Looking for Bigfoot seemed like a good idea, but I've become obsessed."

"You could have told me."

"I know how you feel about folklore. You think it's ridiculous. So it became my little secret."

"Were you dressed in a Bigfoot outfit?" I asked.

His jaw went slack. "What? No. I just go out there with my camera."

"And you were out there last night?"

He nodded. "That's right. I went out late. There's less of a chance of being caught that way. Everyone knows about that hole in the fence that lets people get in and out easily."

"Have you ever seen anything?"

"Not Bigfoot, if that's what you're asking."

"How about something other than Bigfoot? There's been a lot of crime going on there lately."

"There have always been a lot of legends about that property. Jebidiah Reynolds bought it from several families who once owned the land in that area. There were rumors of meteorites hitting the earth there and leaving 'pieces of space dust.' Legends of a fountain of youth by the waterfall. And, of course, stories of Bigfoot."

"But did you see anything last night? It's very important. A college-aged boy was attacked. He almost died."

He cringed. "I don't want to call names."

"Then don't. Just tell me what you saw."

"As I drove down the road, about to park in that small lot, I did pass one other car on my way there."

"What did it look like?"

"It was hard to miss. It was yellow and flashy."

Yellow and flashy? That sounded like . . . "Junior," I muttered.

He nodded. "That doesn't mean he was there at Mythical Falls. But it does mean he was in the vicinity."

I nodded. It appeared that my suspect list was growing longer and longer by the moment.

"You've got some nerve showing your face around here again."

I'd wondered as I'd driven into Mythical Falls if word had gotten back to Nate that I talked to Chief Abel. Apparently, it had, and Nate looked madder than a hornet now. Gone was the laidback, outdoor adventurer, and in his place was . . . one angry Sasquatch.

Riley stepped between us, his hands on his hips and fire flashing in his eyes. "Don't talk to Gabby like that. You're the one who messed up, Nate. If there's anyone to blame, it's you."

Nate narrowed his eyes, backing off only slightly. "The chief came out today and talked to me, like I could be a suspect in a murder investigation."

I raised my hands in innocence. "I didn't suggest that you were guilty of murdering Caleb. But I had to tell law enforcement what I'd learned. It was the right thing to do."

His nostrils flared as he stared at me. "You have it in for me just because I said you were hot when we first met."

That was the most asinine argument I'd ever heard. "That's ridiculous."

He raised his chin. "Prove it."

I threw my hands in the air, feeling like I was back in elementary school. My voice rose in pitch, even though I'd vowed to maintain a level head. "How am I supposed to do that?"

"You said she was hot?" Clarice quipped from the couch.

I ignored her. "Besides, the chief didn't arrest you, did he?"

Nate nudged his chin higher, reminding me of a first grader. "No."

"If he really thought you were guilty, you'd be behind bars."

His shoulders slumped slightly—maybe with relief. "Really?"

I nodded, feeling exhausted from this conversation. "Really. In the meantime, we need to find the real person behind these murders and assaults. That's what I intend to do."

He blinked and brought his shoulders to his head in an obvious sign of cluelessness. "You mean, you want to help me?"

"I mean: I want to find the real murderer. If that means I'm helping you, then, yes, I want to help you."

He let out a long sigh. "I need all the help I can get."

In more than one way.

"How did things go today?" I asked, desperate for a change of subject. It was only when I asked the question that I noticed Chad sitting on the couch with his leg propped up and his ankle wrapped. That wasn't a good sign.

Chad winced as he set his leg on the ground and leaned

forward. "All things considered, I think we got a lot done. We've pretty much finished all the cabins out in Area 51. The landscaping guys are going to come back tomorrow and finish up a few areas. The bathrooms are all working. All in all, we're doing well."

"I'm glad to hear that."

I glanced around again. Clarice gave me a death glare. Nate still paced. Chad looked downright exhausted.

I couldn't deal with any of this drama right now.

"I need to unwind for a little while," I finally said. "I'll be on the back porch in case anyone needs me."

I stomped across the wooden floor and pushed open the screen door. It squeaked, just like always. And, just like always, the sound sent a chill down my spine.

I couldn't wait to be done with this job and go home. I wanted to drink a latte with Sharon, who owned The Grounds across the street from my apartment. I wanted to hear my radio-talk-show-host neighbor, Bill McCormick, tell me his crazy, extreme stories and viewpoints. I wanted to cuddle on my couch with my favorite blanket and relax.

I nearly collapsed onto the wooden chair. My head was pounding, and this whole situation was beginning to get to me.

I had to figure some things out. I'd been living in fear since I got here—in more than one way. I wasn't just fearing this theme park, but I was fearing my future in general. I had to stop. Because living in fear wasn't really living at all.

Life involved taking risks. Taking chances. Experiencing loss and grief. Love and amazing moments. It was a package deal, one that no one was immune to.

I had to learn how to face this head on. To put my fears behind me. To really start living again, and to stop playing it so safe all the time.

Riley appeared at the back door a few minutes later. He slowly pushed it open and gave me a glance that clearly communicated, "Is this okay?" When I nodded, he stepped out and sat in the chair beside me.

"We make a good team, don't we?" I mused aloud.

He nodded slowly. "Yeah, I think we do. Always. In the past. In the present. In the future."

My cheeks heated. He really had been so dedicated since he'd moved back. It wasn't that he wasn't dedicated before. It was just that, after almost losing his life, I think he'd learned what he really wanted in his future and realized life was too short not to go after those things.

Soon, and very soon, we were going to have to have a long talk.

"What are you thinking about?" Riley asked.

Did I even want to go there with him about our relationship? Not now, I decided. There were other more pressing matters. "I'm trying to think this whole murder through."

"Talk it out with me then."

I shifted, still not used to Riley being supportive of my investigations. I wasn't complaining, though.

"Okay, first there's Junior. He was very angry today. He wants to make his dad proud. I think he'd like nothing more than to secure the deal on the land and show his dad he's capable of taking over the family business."

"But would he kill for that?"

I shrugged. "I have no idea. But I don't buy that he just wants this property for no reason. There's something more there. You suggested a natural resource of some sort. That could be the case. But I'd think the man would be more apt to sneak here and try to steal something than to kill over it."

"He could very well have motive, means, and opportunity."

"I agree. I also recognized Marion's husband, Duke, on the video surveillance from last night." I replayed to Riley what had happened earlier.

"That's . . . kind of strange." Riley shifted and leaned back in the ratty camping chair.

"I agree. But people are obsessed with Bigfoot."

"But why would he kill? That's the big question, isn't it? Who has the motive for that?"

I lowered my voice. "Then there's Nate."

"You really think he has motive?"

I licked my lips, uncomfortable with having this conversation with Nate just inside, within easy listening distance. I looked behind me and to the sides, but didn't see anyone. "He's desperate for publicity. Maybe he thinks another murder, just like the one committed here all of those years ago, would bring a weird fascination with people."

Riley twisted his head, not looking convinced. "That's extreme."

"But remember Freddy Mansfield, that guy who was obsessed with serial killers. There are people out there who get a kick out of stuff like this. Or what about Jack the Ripper? Tourists come in droves to visit his old haunting grounds in London—and by haunting grounds I mean the sites of his murders. There's a market for the macabre."

"You have to remember that Nate was with us when Franz was attacked."

"He could be working with someone."

Someone knocked on the door before joining us. I glanced back and spotted Chad. Just as he stepped out, I heard the front door open and voices drift from that direction. The gang had split up, it appeared.

Chad cringed as he started to lower himself on the porch.

"Here, take my seat." Riley jumped up.

"No, I'm okay." Chad grimaced. "I've got to push through this, so please don't do me any favors."

"Be careful or you'll do more damage to your ankle than you already have." I gave him a motherly look.

"Yeah, yeah. You sound like Sierra."

"Speaking of Sierra, how are she and Reef doing?" I missed my best friend, and I missed my godson.

"Reef is feeling better. They're talking about coming on Saturday."

"Saturday? Doesn't she have to be at work on Monday?"

"She's going to bring her work with her. That's the nice part of being the boss, I suppose. She's been working at home a lot more lately."

"At least she can. Childcare isn't cheap."

"She doesn't want to leave him with a sitter. I can't blame her. Before you know it, she's going to want to stay home."

"Are you opposed to that?" I asked.

He shrugged. "No, not really. You gotta do what you gotta do. I just want everyone to be happy, and I want what's best for Reef."

I could read between the lines: It was a complicated issue.

"So, there's been some creepy stuff here, huh? I haven't had a chance to talk with the two of you about things. Clarice and Nate just went for a walk, and Braxton decided to go into town for some fun, so here I am."

"Listen, Chad, I'm not trying to put you in an awkward position," I started. "But I had to tell the police what was going on."

"I understand. You did the right thing." Chad shook his head. "I just can't believe Nate went through all these hoops just to make it look like Bigfoot was roaming these woods. He's always been a little on the crazy and wild side, but I think he took it too far."

"How well do you really know Nate, Chad?" Riley asked, using a diplomatic voice that I admired. I tried to be diplomatic, but it rarely ever worked.

"We were both whitewater rafting guides for a summer. That next winter, we worked the slopes. We worked together one more summer, and then we parted ways."

"How long had it been since you spoke to him before this job?"

Chad shrugged and looked off into the distance. "Probably three years."

"And he called you out of the blue one day?" I asked.

"Now that you mention it, maybe it was a little weird. But, yeah, he called me out of the blue. Said he heard about my business and thought I'd be perfect for this job."

"How did he hear about the business if you hadn't spoken?"

"You know, I don't know. I just assumed it was from mutual friends or something. Maybe from social media. I set up a couple of pages, but never really did anything with them." He shifted. "You think that's got something to do with this?"

I shrugged. "I'm just trying to look at all the angles."

But deep down inside I had to ask: What if there was someone I was missing altogether?

THE NEXT MORNING, all I could think was: the show must go on.

Despite everything that had happened, we still had a job to do. For that reason, Chad worked with the HVAC crew while the rest of the gang finished hanging doors, replacing baseboards, and installing new light-switch covers.

Nate wanted to open this place up in three weeks. The control freak part of me kept dwelling on the fact that taking reservations this early seemed like a big mistake. But, like I'd consistently told myself: it wasn't my call. It wasn't my responsibility. And, if it failed, it wouldn't be my problem.

I was headed back up to Area 51 when I spotted just the person I was hoping to run into: Bill Brunke. I had a few more questions for him. He seemed like just the objective source I was looking for.

"Hey, there," I said, glancing at the path.

The Brunke brothers had poured new cement in the areas that had been broken by tree roots and age. The new trail looked smooth and level—just what this place needed to avoid a lawsuit. Despite the fact that they were pouring cement, the landscaping crew still looked dirty. The thought mildly amused me. How was it possible that they always looked like they'd been digging in the dirt?

"How's everything going here?" I asked.

"Great. We should be finished up with this later on today. Nate said he might want some more help putting up fences around hazardous areas. This place is on the road to opening soon. I know that's gotta make Nate happy."

I shifted, trying not to seem too obvious with my questions. That, however, was not one of my talents. "Listen, the other day when I ran into you guys on Main Street, one of your brothers said something about staying up late. What was that all about?"

He wiped his sweaty forehead on his sleeve as his brothers continued to smooth the cement in the background. "Will, take over for a minute, would you?"

One of the brothers—not Grumpy or Happy—nodded and continued to work. As he did, Bill motioned for me to step away. "Truth is that we're helping Nate plan an opening weekend extravaganza."

"What?" Of all the things I'd expected, that wasn't one of them.

Bill nodded. "Truth is that we used to be one of the acts here. My brothers and I were vaudevillians—hence our name today. First, we got laid off from Mythical Falls. Then we started working at the mines and lost our jobs there also. We've had a bad run of luck. Anyway, we've kept in touch with a lot of the other performers. Nate wants me to bring them back for a big kickoff, but it was supposed to be a surprise. That's why I hushed everyone."

That was their big secret. I let out a breath, relieved it was something so simple.

"So a lot of performers are still around here, huh?"

"Yup. You might be shocked."

His words caught my attention. "Like who?"

"Oh, I don't know. Seamus, for example."

"Seamus was an act? But he was young when it closed down."

Bill nodded again. "Yup. That's true. But he was old enough to wear a pair of stilts and wow the audience. I think his dad put him up to it. It's probably why he's not afraid of heights today and can work on roofs all the time."

Stilts, huh? I imagined Seamus on stilts in a Bigfoot costume, but that was probably too much of a stretch. Certainly I would have noticed Bigfoot walking strangely that day we chased him through the woods.

"How's the big party coming?" I asked.

"Pretty good. My family goes way back in this area, so we've got a lot of pride in Mythical Falls."

I reached into my sweatshirt pocket and found the rock from the gemstone mining. I began tossing it in the air as I talked, hoping the action would make me look laidback. "How well do you know Nate?"

He shrugged. "I've known him since he was knee-high to a grasshopper."

"You support him reopening this park, huh?"

He shrugged again. "I suppose he'll be better at this than he is at finance. I heard he even had to change offices once because no one in the previous town where he worked trusted him with their money."

"Is that right? Isn't that interesting." Funny that Nate hadn't brought that up either. He seemed to like keeping a lot of secrets, and he had the uncanny ability to put a great spin on his life circumstances and decisions.

"It is. Of course, his dad wasn't that great either. It's no wonder Nate wants to open this place. Who wants to do a job they're terrible at?"

"I'm inclined to agree. What about Scotty Junior? Do you know much about him?"

Bill stared at me for a moment as I tossed my rock. "Are you looking into the murders here? Is what the news said true about you being a female Sherlock?"

I shrugged. "I am an investigator, and I have been asked to help find the person responsible. Nate can't open with a killer on the loose."

"No, he can't. My wife will hardly go to bed at night. She checks the windows and doors three times, afraid the Bigfoot Strangler will get her too." He shook his head, the lines on his face deepening.

"I heard Nate and Scotty Junior hate each other," Grumpy called.

I turned my attention to him. "Oh, did you?"

He paused from using a screeding tool to flatten and smooth the cement. "That's right. They can't stand each other. Nate and Junior faced off in a local poker game. Nate won. Junior never forgave him."

"My wife works at the pharmacy." Happy stopped working and looked up at us. Apparently, everyone around here had a theory. "She said Junior is on an awful lot of medications. She'd kill me if she heard me saying this, but she thinks he's a little crazy. Anyone would be after growing up with Scotty Stephens as a father."

"Any other rumors floating out there?" I glanced at all the brothers. None of them bothered to hide the fact that they were listening to the conversation. They had no shame.

And people said women were gossips.

"I heard Scotty Stephens was back in town but remaining on the down low," Sneezy said. At least, I thought it was Sneezy. He wasn't actually sneezing at the moment, but his nose was red.

My eyes widened with surprise. "Really?"

He nodded. "My wife's friend's cousin cleans his house. She said she saw receipts dated this week."

Curiosity spiked in me. "Why would he keep his presence here a secret?"

"Maybe if he thinks he has an alibi, then people won't look at him as a suspect." Bill pointed to the path. "That's gonna dry on us. Keeping working it."

"But you know who I've always wondered about?" Grumpy asked, obviously close enough to listen. "Seamus."

"Why Seamus?" These guys were full of theories.

"He was here when the girl fell off the Ferris wheel."

"What? Are you sure?"

He nodded. "Read the old news articles. His picture is right there. His parents were interviewed. They had to get the poor kid counseling afterward."

"That's . . . very interesting." I remembered when I'd seen him going into the bank with a woman at his arm. Was that in any way connected with this? Was there a reason that Nate always had Seamus around, even though he wasn't that great of a contractor? It was worth looking into.

My phone rang at that moment. It was nearly a miracle that I was standing in range. I pulled it out and saw the number from the police department.

"Excuse me a minute, boys. I've got a call to take."

I leaned back against a tree, far away from the Brunke brothers, and I let the phone call with the chief sink in.

I still couldn't believe it.

They found a match to a fingerprint inside the Bigfoot costume.

It was Duke. Marion's husband. Apparently, his prints were on file after he was arrested outside of Scotty Stephens' house during a protest when the mines had closed.

I wanted to call and break the news to her first, but Chief Abel informed me that he'd already sent men over to question him.

I couldn't believe it. He'd seemed so sincere when he told me about why he'd been in the woods. I'd been convinced he was innocent. But what if I was wrong? Why else would his finger-print be in the Bigfoot costume?

I'd managed to pull one other print from a gas can. The chief informed me that it belonged to Bill Brunke. However, the land-scaper had admitted that he'd stashed some gas used for their lawnmowers in that area, which made sense given their jobs. Bill had suggested that the glove was something someone like Scotty or Scotty Junior would wear.

Wasting no more time, I grabbed the keys and hurried toward Riley's car. I needed answers that I wouldn't get being here on this property. I didn't know where I was going or who I'd talk to, but I needed to get away from this place. In the mean-time, I radioed Riley and let him know what was going on. Riley admonished me to be careful.

Just as I reached the gate, a sleek silver sports car pulled up. I braced myself for whoever was inside—it definitely didn't appear to be the car of one of the contractors.

A moment later, a brunette stepped out. She was slender, stylish in a gray business suit, and she looked as mad as a hornet.

This was the woman I'd seen Seamus with, I realized.

"Are you Gabby St. Claire?" She marched toward me, her finger pointed like she was ready to jab me in the chest.

I cocked a hand on my hip, realizing she looked vaguely familiar. "I am. And you are?"

"Debby Stephens."

"Junior's wife," I muttered. She looked just like the trophy wife I'd expect someone like him to have on his arm. But what were Seamus and Debby Stephens doing together at the bank? The web of intrigue continued to grow, as did my curiosity.

Her eyes narrowed. "He hates being called that."

I knew that already, and it was part of the reason I enjoyed using that version of his name. Why in the world was she here and so upset, though? I crossed my arms and stood by the gate. "What can I do for you?"

"You can leave my husband alone, that's what."

I blinked, processing her words. "You're implying that I've been messing with him."

She wobbled her head, full of attitude that she didn't even try to hide. "I'm not *implying* anything. I'm saying: You're messing with my man, and I don't like it. You need to step back."

I wasn't one for catfights, but I felt one coming on. Debby's in-your-face approach was putting me off—big time. At the moment, I wouldn't mind clawing her eyes out.

That wasn't the most Christlike attitude I could have. I knew that. I was working on it.

"I'm not 'messing' with anyone," I finally said, my teeth partly clenched. "I was merely asking questions."

She raised her chin as she narrowed her eyes. "Is that what you call it?"

"Yes, that's exactly what I call it," I told her matter-of-factly. I had no idea what she was implying, but I didn't like it. And I didn't like her. Irritation continued to build inside me.

"Well, you need to back off." She jabbed my shoulder.

That did it. She'd touched me. *Game on.*

"Do not touch me again." My words sounded menacing, if I did say so myself.

Mischief sparked in her eyes as she leered at me. "What will happen if I do?"

"I'm warning you—you need to stay back and keep your hands to yourself."

She smirked and raised her finger to jab me again. Something came over me and I sprang to life. I grabbed her arm before she reached me and twisted it until she yelped.

"What are you doing? Are you crazy? Help! She's assaulting me."

Footsteps sounded behind me, along with voices. That didn't stop me. I still held onto her arm.

"Gabby! What are you doing?" Riley slipped through the gate and put a hand on my shoulder.

"I kindly asked her to keep her hands to herself and she refused." I didn't take my gaze from Debby.

"Gabby . . ." Riley's voice tapered off in a soft half-warning, half-plea.

Finally, I let go of her arm. She jerked away, sneering at me. "That's what I thought."

At her diva-like words, I started to lunge at her, but Riley grabbed me. "What exactly is going on here?" Riley said.

"This is Scotty Stephen's daughter-in-law, wife of Junior," I said introducing them through gritted teeth. I shook off my anger like a boxer in the ring.

"I told you not to call him—" Debby started toward me, but Riley stopped her with an outstretched hand.

"Ladies, please calm down. What are the two of you even talking about?" He looked back and forth between the two of us and finally stopped on Debby. "You came here for a reason, I assume?"

He was acting like the mediator I always knew he was. And his question was great. Why had she come? Just to tell me to back off? Seemed like an awful lot of effort for nothing really.

"I'm here to set the record straight." She planted a foot and did her little head wiggle again.

"Set the record straight on what?" Riley continued.

Anger flashed in her eyes. "About my husband. He ain't got nothing to do with what's going on here."

"What was he doing here a couple of nights ago then?" I asked, more than happy to have the upper hand here.

A moment of confusion wafted across her pert features. "He wasn't."

"We have a witness who places him here."

She stepped back and did the head wobble again. "He was with me."

"Sure he was." Condescension rolled through my voice. It wasn't my best moment. Queen's "Time to Shine" began playing in head.

"He was."

"His car was spotted."

"That's because his dad—" She stopped herself mid-sentence, but I knew what she was about to say: his dad had borrowed it.

"We know Scotty Stephens is back in town but pretending not to be. That only makes him and your husband look more guilty than they already did." I watched her reaction carefully. "Is that right?"

Something flashed through her eyes—guilt, probably. She knew she'd been caught. "That's ridiculous. Of course, I wasn't going to say that. Don't be stupid."

"So you think your father-in-law is guilty." I nodded slowly, confidently. Maybe—just maybe—I was playing head games with her. Could you blame me?

She visibly bristled again. "I never said that."

"You implied it."

She leered again. "I did not."

"Did too." I leaned closer.

"Ladies!" Riley stepped between us and raised his hands like a referee.

Yes, maybe this was getting out of hand. This woman was bringing out the worst in me. *Forgive me, Lord.*

"She started it," Debby muttered, crossing her arms.

I started to retort, but then realized just how immature it would sound. I bit down instead.

I needed to catch this woman in a lie. People, when emotional, could act in irrational ways. That was what I was counting on now. I had to strike while the iron was hot. "If your husband is innocent, then maybe you could tell me this: Why else would your father-in-law be driving your husband's car?"

"He can't risk driving his right now, of course."

"Why not?"

"That's a secret."

I nodded, realizing good and well that she hadn't realized

her slipup. That was okay. But she'd just admitted that Scotty Stephens was back in this area. Now the question was: why?

"Why is he so fascinated with this property?" Would I be able to get the golden egg twice? I doubted it. I was pushing my luck. But that was okay. As long as I was pushing, I was doing something. "I don't get it. There's a sentimental reason he likes this land, isn't there?"

"You've obviously never met him. He's not the sentimental type. He's the type who likes money. Lots and lots of money."

"I didn't realize retirement villages were that profitable," Riley said.

Debby snorted. "Retirement village? What are you talking about?"

"Certainly the land isn't worth the millions he's offered."

She pulled her lips back like we were morons. "This land certainly is worth millions. There's a load of coal down there by Mythical Falls. But the only way to retrieve it is through strip mining."

"I'D SAY we have a new number one suspect," I muttered to Riley once Debby had left. Riley led me to the pavilion area and encouraged me to cool off before going to talk to Marion. His words were wise.

"It appears this area is ripe for suspects," Riley said, leaning forward with his arms on his knees and taking a sip of water. His sky blue T-shirt was stained, his jeans had a hole in the knee, and his five o'clock shadow had turned into a thin beard. He'd never looked more handsome, I realized.

I pulled out my phone, deciding I'd just wasted entirely too much time on that woman. I had planned on heading into town, but I needed to take a moment to cool off first. "Speaking of which, I need to call Marion. Excuse me a minute."

I dialed her number, and she answered on the first ring. Her voice sounded fraught with anxiety, cracking with every other word.

"Gabby?" she whispered, as if she couldn't believe I would call her.

For a moment I feared that she might hang up. "I just heard. Are you okay?"

She paused a moment before answering. I wondered if she

was crying and trying to collect herself. My heart panged with compassion. "For now. Duke explained everything to Chief Abel. There are no charges against him—yet."

"How did his print get there? Did he tell you?"

"He said he almost tripped on the costume when he was looking for Bigfoot. He picked it up to see what it was. He must have left a print when he did that. It's the only thing that makes sense."

"I'm going to figure out what's going on here, Marion. In fact, I have a new suspect."

"Whatever you do, be careful. This is all getting crazy—and that means a lot coming from a medical examiner."

As I hung up, I saw Clarice walking over with a huge box in her hands.

"You'll never believe what I found today in the old management office." She plopped the box onto a picnic table.

"The old management office?"

She nodded. "Yeah, it's over by Pharaoh's Tomb area. Nate decided he wanted to fix it up. Like, maybe it could be my office one day if I ever decided to come work here." She shrugged and blushed. "Anyway, the plumbers are out to fix up the bathroom there. It was disgusting. While they were working, I started going through some boxes. I found photo albums. Lots and lots of photo albums from when this place first opened. I found Nate's picture, along with his dad's and uncle's. Can you believe it?"

I leaned over as she pulled out one of the albums. "That sounds pretty interesting."

"Yeah, I told Nate we should do something with them—set up a display somewhere or something. I'm still trying to think it through. But maybe we could even blow some of them up and have posters made that we display around the park."

"I think that's a great idea. In some ways, it would even up the creep factor because it shows how the place used to be normal and now it's a shell of what it once was," I said. I flipped through the photos and saw images of the place as it used to be.

Mythical Falls looked like the all-American theme park. Most of the photos had blue skies overhead, people with smiles on their faces, kids holding balloons and with their faces painted. The photos stood in stark contrast to how the place looked today.

"There are even some from when Kiss played here." Clarice handed me some loose photos. "Check these out."

Riley leaned over me, and my heart quickened at his nearness. I kept going, though, forcing myself to remain focused. Sure enough, there on the Pavilion stage was Kiss. The crowds looked like they extended from the stage seating area all the way back through the Bermuda Triangle.

I kept flipping through the pictures and saw other acts. There appeared to have been animal trainers, dancers, a family trapeze act, and a magician, among others. This place really had been hopping at one time.

I glanced around now. Sure, time had diminished its greatness, but over the past week, so much had been renovated. Would it ever return to its former state? No. But it might even turn into something better. Different but better.

A thought caught me, and I sucked in a breath. Maybe more than this theme park had been restored this week. Maybe being here was the proof I needed that restoration could happen. I desperately needed to be restored. I thought once I had Riley back in my life that would happen. But restoration couldn't always come from outside sources. Restoration had to start from the inside.

Maybe that was the lesson I was supposed to learn while I was here this week, because certainly there were lessons I needed to learn in every situation. The world was my classroom, and my learning curve could be awfully steep sometimes.

I continued to look at the faces in the pictures. I paused by a few. Why did some of the people look familiar? The world really wasn't that small, was it? Was Henry among these faces? Was the killer somewhere in here?

If I had weeks and weeks or months and months, for that matter, maybe I could figure it out. But I didn't have that long to pore through these and do the research that I would need.

I couldn't help but think the answers were right here, though.

I straightened. "You know what? Suddenly I'm starving. Anyone want to go to Yuck Yuck's tonight?"

Of course, I had ulterior motives. I was going to find some answers, once and for all.

I was about to leave for Yuck Yuck's when the front door to the cabin suddenly burst open and Chad half-limped, half-stormed inside, his eyes full of fire. He'd gone into town for supplies earlier, and something must have gone terribly wrong.

I braced myself for what was about to come.

"Where's Nate?" he demanded, his hands on his hips and his shoulders tight.

Clarice started to point to a bedroom when that very door opened and Nate stepped out, a look of confusion on his face. "I'm here. What's going on, man?"

Chad thundered toward him, swinging papers in his hands. "What kind of game are you playing?"

Nate raised his hands and stepped back. "Dude, what are you talking about? I'm not playing any game—"

"Cut the garbage, Nate. I just went to the bank. There's no money in your account. There's no money to pay us, Nate."

Nate's face paled. "No, something's wrong. I'll go with you myself—"

"Stop lying, Nate. You're broke, aren't you? You never had any money to pay us."

My stomach dropped. Chad had been counting on this

paycheck. Was his theory correct? Had his friend Nate duped him?

"Nate?" Clarice asked, her voice fragile and on the cusp of devastation.

As she said his name, Nate's shoulders drooped, and I knew Chad had spoken the truth.

I stole a quick glance at Riley, and his expression mirrored mine. This wasn't good. It wasn't good at all.

"You're right." Nate sagged against the wall. "I'm broke. I don't have the money to do this. I ran out."

Chad's eyes widened until the whites all around his irises were visible. "I trusted you! Normally, I take payment up front but, since you were my friend, I decided to take a chance. I put all this junk on my own credit card, knowing you'd pay me back. I have bills to pay!"

Nate stepped closer, his voice low and desperate, even as his shoulders slumped. "I'm going to make all the money back, man. You've got to believe me."

Chad's hands flew in the air. I'd never seen him so angry. "You don't know anything! You're *hoping* you'll make all the money back. Just when exactly were you planning on telling me all of this? I'm set to leave here in a few days. Were you going to drop it on me before that?"

Nate's gaze dipped. "I hadn't thought it through."

"Nate, how could you do this?" Clarice's voice was lined with hurt and disappointment. She'd had the man up on a pedestal and had been envisioning her future here. She didn't even have to tell me—I could see it in her eyes.

Her disappointment seemed to especially deflate him. "I don't know what to say. I was desperate. *Desperate.*"

"I'd say so." I wasn't going to get involved, but how could I not? He'd scammed me too. "First you hired someone to pretend to be Bigfoot. You told the press I was like Sherlock Holmes to get additional attention. Now, come to find out, you were plotting this all along. You had no intention of paying us."

"No, I did!" He sprang to life, his eyes pleading with each of us. "As soon as I made the money back, it was yours. All yours."

"I heard you took money from investors. What happened to it?" Chad asked. "Did you blow through it with your top-of-the-line bathrooms and kitchens?"

"I had to use it to pay the taxes on this place. Some things I paid for myself: the windows and the dumpsters." He frowned and scratched his beard. "I used it for stuff I knew I couldn't convince you to buy."

Chad shook his head and began pacing. I felt sorry for him—I really did. Betrayal by a friend was the worst kind.

"Do you even realize how much money I've put on my card?" Chad rubbed his forehead. It was classic Distress 101. "Do you even realize that I have to pay my employees, that they're counting on me? Do you even realize that I have a wife and a baby at home—that I have my own bills coming in? I'm still paying for the hospital stay for when Reef was born. My health insurance premiums went up. Sierra's going to need a new car soon. Do you think you're the only one who has financial troubles?"

How could Nate have done this to his friend? Didn't he realize that we all had our struggles? That we all needed money to get by?

"I trusted you," Chad continued. "I came out here to help you, as a friend. I gave you a discounted rate. I've worked around the clock, been away from my family, and I've gone above and beyond everything you've asked me to do. And this is how you treat me?"

"Chad—" Nate started.

"No, I'm not finished. You've always been irresponsible. I just never thought you'd take it this far. I was wrong. I've given you the benefit of the doubt for entirely too long. If you think I'm going to let this slide, you're wrong. In fact, the whole reason you asked me out here was so you could use our friendship to your advantage. Isn't that right? There were plenty of local contractors you could have hired, and I made the mistake of feeling honored."

When Nate didn't respond for a moment, it became obvious that Chad had hit the proverbial nail on the head.

"Wait, Chad!" Nate finally said. "I'll make this up to you."

Chad narrowed his eyes. "Like you made it up to me when you stole my girlfriend back when we were rafting guides? Like you made it up to me when you crashed my car and totaled it that one summer? Like you made it up to me when you always conveniently left your wallet at home when we went out?"

"I've grown up since then." Even Nate didn't sound convinced of his words.

"Obviously, you haven't. I'm done." Chad started toward the door.

"No, really, Chad! I'll fix this."

Chad paused. "How?"

"I have investors—"

"They'll be taking you to court soon."

"I'm going to make serious money through this park."

"That's speculation," Chad said. He stormed out the door, letting it slam behind him loudly enough that we all flinched.

The rest of us stared at each other a moment.

"I'll talk to him," I murmured.

I had to make sure he was okay. Because with his level of stress lately, this just might have the power to break him.

I found Chad pacing Main Street, and I had images of an Old West showdown taking place here between Chad and Nate. My bets were on Chad.

"Hey," I called. I walked toward him slowly, shoving my hands into the pockets of my jeans. "Are you okay?"

He stopped pacing long enough to rake a hand through his hair. "I can't believe Nate would do this."

"I can't believe it either. He's your friend, and friends aren't supposed to betray each other."

He sagged against one of the pillars outside the arcade. "What am I going to do, Gabby? I've charged almost thirteen thousand on my credit card, Gabby. Thirteen thousand."

I flinched at the amount. It seemed so unlike Chad. Then again—he'd trusted his friend. "Wow. That is a lot. You could take him to court . . . I know that's not ideal. But, then again, neither is what Nate did to you."

He closed his eyes. "I can't pay you. I can't even pay my bills."

"Sierra's still on maternity leave. She has some money coming in."

"Yeah, but there are hospital bills. And diapers. Do you have any idea how much diapers cost? And we're using cloth!"

It sounded like marriage and fatherhood had overwhelmed him. Was Chad another casualty of commitment? Was life full of more sunshine without the lifelong responsibility of marriage and family?

"Do you wish you were single again, Chad? Do you miss the old days?"

His head snapped toward me. "What? No. I wouldn't change a thing, Gabby."

My lips formed an O. I'd made too many leaps. "I just thought—"

"Yes, I'm stressed out. Yes, it's hard at times. But the benefits way outweigh the negatives."

I swallowed hard, realizing my question had gone deeper than I thought. "They do?"

He squinted. "You're afraid of marriage, aren't you?"

I shrugged, wanting to deny it. "I didn't say that."

"You didn't have to. That's why you keep putting off setting a wedding date."

I opened my mouth, about to argue. But I couldn't. I'd blamed it on fear—and this was one kind of fear. But my issues went deeper than Scum's assault and Riley's traumatic brain injury. They went back to my childhood. "I've had a lot of bad things happen in my life."

"I know. So have I. Okay, maybe not quite as many as you. But life is full of bad things. And good things. I want to cling to the good while I still have time. We're not promised tomorrow, you know."

"I know." Life could slip away in the blink of an eye. I'd seen it happen.

He straightened, distracted from his own problems by mine. For a moment, at least. "Look, Gabby. I'm not a biblical scholar—not by any stretch of the imagination. But I do seem to recall a verse about not worrying about tomorrow for tomorrow will worry about itself. I'm pretty sure that was a command, not a suggestion."

I stared at Chad, dumbfounded. How was it that someone who didn't even go to church was able to realize that before me? He was right. I was worrying too much. I just needed to hold on to the good of today. Focusing on tomorrow had robbed me of the joy in the present.

"Gabby, Riley loves you. I know he messed up. And I know your relationship has had more mountains and valleys than the Appalachians. But I also know that both of you love each other. I have no doubt that you're meant to be together."

I swallowed hard, his words hitting me like a ton of bricks. "You really think so?"

"I know so. Marriage is worth it, Gabby. So are relationships. And we don't know what tomorrow has in store, so why waste time today? We've got to make the most of things, you know?"

I nodded. "Yeah, I do know. Thanks for the reminder. I've been focusing on everything that could go wrong. I need to focus on everything that's right. Be more like Happy and less like Grumpy."

"Huh?"

"Never mind. Just thanks. I didn't realize you were so smart."

"You underestimate me." He rolled his eyes.

"You know, I actually came out here to cheer you up. Somehow the roles reversed."

"I'm a dad now. I need to get better with things like this. I'm going to have to talk through a lot of situations with Reef as he gets older, especially since he's a mix of Sierra and me. I can only imagine the trouble he'll get himself into."

I grinned. "He's really lucky to have you both, you know."

"Thanks. I think we're pretty lucky to have him."

"You ready to go face Nate?"

Chad sighed. "I guess I have to listen to my own advice. There's no time like the present."

CHAPTER
THIRTY-ONE

"I KNOW how he can make it up to you," Braxton said when Chad and I walked back into the cabin. He'd been sitting in a corner the whole time, processing the showdown. Whatever his solution was, he'd be sure to think it was the only way. That was Braxton for you. Chad knew better than to let the two of us work together. We butted heads too often.

As everyone in the room riveted their attention toward him, my gaze found Riley. My heart filled with warmth. I needed to tell him that we should set a date. I didn't want to put it off anymore.

But now wasn't the time or place.

The room crackled with awkward silence as Nate slumped at the kitchen table alone.

"How can Nate make this up to me?" Chad's jaw flexed, and all of my earlier pep talk seemed to disappear.

"Easy. You said he had a Corvette? He can sell it."

Everyone volleyed their heads toward Nate. He shifted uncomfortably, his gaze meeting each person's. Finally, he nodded. "I guess I could do that."

"Then you can take the money from the scrap metal from

some of these old rides," Braxton continued. "It won't be a lot, but every little bit helps."

Nate seemed to hesitantly nod. "Okay."

"Then you can sell the vintage arcade games. I bet investors would pay a pretty penny for them." Braxton spoke as if he didn't have a care in the world and as if he had everything figured out.

Nate wobbled his head back and forth. "I suppose."

"He can also give us partial ownership of the park to make it up to us." Braxton puckered his lips as he waited for Nate's reaction. He didn't have to wait long.

"Partial ownership?" Nate barked. "That's extreme."

"It's either that or you can go to jail for fraud." Braxton shrugged and flipped his hands up. This was one of his few good ideas.

He'd obviously thought this through. I didn't like the man, but I had to give him some credit here.

"As long as the percentage isn't too high." Nate frowned, probably doing some quick mental calculations.

"I don't think you're in a good place to get any sympathy right now," Chad said. "You know if you don't accept our terms, we're going straight to the police—and your investors."

Nate raised his hands again. "Okay, okay. I get it. I was wrong, and I'm going to make it right."

"You're going to make it right. Now." Chad stared him down hard from across the room.

He raised his hands in surrender. "I'll get started on it right away."

"Does everyone here agree to these terms?" Chad asked.

Everyone nodded. If we waited for Nate to pay us back on his own terms, we'd all remain broke.

"The only one who isn't here is Seamus," Braxton said.

I saw an opportunity and grabbed it. Just what was Seamus's story? "Speaking of Seamus, I haven't seen him in a couple of days."

Everyone else added their agreement.

"So where is he?" I asked, glancing at Nate.

"Beats me. He still has a couple of cabins to finish."

"You're not concerned?" I asked Nate.

"Seamus does his own thing. He'll get the job done on his time schedule."

I shifted, not ready to drop this. "You've stayed on top of all of us—almost neurotically. Why not him?"

A shadow crossed his gaze. "He's my cousin, so there's family dynamics to think about."

I shook my head as I processed the bomb he'd just dropped. "Your cousin?"

He nodded. "Not by blood. My great uncle adopted him when he was fourteen."

"Why?"

"His mom . . . she fell off the Ferris wheel. His dad was long gone. Seamus and my uncle never really got along, though. Their relationship was strained. My uncle tried to do the right thing by formally adopting him, but it wasn't exactly a 'happily ever after' story."

"Why keep so many secrets, Nate? Why didn't you just tell us that upfront?"

"Our history is long and convoluted."

"As are many things with you . . ."

Nate opened his mouth to say something when his radio buzzed. It was one of the plumbers he'd left at the old management office. Apparently, there was a water leak there, and they needed back-up.

However, I wasn't done with this conversation. Either Seamus had abandoned this project—that would make him wise —or something had happened to him.

I supposed there was a third option: Seamus was behind the incidents, and he'd hidden himself away to escape detection. He had the perfect motive.

But then again, so did everyone else.

Despite everything that had happened, I still wanted to hear from some of the locals about their memories of this place. That was why I headed to Yuck Yuck's, even after the showdown with Nate the Not-So-Great.

Nate had stayed behind to start "making things right" while the rest of the crew headed to the Area 51 cabins to help with cleanup. Everyone had been a bit begrudging, but Chad had given a pep talk about seeing things through to completion—and he'd reminded everyone that Riley was a lawyer and could slap a lawsuit on Nate if worse came to worst.

I brought the pictures Clarice had found with me to Yuck Yuck's, purchased pizzas and pitchers of soda for anyone who was there, and spread the photos out on over two tables. In the background, a local cover band played folksy tunes using a guitar, bucket drums, and car keys. They actually didn't sound as bad as I'd thought they would as they crooned, "Yesterday Once More" by The Carpenters.

I stood close as locals stopped to reminisce, pointing out familiar faces in the snapshots. They recalled the good times and got far-off looks in their eyes as they remembered those who passed.

Amidst the smell of greasy mozzarella and crusty bread, I asked questions and drew out more recollections. The people who stopped by were mostly blue-collar workers. Many had worked the mines before they shut down. Several were still struggling to find work. But Mythical Falls brought back happier memories.

"Everyone knows Nate is terrible at finance," one man said, picking up an old photo.

The man's name was Alan, if I remembered correctly, and he'd been on the crew with Seamus. He was in his sixties, with thinning hair that had been greased with some kind of gel. The lines on his face made him appear like someone who'd worked in the sun and smoked too many cigarettes. But his voice was soft and kind, as were his eyes.

He'd said Nate was terrible at finance, but he didn't even know the half of it. Not yet, at least. Despite what I already knew, I wanted to hear this man's opinion. I leaned closer and lowered my voice. "What do you mean?"

"He's almost as bad as his dad," the man continued, still holding one of the pictures as he stood by my table. "His dad lost money for some people here in this town. He's the reason Mythical Falls shut down in the first place. People think it was the murders, but those in the know realize the truth."

At the man's statement, I set my pizza back onto a plate. I needed to give my full attention to this man. "I'm not following you. How did Nate's dad shut down the whole place?"

"Nate's uncle—his name was Jebidiah—owned the theme park. He trusted Nate's father, Leo, to run the finances. Leo did a terrible job and, as a result, Jebidiah had to lay off people. Apparently, Leo had invested some of the company's profits, but he invested poorly and lost almost all of it."

"That's interesting." Like father like son.

The man put the picture back down on the table and grabbed his own piece of pizza. He raised it in the air as he spoke. "There's this steadfast loyalty in the Reynolds family, where they refuse to speak poorly of each other. That's why that whole fiasco has stayed relatively quiet. But part of me thinks that Nate wants to do his uncle proud and make things right. That's why he would never sell it to Scotty Stephens, despite all the money he's offered."

"Well . . . that's good, right? I mean, staying loyal to family and everything." I paused. "How do you know all of this?"

"My mother was friends with Jebidiah's wife, so she knew some of what was going on. My father also did magic tricks at Mythical Falls. He refused to call himself a magician because he had no formal training. Anyway, all the acts were the first ones to get let go. Boy, were some of them angry. They'd staked their livelihood on working there."

"Your dad was one of the magicians? I was wondering if the acts were all local or from outside of this area."

He picked up a photo of a man standing on a small stage wearing a Houdini hat and holding a magic wand. "Here he is. You'd be surprised at some of the acts still in town. The Brunkes are trying to get people together for a reunion when Mythical Falls reopens."

"So I heard."

"Jebidiah hired local whenever possible. People around here needed the jobs. Needed the money. Mythical Falls was one of the best things that could have happened to us."

"But what about the murders? Who do you think was responsible?" The man seemed like a wealth of information, so I wanted to keep him talking.

"I personally think it was someone who wanted to ruin Jebidiah Reynolds and his family. They got threats all the time after they began doing layoffs."

"Then why kill Henry if Jebidiah was the one people were angry with?"

"Jeb was young—probably your age. I personally think it was a mistake. Henry and Jebidiah looked an awful lot alike from behind."

"Did you know Henry?"

Alan's eyes welled with tears. "There's one other thing you should know. Henry was my son."

I STARED AT THE MAN. "Henry was your son? Really? I'm so sorry."

He nodded. "It's hard to believe it's been twenty years since he's been gone."

"I can't imagine what you went through." At least he didn't seem overly bitter now. A lot of people would be. Grief could be slow to die.

"It was hard." His voice wavered and he looked away.

I realized that earlier he'd been talking about inconsequential things in order to avoid talking about Henry. My heart panged with sympathy.

I softened my voice, hoping I wasn't being insensitive. "I know this is none of my business, but I heard there was a ten thousand dollar deposit in his account before he passed away. Do you have any idea where that money came from?"

"He got a signing bonus when he agreed to work for Harrison and Buhler after he graduated."

"Come again?"

Alan nodded. "He was an engineering major—top of his class. He was offered a job before he graduated, complete with a ten thousand dollar signing bonus. That's where the money came from. Why?"

I shook my head. "A few people assumed he was paid off."

"That's the hard part about small-town living. People assume a lot of things based on rumors."

"He was dating Debby, right?"

The man actually rolled his eyes. "They went out once. You ask me, she was just milking the situation to get as much attention as she could. She always had her sights set on anyone who was wealthy. That was not my son."

"But why would he have been killed?"

"It's like I said: I think someone who hated Jebidiah accidentally killed Henry."

"Do you have any idea what your son was doing there that night?"

He sighed. "The only thing I can think of is that he was a relic hunter. He'd go out and search for hours for old keepsakes from the Civil War. He was especially fascinated with the area near the Pharaoh's Tomb."

"Thank you so much for sharing, Alan. I know this wasn't easy."

"I still want to see his killer caught."

"I'd love to help you with that."

Before I had time to question him anymore, the front door opened. All the air seemed to leave the room as Nate walked inside.

A woman stood and glared at him. "I just got your email. Is it true? Did you really blow all of our money?"

His arms stiffened. "That's why I'm here. I want to apologize to everyone in person."

Like a riot, almost everyone rose up and began waving their hands and talking all at once.

Normally, I might feel inclined to help. But Nate had gotten himself into this mess, so he needed to handle it himself.

I gathered my pictures and slipped out, realizing I wouldn't be able to get people's focus back now.

But, at least, I had left with something.

I climbed into Riley's car and let out a sigh. What was I missing? What was the connection between these murders? It was there—I felt certain. I just had to put my finger on it.

As I jammed my keys into the ignition, a voice sounded from the backseat. My heart rate ratcheted up higher than the first drop on the Vomit Comet.

"I was hoping to catch a moment alone with you," someone said.

I craned my neck and spotted a man who looked like an older version of Scotty Stephens Junior in the backseat. I started to reach for my gun but stopped myself. "What are you doing here?"

"I couldn't risk being spotted in town." He remained low, as if he didn't want anyone to see him.

"Why not?" Even as I spoke, I thought through my options in case something went wrong. Best case: honk my horn and run. Worst case: use my gun.

He frowned. "Bad facelift."

I squinted, trying to get a better look at him in the darkness. Now that he mentioned it, his face did look a little . . . unnaturally tight, and his eyes drifted upward on the corners.

"Why'd you want to talk to me?" I asked.

"You think I'm guilty of killing Caleb Kidwell."

"Your daughter-in-law said you wanted to strip-mine the land where Mythical Falls is located."

"What? Me? No. That's Junior's plan if he ever gets his hold on my money. That's when I knew I needed to get the property first. That way, when Nate ruins this and is out of money, he won't feel desperate enough to sell to Junior."

"What?" It was my turn to sound surprised.

"The coal market has dried up. It's not as profitable as it once was. Besides, strip mining is viewed by many as despicable."

"So you really want to open a retirement village?"

"Initially, yes. No more."

"So why are you willing to pay millions for the land?"

"I'm getting older. I want to leave a legacy beyond the heart-break I caused when I closed the mines. Do you have any idea how despised I am in town?"

"I have a good guess," I said drily.

"I want to preserve the land. I want that to be my legacy."

"Really? I thought you were all about money." The pieces weren't matching up in my mind.

"With age comes wisdom."

I shook my head. "I don't know what to say. That's quite a change of heart. Almost unbelievably so."

"You want to look at someone? Look at Seamus."

"Why would I look at him?"

"Good old Jeb always favored Nate, even though he adopted Seamus. I've heard Seamus has always held a grudge against his cousin since Nate's the one who inherited Mythical Falls."

"And you think he'd murder for that? Nate hadn't even inherited Mythical Falls twenty years ago, so how do you explain the similarities in the murders?"

He shrugged. "I can't. But I did hear a rumor that Seamus just took off for the Bahamas. Maybe he's running from the law."

The Bahamas? Was that why I hadn't seen him around in a couple of days? And what about his bank trip with Debby Stephens?

"Why would Nate hire Seamus if there's so much animosity between them?" I mused aloud.

"Could be because he feels bad—guilty—about being the chosen one. Or could have something to do with his gambling debt."

"Gambling debt?" Nate had to be the worst financial

manager ever. Yet, gambling didn't surprise me. He seemed like the type.

Scotty nodded. "That's right. He owes a lot of people."

"Does Seamus, by chance, play with your daughter–in–law?" I threw it out there, hoping I might get a hit. I had seen the two together at the bank. And Seamus had been missing for the past couple of days since then.

Scotty scowled. "Why would you think that?"

I shrugged. "Intuition."

"Debby isn't the wisest person in the world. Neither is my son, for that matter."

With that, he jetted out of the car and disappeared into the shadows.

CHAPTER
THIRTY-THREE

RILEY CALLED me as I drove back to the park and asked me to meet him at the old management office. He said he'd found something, and now I was beside myself as I tried to wait to hear what he'd learned.

Patience was a virtue. Not one of my strongest ones.

I rushed toward the office and found Riley sitting at a cluttered desk, poring over several items in a box. The only light was a lantern. Apparently, Braxton hadn't worked on this building yet.

"What's going on?"

He kissed my cheek before sitting back down and picking up some papers. "We had to pull up part of the floor because of a leak. When we did, we found this box. It's full of old correspondence that goes back more than twenty years ago."

"Really?" I sat beside him and picked up a letter. "Interesting."

"You're going to think it's really interesting. Check these out." He handed me a pile. "It's from someone that Jebidiah fired."

I leaned closer to the lantern and scanned the letters. Someone named Richard begged for his job back. He was obviously angry. As the letters progressed, he began making threats, saying he'd burn the place down for ruining his family. He had children to feed, and their whole lives were tied up in this place. Apparently this man's family used to own part of this land.

"He sounds very angry," I muttered.

"Keep reading. It gets even more interesting."

Before I continued, I glanced at the bottom of the paper. The letters were only signed "Richard," but no last name. Strange.

I read the next letter aloud. "I believe there are precious minerals here on this property, and I'm asking for your permission to search for them. Rumors have gone back for years in my family. This would be a great way to make it up to the employees you've fired. You owe it to us. My sons and I deserve to use this land."

I glanced up at Riley before reaching into my pocket and pulling out the crystal Clarice had given me. "I assumed this was nothing. But what if . . . ?"

"It's something worth killing for?" Riley finished.

"Perhaps."

"What if this whole area does have some kind of valuable natural resource—say, for example, a gemstone? Rumors of the Bigfoot Strangler or even the actual Bigfoot would be the ideal way to keep people away from the potential treasure. It would also be the perfect reason for someone to want this park to close down."

My blood raced at the realization that we were getting closer to answers. "And if Henry or Caleb discovered what they were doing—secretly mining for these gemstones at night—that would be reason enough for killing them."

"I agree."

I leaned back in the chair, my thoughts churning. "But who could it be? We can rule Nate out. He owns the property, and he wouldn't have written these letters."

"What about Scotty Stephens?"

I filled him in on our conversation.

Riley twisted his head with doubt. "Sounds fishy to me. He wants to make this a nature preserve? I'm not saying that's not true, but I don't buy it. However, I highly doubt his dad worked here. If these letters are tied in with the murders—"

"Which they probably are, but not necessarily. They do fill in a lot of blanks, though. It's the best motive I've heard yet. Much better than the killer simply being angry about being fired."

"What do we know about the killer?"

"He's agile. He has big hands. He strangles from behind. He has to have a history here that extends more than twenty years." I paused and pressed my lips together in thought.

"What?"

"The one thing I haven't been able to understand is how someone can be such a chameleon. As Bigfoot, he's big. But then there was a clown, who was slight."

"What are you getting at?"

"Remember that night in the woods? How it appeared the sounds were coming from all around us? What if . . . what if the killer isn't just a killer. What if there are *killers*?" My brain began firing on all cylinders.

"So you think Seamus and Scotty Stephens are working together? Or Nate and Duke?"

Things began to click together in my head in a rapid-fire progression. The killer—killers—had a history here. Their father had many sons. They'd want to remain close to the property to keep an eye on it. They'd realized there was a fortune to be made here on grounds that, they felt, rightfully belonged to them.

I didn't know a lot about gem mining. But I had seen a documentary one time on the different types of mining. Some mining was in caves, but there was another type called surface mining. For that, people dug through the dirt and found precious gems in the soil.

It was a dirty job.

Duke had said there was a rumor that a meteorite had hit this area and left something otherworldly on the grounds. Something that could look an awful lot like gemstones maybe? Maybe something that looked like the rock Clarice had found on the ground and given me?

Just then, a hammering sound echoed right outside the building. Was Chad back? Had he found something else to fix?

Riley and I froze.

I walked toward the front door but, when I tried to open it, the door wouldn't budge. "What?"

"Here, let me try." Riley pushed against the door also, but it remained in place. "Is it jammed?"

I shook my head. "I think someone just nailed that door shut, Riley."

"Check the back door," Riley shouted.

I reached it before Riley and threw my weight against it. It didn't move. "It's nailed shut too."

That was when I smelled it. Smoke. Fire.

I realized Riley and I were about to be roasted alive.

THIRTY-FOUR

I WENT to the front window, but it wouldn't budge either. The windows had been nailed shut also. Someone had planned this . . . this . . . attack well in advance.

"Watch out!" Riley raised a chair and tossed it into the back window. Glass shattered. Riley used a lamp to remove the sharp edges at the bottom before grabbing my hand. "We've got to get out of here."

As I sucked in a deep breath, the smoke nearly choked me. The heat from the fire already caused perspiration to cover my skin and dampen my clothes.

Memories of the very first case I ever solved rushed back to me. I'd been trapped in a fire then also. I'd thought I was going to die.

But I hadn't.

And I wouldn't die now either.

Riley tugged me toward the window.

Orange flames danced at the edge of my line of sight. The fire was spreading. But we still had a chance. A good chance.

"Climb out, Gabby. We don't have much time."

I swallowed hard before lifting my leg up toward the windowsill. Carefully, I maneuvered over the broken glass shards. As soon as I cleared the frame, I let myself go, landing with a thump on the ground below.

Riley gracefully climbed out behind me. He grabbed my hand and pulled me to my feet, urging me farther away. "We've got to get away before this whole place goes up in flames."

Just as we reached the stream, the whole building collapsed in the flames.

I glanced into the woods and spotted a shadow moving there.

The killer. He'd waited to see what would happen, to see if the fire would consume us. Now he was on the run.

No way would I let him get away.

"I'm going after this guy." I still had my gun tucked into my waistband. I wasn't missing this opportunity.

"I'm behind you," Riley muttered.

Without wasting any more time, we darted through the woods. My gaze scanned the area in front of me. I didn't want to lose sight of the man, but he obviously knew these woods better than we did. He wove in and out of the trees, in and out of shadows.

He was far enough ahead of us that catching up would be challenging. But I had to try. People's lives depended on it.

I paused as the mountain became steeper. At least, I tried to pause. Before I could, momentum pulled me downward and I began to slide.

Riley followed, but his motions were purposeful and controlled. I landed on my rear, and mud covered my jeans, my shoes, and my hands. Grace should be my middle name, because I was full of it.

"You okay?" Riley helped me to my feet.

My heart pounded in my ears as I realized how close that had been. I could have easily broken something. Thankfully, I hadn't.

A branch snapped in the distance. That had to be the man who'd set the building on fire. We still had a chance to catch him.

Riley grabbed my hand. "Come on."

He pulled me through the woods. I could barely keep up with his pace, and it was all I could do to prevent branches from slapping me in the face or tree roots from tripping me.

Finally, we stopped at a clearing to catch our breath, and we both scanned the area around us. Mythical Falls roared in the distance, and the air was crisp with an autumn chill.

"Where do you think he went?" Riley asked.

I continued to survey the area, hoping desperately for a sign of where the man had gone. I didn't see him anywhere. I couldn't help but feel like I was being watched, like the man knew just what he was doing.

My skin prickled as I searched for the person whose eyes were on me. I was certain he was out there, trying desperately not to be discovered.

I took a step forward, searching behind trees and between rocks. My hand went to the gun at my waist, and I pulled it out.

Please don't make me have to use this. Please.

I kept heading forward, certain this was where the man was hiding.

As I took another step, a figure darted away in the distance.

Riley and I took off after him. I raised my gun. Should I shoot?

No, I couldn't do it. I didn't have a clear shot. I had to be certain. Instead, I sprinted after him.

Suddenly, the man disappeared.

Then the trees in front of me disappeared.

And so did Riley.

The cliff, I realized. Was this where the cliff was?

My heart plunged as I raced toward him.

"Riley!" But it was too late. He was gone.

CHAPTER
THIRTY-FIVE

MY LUNGS TIGHTENED with every step closer I got to the cliff. What would I see on the other side? Did I really want to look?

I had no choice. I had to check on Riley. Maybe—just maybe—he was okay.

Please, Lord.

I paused at the brink, wobbling off balance for a moment and fearing I might go over too. My head swam at the thought. Holding my breath, I peered over the edge. My neck muscles clenched.

I blinked at what I saw. Riley had grabbed onto a ledge, and he literally held on by his fingertips.

He was alive. Alive!

"Riley!" I lowered myself to my belly and reached down. It was no use—there was still at least five feet between us.

"I've got this, Gabby." Riley's voice sounded tense, but his gaze looked focused.

"You've got this? What do you mean? I can run back and get help." Even as I said the words, I knew there wasn't enough time. His fingers would cramp after holding on too long. There wasn't enough to grip onto on the rocky cliff.

"Riley . . ." My voice sounded desperate, even to my own ears. I tried to reach for him again, but it was no use.

"Gabby, it's okay." He raised his hand and grabbed a rocky ledge above him. His muscles looked taut—from his arms all the way to his jaw.

I didn't want to move—not even swallow. One wrong move and Riley would fall to his death. This part of the cliff didn't have water below it. No, it was a rocky patch of boulders.

Please, Lord. Have I said that yet?

Riley pulled himself upward. He managed to find a foothold, making the climb a little easier.

I released my breath. He still wasn't close enough for me to touch, but he was getting closer.

Thank You!

All these crazy fears I'd had since Riley had come back into my life suddenly became amazingly clear. I couldn't lose him again. Even if that meant risking getting hurt. Risking my heart and disappointment and being let down.

Love was worth the risk. And, as much as we liked to think we had all the time in the world, the truth was that we didn't. We weren't promised tomorrow. If we didn't seize opportunities as they arose, those opportunities may not even present themselves to us again.

Riley continued to move upward with amazing ease.

"How . . .?" I whispered.

"I've been learning rock climbing as a part of mixed martial arts and parkour."

"It's . . . incredible. Thank goodness for that."

"This isn't exactly the way I wanted to test my skills."

"But, boy, am I glad you've been studying up."

He grimaced and pulled himself up toward the ledge.

Finally, he was close enough for me to reach. I grabbed his arm and helped him back onto solid ground. He collapsed beside me, his chest rising and falling from exertion and adrenaline.

Before I could properly show him how thankful I was that he was alive, I had to check on the man we'd been chasing. Carefully, I peered over the edge and saw a shadow climbing with ease toward the bottom.

He'd intended to let Riley die by purposefully leading us into this trap.

Anger surged through me. I'd have to address that later. Right now I had to check on Riley.

I crawled his way and collapsed beside him. We stared up at the trees together, my hand reaching for his until our fingers intertwined. I couldn't stop touching him. I had to know he was still there.

At the moment, I felt so incredibly grateful. To be here. To be with Riley. To be alive.

How many times did I need to be reminded of all of this? Why was I so hardheaded?

"You never told me who we're chasing," Riley said.

"I can't believe I didn't see it earlier. It's the Brunke Brothers."

He shoved his eyebrows together. "What?"

"They were an act here. I believe their father wrote those letters. Their entire family depended on their income from Mythical Falls. You think Chad is stressed out over providing for Reef? How about for seven sons?"

"They were an act here, right?"

"Yes—a vaudeville like act. I guess part of them juggled, another part did contortion work. People who are a part of acts like these are flexible. A lot of times they have double joints. That could explain why the hands looked so large."

"So their father told them about some kind of gemstone he thought was here at the park?"

I nodded. "That's right. Finding those gemstones would solve their family's financial problems. Maybe Henry walked in on them doing that, and they had to kill him to stay quiet. It was a family affair. After a while, I'm guessing they gave up on trying to find these gemstones. But when they lost their jobs at the mine, they became desperate for money again. I have a feeling Caleb saw something he wasn't supposed to. Maybe he even bribed them for their silence. Maybe he came back wanting more and that's when the brothers killed him."

As I finished my sentence, a bullet rang through the air.

"Now someone's shooting at us," Riley muttered. "What in the world . . . ?"

"If I had to guess—it's either Bill, Phil, Will, Hill, Dill, Quill, or Gill."

He let out a slight moan. "We've got to get out of here. There's no telling how many of them are out here."

"On the count of three?" I whispered, bracing myself for whatever was to come.

"Three!"

We darted from the ground and took off away from the shooter. The thick trees blocked the bullets—but plenty came our way.

"I know where we are," Riley yelled. "Do you trust me?"

"Of course, I trust you."

"Then I have a way out. I promise you, this will work."

My heart lurched. What in the world was he talking about?

When he stopped in front of me, I knew.

The alpine slide.

Riley wanted me to go down it with him.

As I imagined my body hitting numerous obstacles on the twenty-year-old ride, I cringed and took a step back.

I wasn't sure if I could do this.

CHAPTER
THIRTY-SIX

"YOU SAID YOU TRUSTED ME, GABBY." Riley stretched out his hand.

I swallowed hard. I did trust Riley. I did.

I was going to prove that to him today. And for the rest of my life.

"I do." I took his hand. "Let's go."

He grinned—but only briefly—before sitting on the slide and motioning for me to sit behind him. Just as I lowered myself there, another bullet rang out. I turned and saw one of the brothers running with a crazy Geronimo expression on his face.

Grumpy. It was Grumpy.

Riley grabbed my legs, and I grabbed his waist as we pushed off. I pressed my face into his back, closing my eyes as we slid downward. I waited for pain. For derailment. For the fire or a bullet to catch up.

After a few seconds, nothing happened. We continued to glide down the mountain in an amazingly smooth ride.

I actually popped my eyes open. Trees whizzed past, the slide dipped and turned. Its thick plastic base kept us well-covered.

"This is actually kind of fun," I whispered. "I mean, other than the bad guys shooting at us and everything else."

"Alpine slides are great—under different circumstances. We've got to think about what we'll do when we get off this thing."

I looked behind me, just out of curiosity. What I saw made my blood go cold.

"Grumpy is on the slide!"

"What?" Riley glanced over his shoulder.

"We're still being chased." As Grumpy got closer, I reached for my gun. Just as I grabbed it, we hit a bump and the gun flew from my hands, landing somewhere behind us. "Oh, that's not good."

"What happened?"

"I lost my gun, and Grumpy is getting closer. At the moment, he reminds me a bit of an angry gnome."

"What?"

"Never mind. Where does this lead?"

"Near Pharaoh's Tomb. I have an idea, Gabby. I'm going to get off. But you keep going down. If you don't, my plan won't work, so you have to promise me you'll do it."

My mind raced with possibilities. "Okay. I'll do it."

Just as we started slowing down and the incline lessened, Riley reached up and grabbed one of the branches overhead. He lifted his legs and I slid under him.

I jerked my head back to see what he would do next. He managed to turn himself around so he faced the top of the mountain. As soon as Grumpy got close enough, Riley kicked him in the chest.

The man moaned and fell from the slide, dazed.

All of a sudden, I hit the end of the slide with an *oomph*. Riley helped me to my feet, and we kept moving. As we did, I heard movement in the distance. From more than one direction.

My heart raced. This wasn't good. I knew exactly what was happening. We were outnumbered. But we had to keep moving.

Movement could save lives. I'd learned that in a self-defense course one time, and I had to believe it now.

As someone stepped into our path, we threw on the brakes. Bill.

We took a step back. I glanced behind me, ready to run in the opposite direction. But it was just as I feared. The other Brunke brothers had surrounded us. We were trapped.

"Bill, why are you doing this?" I started. "There's got to be a better way. I always thought more of you."

He sneered, all indications of his earlier laidback personality gone. "My dad always talked about diamonds in this area. People laughed at him. Diamonds in West Virginia? We could talk all we wanted about Punch Jones. We'd given up too—until we lost our jobs at the mines."

"I didn't think this area had the right conditions for diamonds," Riley said. He moved closer to me, nudging me behind him slightly.

That's right. Keep them talking. Buy time before they kill us.

"There's an ancient, diamond-bearing volcanic pipe that runs through here," Bill continued. "I researched it. It's probably from volcanic activity that happened in this area who knows how many thousands of years ago."

"That's really fascinating."

He pulled a rock from a pouch at his waist. "This one? It's probably five karats. If I get it cut, it could be worth $10,000."

"That's incredible. It really is. But why kill Caleb?" I asked.

"Easy. He stumbled on us collecting these gems. He knew immediately what we were doing and threatened to tell Nate. We gave him a cut—$15,000. We thought we were good. Then he came back demanding more for his silence. That's when we knew we had to take action."

I nodded, my throat tight as I realized the other Brunke brothers were now close enough to touch. They surrounded us completely. How were we going to get out of this?

"So you killed him like you killed Henry?" I said.

Bill deposited the gem back into his pouch before pulling out a hammer on his tool belt. He hit it against his palm. At once, I had visions of him slamming that hammer into us. I cringed, imagining the pain it would cause.

"Henry was a mistake," he growled. "He was out here relic hunting when he found a diamond. He showed us what he'd found, and we knew he'd hit the mother lode."

"So you killed him? Isn't that extreme?"

"This land used to be our family's until Jebidiah bought it from us for dirt. My father was desperate, and he was promised a job here. But we were the first ones let go. Then Henry showed up. He had a nice job and life ahead of him. And he wanted to pocket the money from it. We couldn't let him do that."

"You've been mining the area for the past twenty years? I'm surprised the supply hasn't dried up," Riley said.

Bill scowled. "We spent the next two decades looking for more diamonds like the one Henry found. It wasn't until it flooded in this area last summer that we located the mother lode. Apparently, all of these beauties are located near the Pharaoh's Tomb area."

Keep them talking, Gabby. Keep them talking. "You didn't want this place to open up, did you?"

"We had to keep it out of Scotty Stephens' hands," Happy said. "Scotty has an endless supply of money. He would have put up fences and added security. Nate didn't have those advantages. We really didn't want to hurt anyone. But it happened, and we've had to live with that."

"I thought more of you, Happy." I had to play on his kindness. "I thought more of all of you, for that matter. I didn't realize your brotherly bond ran so deeply."

"Happy?" he repeated, scratching his head in confusion at my nickname.

"We are all each other has," Bill growled. "We have to stick together. My dad taught us that lesson. You don't snitch on family."

"And Bigfoot?" Riley asked. "Do you have anything to do with the sightings in this area?"

"We initially dressed up to keep people away," Bill said. "It was the perfect disguise and a great way to keep people off this land. Then people started getting interested. They started coming out here because they were fascinated with Bigfoot instead of scared of him."

"You don't have to do this, Bill," I said, feeling smothered as the circle squeezed tighter. "There are better ways."

"We've come this far. We can't lose everything. These diamonds are rightfully ours. We've made enough money on them since this summer that we've been able to actually pay our bills and buy groceries—even dentures. There's nothing wrong with providing for your family."

"No, but there's a lot wrong with stealing and murder."

Bill growled.

"What's with the hammers?" Riley asked. "I've noticed you all had them while doing landscaping work at the park. I didn't think anything of it, at first, but now it's starting to seem weird."

"It's how our dad taught us to mine," Happy said. "You dig into the ground with the hammer. And then you fill in the dirt using the side of the hammer. It works perfectly."

"That explains why you all looked so dirty all the time." Everything suddenly made sense. All of the puzzle pieces fit. Well, almost all of them.

"What were you doing in the clown house that day?"

"We hid some of our loot in there in between jobs. We weren't expecting you to go inside, so we had to think quickly. That was Dill. He always liked being a clown. We thought it would be a good chance to scare you away also, but nothing worked. Then we heard you were Sherlock, and I saw the diamond you'd found. I knew we needed to get rid of you. And those silly college boys that Nate Reynolds hired."

"It looks like the Bigfoot Strangler is about to strike again," Bill said, raising his hammer. "Sorry about this. You seemed like a nice girl."

Suddenly, someone jumped on my back, his hands going to

my throat. Just like on the old Mythical Falls commercial, I realized. The one where the small clown jumped on the bigger clown's back.

I was going to be the Bigfoot Strangler's next victim.

CHAPTER
THIRTY-SEVEN

RILEY GRABBED MY HAND AND, in one quick motion, he burst through the circle, pulling me behind him. The Brunke on my back tumbled to the ground.

Before anyone could realize what was happening, he led me through the wilderness. We moved so fast that I couldn't tell which end was up or which direction we were headed.

I heard shouts behind us. Footsteps pounding. A gun being fired.

"Hold your breath!" Riley yelled, gripping my hand harder.

What in the world was he talking about? Before I could voice the thought aloud, the ground disappeared beneath me.

I sucked in a breath.

The cliff. We'd just jumped off the cliff.

What in the world was Riley thinking?

The next instance, cold water surrounded us. My body went into shock. But, before I succumbed to my panic, arms reached around me and pulled me to the surface.

I gasped, sucking in air. Before total fright could set in, Riley's face came into focus.

"Are you okay?" he asked, water covering his eyelids and dripping from the tip of his nose.

I did a quick self-assessment. "I think so."

"Good. Because we need to keep moving. Can you swim?"

"Usually."

His lip curled in a half-smile. "If we can make it halfway down this river, we can reach Area 51 and run for help."

"I can't feel my arms."

"We don't have a lot of time, Gabby."

I nodded. "Okay, then. Let's go."

I forced my limbs to move through the water. I wouldn't let Riley out of my sight. My life depended on it.

Who knew where the Brunke brothers were at this point. They could be chasing us downstream. I couldn't let them catch us again. We were too outnumbered.

We reached an area where the stream became too shallow to swim through. But as I rose out of the water, my shivers overwhelmed my body. The cool night air mixed with the frigid mountain stream would mean hypothermia could easily set in.

My breath froze as I expelled air from my lungs.

"I wish I had something to keep you warm," Riley said, putting his arm around me.

"Me too."

"We have to keep moving, okay?"

I nodded. "Okay."

We slogged through the stream and onto dry land. "Just up this hillside is Area 51. We can make it. The buildings will offer us some warmth. In the meantime, I can go find the rest of the gang."

Sirens sounded in the distance. Thank goodness. Maybe help was on the way. For all of us.

"How'd you know it was safe for us to jump off that cliff?" I asked, trying to keep my thoughts focused.

"I wandered one day while we were working on the alpine slide. I couldn't resist exploring a little. It paid off."

"Yes, it did."

My legs burned as we climbed the incline. In the distance, I spotted a gigantic spaceship. We were almost there.

There were no signs of the Brunke brothers.

Praise God.

Finally, we reached the metal structure. Riley started to pull me inside, but I shook my head. "We've got to find help."

"Can you make it much farther?"

"I'm going to have to."

Just as I said the words, someone emerged from a cabin in the distance. Chad. It was Chad!

Finally, maybe we were safe.

He hobbled toward us as quickly as possible with his hurt ankle. "Where have you been? Nate just radioed me and told me about a fire. I came up here to check and see if you'd ventured this way to work. I was hoping."

"We got out just in time. But Chad—the Brunke brothers," I said.

"The police have them in custody."

"What?"

Chad nodded. "Marion Edwards called. Duke was out here searching for Bigfoot when he saw everything happen. He hurried back and called Sheriff Abel. The police found the brothers coming out of the back entrance to the park and took them in for questioning."

"How about the fire?"

"Firefighters are on their way." As if on cue, I heard another siren in the distance, growing closer by the moment. "It's contained to the old office. Thankfully." He paused. "I think we need to get you guys some blankets and coffee before you get sick. Come on."

THIRTY-EIGHT

BY THE TIME Chief Abel let us go, sunlight filtered through the trees in misty rays that inspired the imagination. Slowly, Riley and I trudged back toward the cabins. I looked like a wreck. A total and complete wreck. I was still partly covered in mud. My hair had twigs in it. I could only guess what my face might have picked up—dirt, dust, pollen. The possibilities were endless.

Riley didn't really look all that worse for the wear. Sure, he had dirt smudges here and there: on his knee, his elbow, and a small smudge on his cheek. But, overall, he still looked great.

In the craziness of the past several hours, we'd learned several things. Seamus had been involved with a poker ring in the area. Apparently, he'd won big-time against Junior and Debby Stephens. He won so much money, in fact, that he decided the job here at Mythical Falls wasn't worth finishing and he'd taken off for the Bahamas.

Caleb Kidwell's parents had stopped by and thanked me for solving the case. Word traveled quickly in such a small town. They'd even cut me a check, which would help greatly with purchasing a new car. Though insurance would cover most of my loss, the extra would provide for anything I would have had to pay out of pocket.

It had also come out that the Brunke brothers had been troublemakers when they were younger, but most people thought they'd mellowed out. They'd been stockpiling the diamonds they'd found, waiting to cash them in and get out of town. Thankfully, there was plenty of evidence to convict them, especially since none of the brothers were talking or ratting each other out.

In the back of my mind, I wondered if Scotty Stephens had secretly known about the diamonds. If he'd heard rumors. He'd probably never admit to it.

Now it was time to move on to the most important matters of all.

Just as we crossed the arched bridge leading into Bigfoot Woods, I turned toward Riley. I was ready to finish the conversation I should have wrapped up months ago.

"Riley, can we talk?" My voice cracked with some kind of emotional strain that surprised even me.

"Of course. What's going on?"

I sucked in a deep breath, realizing just how scary it was to put my heart out there. "You know how you've been asking me if something is wrong?"

He nodded and took my hands in his as we faced each other. "Because I knew there was something wrong. I also knew you'd tell me when the time was right. I was trying to give you space."

My heart filled with gratitude. I loved this man. I really did. "Well, I guess there's been a part of me that's been holding back. I've been afraid of getting hurt again. I mean, every time things seem great between us, something happens that tears us apart. The fact that we're together right now has seemed too good to be true. So I thought that maybe if I didn't wish as hard or hold on as tight that maybe this time things would be different."

"Oh, Gabby." He pulled me closer and kissed the top of my hands tenderly.

"I know it probably sounds crazy—"

"We have been through a lot. Way more than most couples. The fact that we're still together says a lot."

I nodded, feeling calmer by the moment. "I agree. There's no one else I ever want to be with, Riley. Just you."

A huge grin spread across his face. "I was hoping you'd say that one day. Because I feel the exact same way about you."

I wanted to rejoice, but I needed to finish what I had to say first. "I'm sorry I've been distant."

"After how I acted the months following the ordeal with Scum, I have nothing but forgiveness. Life is hard, Gabby. We've changed. We're going to continue to change as we grow. But that's okay. As long as we're committed to each other."

I grinned, feeling immense relief after getting that off my chest. "There's one other thing . . ."

He put his hands on my waist and pulled me closer, close enough that I could see the flecks in his eyes. "What's that?"

I rubbed my lips together, collecting my thoughts before launching into my announcement. "You know how you've been wanting to nail down a date, and I've been putting you off?"

"I have noticed that."

"Let's set a date. Right now. I don't want to waste any more time."

A wide smile stretched across his face. "Sounds great to me. When do you want to get married?"

Excitement sparked inside me—it burst to life, for that matter. "How about today?"

"Today?" His eyes widened.

I nodded, my thoughts coming together quickly. "Down by Mythical Falls. I think it would make a beautiful backdrop." Thanks, Clarice, for the idea. "Sierra's on her way with Reef. My father is coming to paint. It's the perfect timing."

His intense gaze wrapped around me and made me forget everything else around. "Is that what would make you happy?"

"Immensely."

"I was hoping you might say that." He reached into his pocket and pulled out wedding rings.

My breath caught. "You still have these?"

A smile teased his lips. "I've been carrying them around, waiting for you to give me the word."

I threw my arms around him. "That's just about the sweetest thing I've ever heard. How long have you had these?"

"Six months."

"But we weren't even back together then!"

He shrugged. "I know."

"Oh, Riley." I planted a kiss on his lips, a kiss that I didn't want to break.

"Let's do this," Riley said, pulling away from the kiss but pressing his forehead against mine. "You want me to call Pastor Randy and see if he's available?"

"That would be perfect."

His eyes turned serious. "Gabby, you make me feel like the luckiest man alive."

"Luck's got nothing to do with it."

"That's for sure." He leaned closer and brushed his lips against mine again. "Now, let's get ready for a wedding!"

CHAPTER
THIRTY-NINE

SIERRA SQUEALED when I stepped from the bedroom, wobbling slightly in my high heels. "Gabby, you look gorgeous!"

"You think?" I smoothed the skirt of my gown, feeling a touch overwhelmed—but in a good way.

"I know."

Clarice stepped out behind me. "I did her makeup and hair, but that's all I can take credit for. The rest of her beauty is all natural."

I felt myself beaming. I felt beautiful. Like, really, really beautiful.

Sierra had brought the wedding dress I'd tried on the first time Riley and I were engaged. My future step-mom had purchased it for me before Riley and I called things off. I'd stuck it in my closet, figuring I'd never get a chance to use it.

But now here I was. The bodice of the white gown was fitted, sleeveless, and simple. Waves of fabric flowed from the waist. I skipped the veil, and, instead, Clarice had smoothed my hair, adding gentle curls.

"This is really happening," I whispered.

Sierra, holding Reef in her arms, gave me a hug—and she didn't give hugs easily, so I knew this moment was special. "I'm so excited for you. You deserve all the best, Gabby. And I really believe that Riley is the best for you."

"I do too."

"You'll have quite the story to tell your kids one day. Most of us just meet and fall in love. You and Riley . . ."

"It's been a thrill ride."

She smiled and pushed her glasses up higher as Reef tried to grab them. "Exactly."

I stared at my tiny Asian friend. My best friend. The two of us were unlikely BFFs, but I was so glad she was here. "I never thought this day would really come."

"We all knew it would happen. We were just waiting for you and Riley to realize it."

"Sierra, we're both going to be married now. We're growing up. Isn't that . . . weird?"

She shrugged. "Maybe. But it's exciting."

A knock sounded on the door, and Sierra hurried to answer. A moment later, Nate peeked his head inside. "Can I chat with you a minute, Gabby?"

I nodded, and Sierra and Clarice disappeared to the back. "What's going on?"

"First of all, let me say that you look gorgeous. Riley is one lucky man."

"Thank you."

"Secondly, I'd like to give this to you." He pulled something out from behind his back. It was a giant rock. "It's a diamond. We think it's worth around five thousand dollars. It should be more than enough to make up for the wages you lost because of my neglect."

My eyebrows shot up. "Wow. That's amazing, Nate."

"I'm going to give one to everyone who's worked here on the job. It's the least I can do."

"Has anyone certified that these are the real thing?"

He did the woodpecker laugh. "Oh, you. You're always thinking, aren't you? As a matter of fact, a gemologist just got here and confirmed that these are the real things. They're some kind of freak phenomena in this area. There's more than enough out there to make amends with. I'll be able to pay my investors and workers. Everyone. And Riley has agreed to oversee it. It was a stipulation so people wouldn't bring lawsuits against me."

"That's great."

He lowered his gaze. "What about Clarice? Do you think I ruined my chances?"

"I know she really likes you, and I know that, for some crazy reason, she's thrilled with the possibility of helping run this place. I think she's forgiving. Just be real with her. And stop keeping so many secrets."

His eyes lit again. "Okay. Thanks, Gabby. And congrats. I think the ATV is waiting to take you down to the falls."

A wave of nerves rushed through me. This was normal— having a few jitters on your wedding day. I'd be strange if I didn't.

"Girls, I'm ready to go." Almost as if they'd been waiting with their ears pressed against the door, they emerged from the back. Clarice's gaze went to Nate.

"Gabby, can I meet you down there in a few minutes?" Clarice asked.

I glanced at Nate and smiled. "Of course."

Sierra and I climbed in an ATV driven by Chad.

As we reached the bottom of the hill, I spotted white chairs set up facing the waterfall. Beyond the seating area, mist rose from the falls. The leaves couldn't be prettier in their autumn glory.

This was going to be a great day.

My dad met me at the start of the trail. He'd dressed up in his finest suit. His long hair was brushed back neatly. It was the best I'd seen my father look in a long time.

"Gabby . . . you look . . . you look gorgeous."

"Thanks, Dad."

His eyes grew misty. "Your mom would be so proud of you.

You know that, don't you? You've turned into a wonderful young woman."

Tears pushed to my eyes. "Thank you. I wish she was here."

"So do I, Honey. So do I. I wish every day that I could turn things around and do life differently. But all I can do is try not to make the same mistakes twice."

The folksy band from Yuck Yuck's began playing the Wedding March. Nate had been able to convince them to play here at the last minute.

"Here goes nothing!" my dad said.

"Actually, here goes everything."

"You got that right."

As the music played, I started down the aisle with my father. I couldn't believe this was actually happening. It was *really* happening.

My heart felt like it might burst with joy.

I passed the Squeaky Clean crew, Marion, my brother, Sierra and Reef. Riley's parents had even come from the DC area. I had everyone here I needed to have here.

Pastor Randy stood at the end of the aisle, Riley beside him. Riley's eyes lit when he spotted me, and I tried to memorize every part of his gaze. I'd never seen him look like that before. His eyes were wide and mesmerized. His breath looked baited. His lips parted in awe.

He'd borrowed a black tux from Nate, and he looked good enough to be on the cover of *GQ*. My heart pounded at the sight of him. He was going to be my husband. My *husband*!

This was it. This was my moment. The one I'd dreamed about for so long. The day that Riley and I became one. Forever.

I drew in a deep breath, praying I didn't trip on my walk down the aisle, and I continued until I reached Riley and Pastor Randy. Riley winked as I looked at him, the action setting my heart aflutter.

"Who gives this woman to be married to this man?"

"I do," my father said.

My dad kissed my cheek before joining his fiancée, Teddi, in the front row.

Riley and I joined hands and faced each other. I felt giddy enough to squeal. All the fear I'd been feeling somehow seemed like a distant memory.

"I understand you've written your own vows?" Pastor Randy said. "Riley, please start when you're ready."

Riley pulled out a piece of paper from his jacket. His hands shook ever-so-slightly. The sight of it actually made me feel better. I wasn't the only one feeling anxious about our big moment.

"Gabby, from the moment I first saw you, I knew there was something different about you—and it wasn't because you'd just come from a crime scene."

The audience chuckled. I couldn't help but grin.

"I thought you were beautiful. And the more I've gotten to know you, the more beautiful you've become. You're the strongest woman I know. You face danger—sometimes to a fault, but it's because you stand up for what you believe is right. You act as a voice for those who don't have a voice."

I squeezed his hand as I felt tears rushing to my eyes and then whispered, "Thank you."

"I can't wait to spend the rest of my life with you. I'm certain it will be an adventure. An adventure I don't want to miss. I vow to always be there for you. In sickness and in health. For richer, for poorer. In the good times and the bad. I love you, Gabby St. Claire."

"Gabby," Pastor Randy said.

I wiped away the tears that had popped to my eyes. I didn't even realize they were there until a wayward one raced down my cheek. Sierra handed me a tissue, and I dabbed the moisture there.

I sucked in a deep breath and pulled out my own vows from my wedding bouquet. I'd spent most of the morning trying to compose what I wanted to say, and it still didn't sound right. I took one glance at my words and shook my head. I put the paper back into the bouquet.

"If it's okay, I'll just speak from the heart."

Riley squeezed my hands. "Please do."

I pulled in another shaky breath, more nervous than I'd envisioned. Not because I was uncertain, but because I realized just how serious this was. "Riley Thomas, from the moment I met you, I was fascinated. I wanted to get to know you more. I wanted to know what was different about you. Then I realized what it was: I've always felt safe around you. I've always felt like you cared. We've had our ups and downs—we're going to always have those . They're a part of life. But it's always been you. Even when we were apart, it was you. And it always will be. Forever."

"I love you, Gabby," Riley whispered.

"So I vow to be there for you in chaos and in peace," I continued, my voice catching. "When we're scraping by or when we're prosperous. When life feels clean and tidy, and when life gets messy. When we're facing death, and when we're facing life. I'll always be by your side."

"Is there really anything else to say?" Pastor Randy chuckled, and everyone joined him. "I think we can all agree that we've been praying for this day. Long before the two of them knew they were meant to be together, many of us did. We could see it from the start. I see them having a wonderful life together, a life where they focus not only on themselves but on giving back to other people. That said, I now pronounce you husband and wife. You may kiss the bride."

Riley grinned and leaned toward me. Our lips met. Lingered. Relished.

I was going to have the rest of my life to feel his lips against mine.

That meant I was the luckiest woman alive.

"Everyone, I now present to you Mr. and Mrs. Riley Thomas!" Pastor Randy announced.

The band began playing Jason Mraz's "I'm Yours."

I was so glad that my soul was being restored piece-by-piece —just like this old theme park. It seemed only fitting that we had gotten married here in a place once dead but now revived.

With the ceremony over, the band continued to play. Yuck Yuck's had catered for us—pizza, soda, nuts, chips. No Appalachian oysters, however. Clarice and Nate had managed to set up a makeshift dance floor with string lights dangling overhead. As the sun sank below the tree line, the lights formed a perfect backdrop.

"Hey guys, check out this picture on my camera phone," Clarice said.

Riley and I gathered behind her to see the photo. Riley and I grinned from ear to ear in the picture, looking happier than we'd ever been.

"That's a great picture," I told her.

"Well, yeah. But that's not what I wanted you to look at." She rolled her eyes. "Look at this."

She enlarged something on her phone and pointed to a shadow in the background.

Only it didn't look quite like a shadow. It almost looked like .

. .

Bigfoot.

Riley and I glanced at each other and then shook our heads.

"He's not real," Riley said.

"That's just our eyes playing tricks on us."

Nate snaked his arm around Clarice's waist. The two of them had obviously made up. "Say what you want—I'm a believer."

"Are you sure you didn't hire someone—?" I started.

He raised his hand. "Never again. By the way, when this place opens, you should come back here. On me. As a late honeymoon."

Riley and I glanced at each other.

"I think we'll pass," Riley finally said, speaking for both of us. "I've had my fill of Mythical Falls."

Nate shrugged. "Have it your way. But don't say I didn't offer. Besides, you'll have two percent ownership."

"I'll be back," Clarice said, looking up at him and rubbing noses.

I was feeling all sentimental and romantic at the moment, but that was crossing some kind of affection meter. Could Nate and Clarice actually have a chance? I supposed we'd be finding out.

I looked up at Riley as the band began to play Shania Twain's "You're Still the One." "I couldn't be happier than I am right now," I whispered.

"You and me both. We're going to make it, Gabby. Together."

"I agree."

He leaned closer. "I love you, Gabby Thomas."

I grinned upon hearing the name. "I love you too, Riley. Forever."

~~~

Thank you so much for reading *Thrill Squeaker*. If you enjoyed this book, please consider leaving a review!

Keep reading for a preview of *Swept Away*.
~~~

NOW AVAILABLE

SWEPT AWAY: CHAPTER ONE

"I had to search far and wide, Gabby, but I finally found the perfect location," Riley said.

Something close to pure delight oozed through my chest at the sound of Riley's—no, make that *my husband's*—voice. I couldn't wait to enjoy seven full days of alone time with him.

"The perfect location, huh?" I said. "I hate to say this, because I know you worked hard on our honeymoon plans, but anywhere with you is perfect."

"I feel the same," he said.

Riley squeezed my hand as we cruised down the road in a rental car. I had no idea exactly where we were since a blindfold covered my eyes, but I was okay with that. We'd gotten married quickly two weeks ago at the end of September, and I'd figured we might get around to honeymooning next summer at the earliest, due to both of our crazy schedules.

"You have no idea how challenging this was," Riley said. "But I knew an island far off the coast was out, especially after the whole Cemetery Island fiasco."

"True." A secluded island and being cut off from the outside world had scarred me for life.

"I knew a resort was out of the question after the whole Healthy Springs episode."

"True again." A missing woman in a highbrow resort had made me never want to go to another one.

"A mountain cabin just didn't seem appropriate after Mythical Falls."

"I can't argue with that." A creepy abandoned theme park and Bigfoot sightings were enough to give anyone nightmares.

Riley pulled the car to a stop and cut the engine. "So, I pulled a few strings, and here we are."

Anticipation sizzled through me. I couldn't wait to see what he had planned. Something about the surprise of it all made me feel like a detective at her first crime scene.

"Can I take my blindfold off yet?" My fingers reached for the soft cotton hankie.

We'd gotten off the plane in Florida, so I knew which state I was in, at least. But as soon as we'd rented a car, my eyes had been covered, and I'd placed myself in Riley's capable hands. As the blare of the AC faded and silence filled the air around me, another ripple of excitement rushed through me.

It had been ages since I had a real, genuine vacation. Come to think of it . . . had I ever had a real vacation? I couldn't remember. I'd traveled, but it was always for work or purposes other than relaxation and fun.

"Stay right there. I'm coming around to get you." Riley's door opened, and a whiff of heavy, salty air drifted into the car along with the sound of seagulls.

I'd been trying to use my detecting skills to figure out where we were. Based on the sun's location, I figured we were headed west. Based on traffic, which had started out as heavy but gradually eased, I figured we were outside the city limits. Based on the smell and the sounds, I'd guess we were on the Gulf Coast somewhere.

My door opened, and Riley clutched my arm, gently easing

me from the sedan. Once I stood on solid concrete beneath my feet, I expected him to take the handkerchief from my eyes.

He didn't.

Instead, he tugged me across the ground until my feet hit something soft. Sand, probably. The scent of salty air hit me even stronger. Since I lived near Virginia Beach, the smell made me feel right at home.

"You ready?" Riley stood behind me, his touch making my skin come alive.

He sounded so cute in his excitement. All of this just reaffirmed how much I loved this man. I couldn't wait to spend the rest of my life with him.

"I'm ready," I told him, not bothering to hide my smile.

He carefully untied the cloth, and my eyelids fluttered open, adjusting to their newfound freedom. I sucked in a deep breath at the sight before me.

The sun sank in front of us, as if it had waited for us to arrive before putting on its show. Pink and purple smeared across the sky. The Gulf waters, though late in the day and absent of any bright sunshine, were still crystal blue and clear. The sandy beach looked white and pristine.

It was one of the most beautiful sunsets I'd ever seen.

"Do you like it?" Riley asked, his breath warm on my ear as his arms circled my waist.

"I love it." I turned and wrapped my arms around his neck. We both pivoted so we could still see the spectacular display on the horizon. "I grew up near the beach, so I thought I'd seen and experienced it all."

"There's something different about the waters down here. And watching the sunset on the Gulf . . . it's amazing."

"I agree." I glanced behind us and spotted a three-story house with an entire wall of windows facing the water.

The place looked grand and fancy with multiple porches and decks and even a little gazebo, all trimmed in a neat white. The building itself was covered in a rich coral-colored siding. Colorful Adirondack chairs rested outside, beckoning people to sit and enjoy the scenery. The bottom level appeared to be mostly pilings that set the residence up high in case floodwaters came.

The nearest house looked to be a good three hundred feet away, and it was a monster, surrounded on two sides by water as the land jutted out into a point. We seemed to be in an exclusive residential area, but just a little farther down the shoreline I spotted a marina and a small town.

"Where are we exactly?"

"Crystal Key," he said. "It's not actually a part of the Florida Keys. We're still a couple of hours away. But we're on an island off the west coast of Florida, about an hour south of Clearwater."

"I love it."

Riley looked back at the house. "A friend owns this place and offered to let us use it. I couldn't come up with a single reason not to. It fit all my criteria."

I turned to face him again, not really wanting to look at the house or the sunset anymore. Just Riley. My husband. The man I loved. Heartache had pulled us closer and pushed us apart only to eventually solidify our relationship for good.

My heart quickened at the sight of him. He looked so handsome. Since he'd taken up mixed martial arts last year, his slim, tall frame had turned into all lean muscle. He had dark hair and was usually clean shaven, but whenever he had the chance lately he let a five o'clock shadow form. I actually liked the look. His blue eyes were kind and wise, he had an easy smile, and he was a great listener. In other words, he was everything I'd ever wanted.

"I'm glad you picked this place. It's nice."

His eyes twinkled. "I planned this carefully, you know. We're staying by ourselves, so there's no one else around to distract us. There's no mysterious history haunting the place. The crime rate is practically nonexistent. There have never been any murders—yes, I researched it. The biggest excitement around here was when the grill didn't work during a local fish fry about a month ago. I think we should actually be able to enjoy our honeymoon like two normal people."

I raised an eyebrow. "Whoever said we were normal?"

"True that." He leaned toward me and planted a soft kiss on my lips. "You ready to grab our bags and get inside?"

My heart fluttered again. I hoped that feeling never left me when I looked at Riley. "Let's go."

We'd only taken one step toward the door when a sound caught my ear, and I stopped.

It sounded like an army was rolling into town somewhere in the not-so-distant distance. Riley's grip at my waist tightened, as he seemed to anticipate the worst also. We both sensed something on the horizon was threatening our plan for peace and solitude.

A convoy of probably ten vehicles—all kinds, from SUVs to vans to limos—appeared on the road and stopped at the massive house beside ours. All at once, people began pouring from the vehicles. Mostly girls. Giggling. In bathing suits. *Tiny* bathing suits.

I was tempted to cover Riley's eyes—the last thing I wanted was Ms. America swimsuit models lounging beside me on my honeymoon. But I trusted Riley. He wasn't the type to gawk.

Three men with cameras also appeared, along with a couple of people with clipboards and other people hauling out equipment of some sort.

The girls continued to giggle as they hurried toward the beach. I halfway expected to see Annette Funicello and Frankie Avalon appear singing "Beach Party."

Riley and I glanced at each other, and neither of us had to say a word.

This had not been on Riley's agenda. *They* had not been a part of the plan.

One last car pulled up. A limo constructed from a Hummer, at that.

A man stepped from the back wearing a white suit and sunglasses. He had curly dark hair and an air of charisma about him.

As soon as he cleared the vehicle, the women went crazy. "Ricky! It's Ricky! Hi, Ricky! Over here, Ricky!"

He grinned a Hollywood type of grin and sauntered toward them. As soon as he reached the sand, the women surrounded him and began fawning over the man. He didn't seem to mind.

All I could think of was "harem."

Maybe, if I blinked, all of these people would be gone, and Riley and I could have our nice, quiet honeymoon. We deserved that much, didn't we?

One of the men toting a clipboard sauntered across the grassy sand toward us. He had a sun-kissed face with thinning, light-brown hair, and a smile that screamed "salesman." His clothing was an updated throwback to the old show *Miami Vice*: a light-colored sports coat, a pink T-shirt, and aviator sunglasses.

"Wally Walker." He extended his hand, a businesslike smile on his face. For some reason, the man looked slightly familiar.

Riley seemed to hesitate before returning the gesture. "Riley Thomas. This is my wife, Gabby."

"Pleasure to meet you both." He nodded toward the house behind us. "You staying here?"

"Yes, we are," Riley said. "On our honeymoon."

The man grunted. "Interesting. We were told no one would be here."

"Who told you that?" Riley asked.

"The owner. We called him about a month ago when we were scouting out locations."

"Well, this was last minute," Riley said. "He must have forgotten."

The man grunted again. "We can work around you two."

"Work around us?" I asked, totally confused or maybe just in denial. I gripped Riley's arm more tightly as anticipation of bad news built inside me.

"Sorry. I'm the host and one of the producers for *Looking for Love*. You heard of us?" Before I could answer, he continued. "We're a reality show. Ten women. One rich, handsome man looking for a soul mate . . . or a trophy wife. Nobody really knows nowadays." He let out a canned laugh. "Anyway, we'll be filming here on Crystal Key this week."

Wasn't that just perfect? Like I'd thought earlier: harem. That had always been my opinion of those reality dating shows.

I had watched the show a couple of times. There was always a handsome bachelor who was called Mr. Eligible, or, during the seasons when a female was the lead, she was called Ms. Eligible. The show's star went on exotic dates with contestants, mostly after they won crazy competitions where time alone with Eligible was the prize. The contestants were given dance cards that promised them a place on the show for another week.

"What's that mean for us?" Riley asked, pulling me closer in a silent apology. He didn't have to say it. I knew him well enough to read the gesture.

Wally thrust a clipboard toward us. "Would you mind signing these release forms?"

"Why would we need release forms?" I asked, staring at the very detailed paper in front of me. The fine print was over-whelming, to say the least.

"Just in case we're filming and we catch you on camera. We hope that doesn't happen." He leaned closer. "Like, we *really* hope that doesn't happen. Like, if you could try to stay out of our way, that would be the best."

We both stared at him until he shrugged without a mere hint of shame.

"But, just in case, we want to cover all our bases. Lawsuits are not our friend." He let out a long, fake laugh.

"I only charge ten thousand for appearances on camera," I said, keeping my expression neutral. "Can we put that in the contract?"

The man's eyes widened, and he let out another forced laugh. "Wh . . . what?"

I smiled, big and broad. "Just kidding."

It's actually twenty thousand. I mentally laughed at myself and then patted my own back for not saying it out loud.

His laugh deepened. "You're a funny one. You two looking for limelight? I have some other shows I'm producing, and we're always looking for camera-worthy faces—"

"No," Riley and I both said at the same time.

Wally raised his hand. "That was loud and clear. Now, about these forms . . . ?"

"I'll read them over," Riley said. He was an attorney, so at least he knew what to look for.

"Fine. I'll come back tomorrow morning to pick them up. How's that sound?"

"Not too early," I pleaded with him

"Sure, sure." He took a step away. "Oh, and by the way—I'm sorry."

"Sorry for what?"

He shrugged apologetically. "You'll see."

I was sleeping in Riley's arms, dreaming about paradise and happy-ever-after when a sound jerked me from my happy slumber.

Thump, thump, thump.

I tried to ignore it and enjoy this moment I'd been dreaming about for so long—being married to Riley. Being here. Being with him.

Maybe I'd been hearing things. Maybe it was a dream. After all, it was the middle of the night in the town without crime.

Thump, thump, thump.

The sound became more urgent, and I couldn't pretend I was hearing things.

Somebody was pounding on the door to our beach house.

If I had to guess, this had something to do with the reality show next door. The ladies over there had partied hard until two in the morning, with music blaring and loud, loud talking. It had sounded like festivity central.

What could be happening now to pull me out of my slumber?

Option one: Someone didn't get a dance card.

Option two: Someone had a clothing malfunction.

Option three: Someone found out Ricky the Gigolo was dating someone else.

Riley stirred beside me. "What is that . . . ?"

"I'm not sure. But I guess we should go check it out."

He kissed my shoulder. "Do we have to?"

Just then, someone screamed in the distance, "Please. Help me!"

Riley and I threw off the soft down comforter and jumped out of bed. I grabbed a robe and quickly tied it around me as Riley and I rushed toward the sound. The scream sounded like more than *Looking for Love* gone bad. Someone sounded scared.

I glanced at the bedside clock. Four a.m.

At the front door, Riley pushed me behind him and finished pulling on his T-shirt. As he jerked the door open, tension crackled in the air. The ocean breeze drifted inside, deceitfully peaceful and balmy.

A woman stood there. Mascara streaked her cheeks, and sand clung to her itsy-bitsy black dress.

"You've got to help me. Please!" She tumbled inside and fell against Riley, heaving in deep gulps of air.

"What's wrong?" Riley grasped her arms. If he let go, she'd surely slip to the ground.

She looked up at us, her eyes wide and tear-rimmed. "They took her."

I touched her arm, concern ricocheting through me. Something had happened to traumatize the woman. Something bad.

I glanced outside beyond the woman and saw nothing but a dark beach. Nothing else was discernable through the blackness of the night. Just what was hiding out there in the nighttime?

"Took who?" Riley asked the woman.

"Vivian." She sobbed again. "We were walking down on the beach when these men pulled up in a boat. They jumped out, grabbed Vivian, and took off. One of them started to come after me, but I got away. This was the first house I found. Please, you've got to do something!"

Riley and I exchanged a glance.

So much for a peaceful honeymoon.

Click here to continue reading.

ALSO BY CHRISTY BARRITT:

BOOKS IN THE SQUEAKY CLEAN UNIVERSE

On her way to completing a degree in forensic science, Gabby St. Claire drops out of school and starts her own crime-scene cleaning business. When a routine cleaning job uncovers a murder weapon the police overlooked, she realizes that the wrong person is in jail. She also realizes that crime scene cleaning might be the perfect career for utilizing her investigative skills.

SQUEAKY CLEAN MYSTERIES

#1 Hazardous Duty

Half Witted (Squeaky Clean In Between Mysteries Book 1, novella)

#2 Suspicious Minds

#2.5 It Came Upon a Midnight Crime (novella)

#3 Organized Grime

#4 Dirty Deeds

#5 The Scum of All Fears

#6 To Love, Honor and Perish

#7 Mucky Streak

#8 Foul Play

#9 Broom & Gloom

ABOUT THE AUTHOR

USA Today has called Christy Barritt's books "scary, funny, passionate, and quirky."

Christy writes both mystery and romantic suspense novels that are clean with underlying messages of faith. Her books have sold more than three million copies and have won the Daphne du Maurier Award for Excellence in Suspense and Mystery, have been twice nominated for the Romantic Times Reviewers' Choice Award, and have finaled for both a Carol Award and Foreword Magazine's Book of the Year.

She is married to her Prince Charming, a man who thinks she's hilarious—but only when she's not trying to be. Christy is a self-proclaimed klutz, an avid music lover who's known for spontaneously bursting into song, and a road trip aficionado.

When she's not working or spending time with her family, she enjoys singing, playing the guitar, and exploring small, unsuspecting towns where people have no idea how accident-prone she is.

Find Christy online at:
 www.christybarritt.com
 www.facebook.com/christybarritt
 www.twitter.com/cbarritt